"Isaac of Girona, a good man in a bad time, should delight readers in this tale of court intrigue and religious tension in medieval Spain—a rich, spicy paella of a book."

—Bruce Alexander, author of *Blind Justice*

A Suspicious Substance . . .

Isaac shut the door behind him. "Yes, Sister?" he murmured.

"The Abbess instructed me to tell you directly, Master, as soon as she heard of it," said Sor Agnete. Her words tumbled out of her, scrambling in their haste.

"Tell me what?"

"Of the vial. Here. That I have in my hand."

"What vial, Sor Agnete?"

"I discovered it in Dona Sanxia's clothes. As I prepared the body. You had spoken of perfume, and so I uncorked it, but it doesn't smell at all like perfume."

Isaac reached out his hand for the vial. He rolled it about on his palm, sniffed it, and then removed the cork. He sniffed that, touched the wet end, and frowned. He rubbed the liquid between his thumb and middle finger, and then very delicately touched the end of his tongue to his fingertip. It was bitter to the taste. "Not something I would recommend drinking," he remarked dryly, extracting a cloth from his robe and vigorously cleaning off his hand . . . Isaac walked up and down the room, taking its measure, all the while touching his tongue to the roof of his mouth, and considering the problems raised by the presence of the vial.

MORE MYSTERIES FROM THE
BERKLEY PUBLISHING GROUP . . .

SISTER FREVISSE MYSTERIES: Medieval mystery in the tradition of
Ellis Peters . . .

by Margaret Frazer

THE NOVICE'S TALE	THE BISHOP'S TALE
THE OUTLAW'S TALE	THE BOY'S TALE
THE PRIORESS' TALE	THE MURDERER'S TALE
THE SERVANT'S TALE	

PENNYFOOT HOTEL MYSTERIES: In Edwardian England, death takes
a seaside holiday . . .

by Kate Kingsbury

ROOM WITH A CLUE	EAT, DRINK, AND BE BURIED
SERVICE FOR TWO	GROUNDS FOR MURDER
CHECK-OUT TIME	PAY THE PIPER
DEATH WITH RESERVATIONS	CHIVALRY IS DEAD
DO NOT DISTURB	RING FOR TOMB SERVICE

GLYNIS TRYON MYSTERIES: The highly acclaimed series set in the
early days of the women's rights movement . . . "Historically accurate and
telling." —Sara Paretsky

by Miriam Grace Monfredo

SENECA FALLS INHERITANCE	NORTH STAR CONSPIRACY
BLACKWATER SPIRITS	THROUGH A GOLD EAGLE
THE STALKING-HORSE	

MARK TWAIN MYSTERIES: "Adventurous . . . Replete with genuine
tall tales from the great man himself." —*Mostly Murder*

by Peter J. Heck
DEATH ON THE MISSISSIPPI
A CONNECTICUT YANKEE IN CRIMINAL COURT
THE PRINCE AND THE PROSECUTOR

REMEDY
◆ *for* ◆
TREASON

Caroline Roe

BERKLEY PRIME CRIME, NEW YORK

REMEDY FOR TREASON

A Berkley Prime Crime Book / published by arrangement with the author

PRINTING HISTORY
Berkley Prime Crime edition / May 1998

The Penguin Putnam Inc. World Wide Web site address is
http://www.penguinputnam.com

ISBN: 0-425-16295-8

Berkley Prime Crime Books are published by
The Berkley Publishing Group, a member of Penguin Putnam Inc.,
200 Madison Avenue, New York, N.Y. 10016.
The name BERKLEY PRIME CRIME and the
BERKLEY PRIME CRIME design are trademarks
belonging to Berkley Publishing Corporation.

PRINTED IN THE UNITED STATES OF AMERICA

10 9 8 7 6 5 4 3 2 1

This book is dedicated to the memory of

PROFESSOR ULRICH LEO

of whose vast learning it is one small fruit

This book could not have been written without the expertise and knowledge of my research collaborator, Deborah Schlow, nor without the help of many, many friends in the world of medieval study and research. Amongst them, I would like to acknowledge particularly Professors Jocelyn N. Hillgarth, Joseph Goering, and Giulio Silano. I am very grateful to the staff at the library of the Pontifical Institute for Mediaeval Studies, and to numerous other individuals who read the manuscript and offered criticism, comfort, and expertise: especially Eric Miltenburg, Anne Roe, Dina Fayerman, Jacqueline Shaver, and, as ever, Harry Roe, whose knowledge and support inform every aspect of the project.

The errors and oddities are all my own.

THE CITY OF GIRONA IN 1353

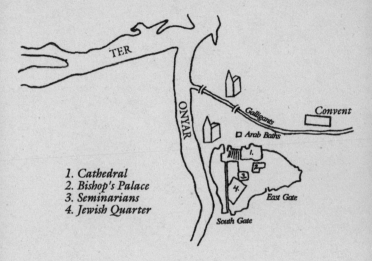

TER

ONYAR

Galligants

Convent

□ Arab Baths

East Gate

South Gate

1. Cathedral
2. Bishop's Palace
3. Seminarians
4. Jewish Quarter

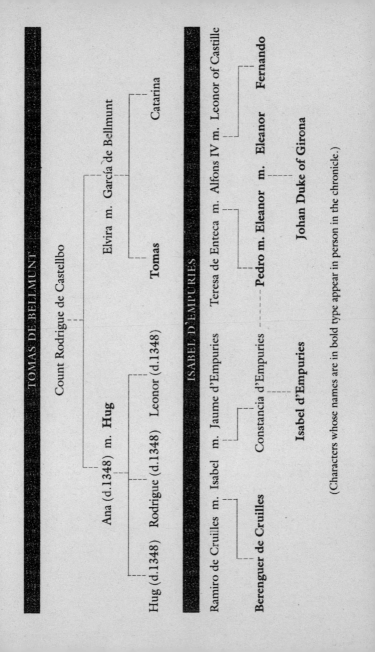

TOMAS DE BELLMUNT

Count Rodrigue de Castellbo

Elvira m. García de Bellmunt

Ana (d.1348) m. **Hug**

Catarina

Hug (d.1348) Rodrigue (d.1348) Leonor (d.1348) **Tomas**

ISABEL D'EMPURIES

Ramiro de Cruilles m. Isabel Jaume d'Empuries Teresa de Enteca m. Alfons IV m. Leonor of Castille

Constancia d'Empuries ------ **Pedro** m. Eleanor m. **Eleanor** **Fernando**

Berenguer de Cruilles

Isabel d'Empuries

Johan Duke of Girona

(Characters whose names are in bold type appear in person in the chronicle.)

PROLOGUE

Death visited Girona in the summer of 1348. It was said—with little exaggeration—that during those scorching-hot months, a man who rose at dawn full of strength and vigor could easily be in his grave by sunset. Before the arrival of the plague, there had been one hundred and fifty hearths—some seven hundred and fifty souls—in the *aljama,* the thriving Jewish Quarter of the city of Girona. When the epidemic finally retreated, one hundred and thirty survivors remained.

The pestilence—the Black Death—was everywhere: wherever ships touched land and sailors disembarked, and wherever people traveled from town to town. She leapt and raced around the Mediterranean, carving a path inland through Italy and France, and pouncing on the eastern coast of the Spanish peninsula. In spite of prayers, and spells, burning herbs and incense, and the performing of penitential exercises, she tore into the Spanish kingdom of Aragon, devastating the province of Cataluña, attacking Barcelona, and then springing on Girona like a lion striking a gazelle. The city reeked of death and dying; its air rang with the wails of mourners. Death was no respecter of rank or virtue. To her, all were equal: the laborer collapsing in the field;

the beggar dying in the street; the rich man shivering in silk bedclothes.

Pedro, King of Aragon, wept for his young bride, who had died of the plague before she could give her lord a much-desired successor to the throne.

Count Hug de Castellbo, whose wife, two sons, and a daughter had died the week before, walked seven miles to the Cistercian abbey, barefoot and clad in sackcloth, carrying a chest filled with silver coins, before riding off to Valencia in service of the King. For without expiation of his sins, who knew what further hideous retribution lay ahead of him?

Lady Isabel d'Empuries, twelve years old, placed a meadow flower on her mother's newly sealed tomb, and left for the convent of Sant Daniel, to join other bewildered orphaned girls being looked after by the Benedictine sisters.

In the house of Isaac the physician, a young man writhed and shivered and sweated, crying out for help to Isaac and to the Lord, and finally, in the irony of delirium, to his dead mother, from whose bedside he had brought the disease.

"Can you do nothing for him, Papa?" The girl standing in the doorway took a step forward into the room.

Her mother's strong arm caught her around the waist and pulled her firmly out into the courtyard. "Stay out of that room, Rebecca," she said.

"But, Mama, it is *Benjamin* who suffers." Her voice rose to a shriek and she broke into a storm of weeping. "Let me bathe his forehead to cool the fever," she whispered. "I don't care if I die with him."

"Rebecca, you are being foolish," said Isaac. His habitual calm control gave way to exasperation. "The only thing we can do is not take the contagion ourselves. I would save him if I could, I swear to you."

Rebecca succumbed to a further outburst of weeping.

"Indeed, I do not know what I will do without him, Judith, my dear."

"You will find another apprentice, husband," said the

physician's wife in her best soothing voice, while retaining a firm grip on her daughter.

"Where?"

The question hung in the air unanswered for the space of a long moment. "Has death taken so many?"

"It has. And I do not know why our household has been spared, with the exception of your foolish nephew here." As he spoke he laid his hand on the young man's chest. He listened intently for a moment, and then laid his ear where his hand had been. After a few moments he raised his head again. "Send for Naomi, Judith. He is dead."

His fifteen-year-old daughter caught her breath in her throat and turned on her mother. "You wouldn't let me go in the room and comfort him. And now he's dead. My Benjamin is dead." She broke free of her mother's grasp and fled across the courtyard to the stairs that led to the rest of the house.

"*Your* Benjamin, Rebecca?" said Judith, startled, and headed toward the stairs. "Raquel?" she called, and waited for her younger daughter to appear.

"Judith?" called Isaac through the door. "Where are you?"

"I am here, Isaac," said his wife, moving briskly back across the courtyard. "I have sent Raquel to fetch Naomi and to comfort her foolish sister. But is it true? Benjamin is—" Her voice failed.

"Dead, yes," said Isaac wearily. "Like all the others." He peered uncertainly into the brightness of the courtyard. "His body must be stripped and washed at once," he said, stooping automatically to get his tall frame under the doorway and walking over to the fountain. "Then put his clothing and bedclothes in the fire. Tell Naomi to set bundles of purifying herbs alight, and seal up the room until the contagion is over. And Judith, if you will bring me my loose fustian robe, I will wash and change here."

"Is this necessary?" asked Judith, pale with fear.

"Until now, our house has been free of the pestilence, my dear. I hope we may keep it so." Isaac stripped off all his clothing, and threw it in a tub full of water next to the fountain. Then he picked up a large dipper and poured cold water liberally over himself.

"But you have kept us all away from the room where he lay. Surely—"

"Some say that the contagion can rest on the smallest trifle—a ring, a piece of clothing—that has been near an infected person. If it is true, my tunic can carry the disease from me to you, Judith, from our house to another's. That is why I leave potions for the afflicted, but never enter their houses."

"Are you saying the contagion can be washed away, like dirt?" Her voice rose skeptically. "I don't believe it."

"No one knows. I hope so."

"Then how was Benjamin afflicted? He's always been a clean boy."

"He went to Hannah while she lay mortally ill. He confessed it to me," said Isaac, "when the fever struck him."

"My poor sister," said Judith soberly. "It is hard when a son is punished so for honoring his mother."

"It is," said Isaac, grimly, and poured more cold water over his back to rinse away the soft soap. "But the pestilence has its own laws. His wretched filial piety has killed him and brought the disease into our house. We must do what we can to hold it off."

"I will fetch you a clean coat."

The body of his apprentice was brought out on a hurdle to be washed and shrouded in clean linen. Already the cleansing fires were burning, and the room in which he died was filled with dense smoke. Naomi closed the door and held out the key to her master.

"Isaac," said his wife, from behind him. "Here is your robe. Clothe yourself. You shame Naomi with your nakedness. I will take the key."

"Naomi has seen me naked before this," said Isaac.

"But that was when you were a child, not a very handsome man, at the height of his powers—" said his wife, with an involuntary giggle. "Such thoughts—with Benjamin lying dead a few paces away," she added, blushing. "Here . . . Put on your robe. I will lock the door."

Isaac stood by the fountain, fastening the many buttons on his loose tunic, worn long as befitted his status as physician to some of the wealthiest and most powerful families in Girona. Again he looked around uncertainly. "Judith?" he said tentatively. "Where are you?"

"I am here, Isaac. By the stairs. Whatever is the matter?" With alarm on her face, she walked quickly over to him.

"Stay with me in the courtyard for a moment. My dearest, my beautiful Judith, stand here, with the light upon your face. I want to look at you."

"It is not only that my eyes grow weak," said Isaac, after they had settled themselves on a bench under the arbor. "You knew that. But every morning brings further deterioration. For days now, I have lived in a world of shadows, and I fear that soon the distinction between light and darkness will be gone. Until he fell ill, Benjamin was able to describe anything I could not see clearly, and his hand was steady on the knife where it was required, but now he is dead." He took his wife's hand in his, and held it firmly for a moment. "If he brought contagion into the household, it matters not. We will bar our doors to the unafflicted, pray, and comfort each other in our final days."

Judith sat silent under the arbor beside her husband. She picked up her work, and set it down again. "When will we know?"

"Soon. It is Wednesday. Before the Sabbath ends, we will know. For those days, we shall keep ourselves apart. But if, by some miracle, we have escaped, what will I do?"

Judith waited until her voice was steady. "You will find another apprentice."

"And how do I find one in the midst of death and desolation? He must be clever with his hands, and quick to learn. I cannot afford to spend two or three years teaching an empty-headed boy to open the gate to a patient, or carry the basket of herbs without dropping it. Think of all the families in the Quarter. There is no one. Everyone who isn't dead is doing the work of two or three."

"Then I will be your apprentice. I will go with you into the woods to gather herbs. There was a time when I did. You will tell me what you need, and I will find it. You can still smell and taste to approve my choice."

"Ah, Judith, my love. As strong as a lion, and as brave. But you cannot come with me to visit my patients," said Isaac. "It would not be seemly."

"Then I shall send Rebecca with you. She is quick and clever with her hands. You will have to make do with daughters until Nathan is old enough to study at his father's right hand."

A golden-eyed brown-striped kitten climbed into Judith's lap. She brushed it off impatiently. "Among all our troubles, Isaac, whatever prompted you to bring these creatures into the house?"

"Naomi complained of mice in the kitchen, and thought she saw a rat in the pantry. You will admit that the kittens have chased the rats and mice away. And besides," he said, in his old teasing voice, "old Mordecai claims that golden-eyed cats bring luck. The houses that have one suffer less from the effects of the pestilence than do their neighbors. But say not a word of that to anyone, or they will steal our cats."

Judith rose, and looked at her husband with affection and exasperation. "Do not jest, husband, not with Benjamin lying dead not twenty feet away. And a sentence of death hanging over us all."

Isaac caught her hand. "I do not jest, my love. And it may be true, as true as anything that men believe about this terrible affliction."

"I'll send Rebecca to you. If she's to be your apprentice, she should begin now. She needs a useful occupation," said her mother sharply.

And the plague raged from Granada to Girona that summer until the cool winds blew down from the north, cleansing the infection from the city. At the end of her reign of terror, she had snatched away one out of every three souls, leaving every craft and profession and trade in the city, from cobblers to scribes to physicians, empty of its skilled practitioners.

But she did not touch the household of Isaac the physician again.

ONE

Girona
Sunday, June 22, 1353

The cathedral was cool and dark, in spite of the dazzling midsummer sun that filtered through its high arching windows, and the brilliant colors that ornamented its interior. Bells rang for Mass, and the faithful poured in, laughing and talking. Young women preened in their best gowns of brightly colored silk layered on silk, or simple dark modest cloth. They tossed shiny hair dressed in loose curls over their shoulders, or pushed back veils to reveal elaborate braids. For love was in the air. Tomorrow was the Eve of Sant Johan, when young women searched for their suitors' faces in pools of clear water, as well as in distant meadows and other private spots. A good many suitors were in the cathedral at that very moment, distracted from the state of their souls by the attractions of nearby bodies. A flirtatious glance, a giggle, a reproving hiss, and the congregation began to settle itself.

In the farthest corner from the altar, two strangers, a man and a woman, were deep in conversation. The man was arrogantly handsome, showily clad in bright, exquisitely fit-

ting hose, and a closely fitting tunic with sleeves that bil-
lowed with slashes of color.

"Is everything arranged?" he asked. He leaned over her,
demanding, urgent in his manner, and she stepped back in
alarm. Her veil slipped, revealing thick plaits of rich red
hair dressed low over her ears, in the complicated fashion
of the French court.

"Nothing has changed," she said, avoiding her companion's eyes. "I haven't convinced her yet, but I think she's
bored with the convent, and the adventure intrigues her.
They say she's fearless."

"Then she'll make him an uncomfortable wife," said her
companion. "But that's his concern, not ours. Willing or
unwilling, she is to be brought out between matins and
laud." He paused, apparently intent on the service. "Give
her this if necessary," he said, handing the woman a small
packet. "A drop or two in wine, no more, and she will
sleep like the dead. Someone trustworthy will be stationed
outside the small gate to help you with her. But you must
get her that far."

"What if I am seen?"

"You won't be. There will be such a disturbance in the
town, no one will have time to notice you."

"A disturbance? How do you know?" She gave him a
startled glance and paused. "Am I still to bring her to the
Arab Baths?"

"Yes. Where else is so close and private? We will leave
from there. And this is no game, my lady," he added. "If
you do not bring her, we are all ruined."

Monday, June 23

On the eve of the feast of Sant Johan, the unofficial patron
of midsummer revels, the bells of the convent of Sant Daniel rang for compline, and the nuns filed into their newly
built chapel for the last service of the old day. Darkness
seemed reluctant to fall, despite the hour. The lingering

glow of the sun competed with a waxing moon to light the convent and the town. As the voices of the sisters rose in a chant of melancholy beauty, commending soul and body to the Lord until day returned, the music to awaken the town to its celebrations began its own insistent rhythm.

In Rodrigue's tavern down near the River Onyar, the crowd was restless and moody, as if nightfall had increased their expectations of pleasure without fulfilling them. The room was oppressively hot, and thick with smoke from flickering lamps. Conversation had become desultory, the sullen drinkers irritable. Then quick footsteps sounded on the stairs and the stranger who had been at Mass at the cathedral walked in, bringing the dank air of the riverbank in with him. The room fell silent.

The stranger's appearance had altered since the day before. The coat he now wore was not so fashionably cut, nor were his hose so elegantly fitted. His smile was more open, his glance less arrogant. One or two men admitted to recognizing him; they nodded cautiously and waited. He flashed a bright and reckless smile on the assembled crowd.

"Josep," he said, in the silence, with a nod at a square, powerful-looking man with a prosperous air. "Pere, Sanch." He acknowledged them in turn. Still no one spoke. "Landlord," he said, "a jug of wine for my friends to celebrate the saint. No—that will not be enough. Three jugs to start. Blessed Johan has brought me luck, and I must repay him."

"Thank you, sir," said a man who lounged comfortably in the window. "And to whom do I pay my thanks? Other than the blessed saint."

"Romeu," he said. "Romeu, son of Ferran, born in Vic, soldier, traveler, wanderer, and only last week returned to my native land."

The jugs were carried out and set on the long tables. Romeu filled tankards and cups, called for another jug, and then filled his own cup. He raised it. "To the fairest city in the world," he said, "long may she thrive," and drank. They all drank; he filled their cups and tankards; they drank again, this time to fortune. He pushed the jug along the table nearest him, and as suddenly as it had stopped, conversation started again. Romeu ambled over to the other long table, and pushed a jug down in the direction of a giant of a man, who was listening with awe, if not comprehension, to a thin, lithe man with a sulky face and a brooding eye.

"Let me fill your cups," said Romeu to the two, pouring wine into the big man's tankard, and reaching for the thin man's cup.

"I do not drink," said the thin man, snatching it away. "Not having the coin to repay your hospitality."

"He was telling me his troubles," said the big man, and subsided once more into silence.

"Big Johan is a patient listener to the woes of others," said his friend.

"A patient listener is a rare thing," observed Romeu, absentmindedly filling the thin man's cup. "I, too, have come through bad times." He dropped his voice to a conspiratorial level. "Through the wiles of others, whose names would surprise you, I lost my post, my good name, and my modest fortune. I spent three years penniless and in exile. But, as you can see, the wheel has turned. Those who plotted against me were found out. My position has been restored to me, and my good name." He refilled the thin man's cup.

"I am a bookbinder," said the thin man. "Martin by name."

"An excellent trade," said Romeu. "Are there no more books in Girona, that you cannot raise a cup to the blessed saint?"

"Ah—plenty of books. Not long ago, I had all the binding at the cathedral, and the ecclesiastical courts, as well as casual work for certain gentlemen in the town. It was an excellent living. I am no older than yourself, sir, and I kept a journeyman and two apprentices busy all the time. And then some malicious canon—and I know who he was," said Martin, filling his own cup this time. "He complained about carelessness. It was the apprentice—you can't get

apprentices these days. Not since the pestilence killed off
so many. Now every careless, lazy good-for-nothing thinks
he's worth a purse of gold and his keep for sleeping all day
at his bench in the workroom." He shook his head. "Well,
I was busy and the Canon Vicar—there's a hard man—he
gave some of his work to another, a Jew, and they said he
did it better, and at a better price."

"And they gave your work—"

"They did, sir. They gave all the work to him. A Jew.
Working for the bishop." He dropped his voice. "They say
he has slaves. He keeps them locked up in the bindery,
feeds them on slop, and keeps his expenses down. It's not
right. The Bishop should have his work done by Christians,
not by Jews and their Moorish slaves."

"Did you hear that, Josep?" asked Romeu. "What will
happen when paper making is taken over by the Jews?"

"It won't come to that, friend," said the prosperous-
looking man. "I know how to protect my interests."

"It's time we did something about it," said another voice
from across the table.

"We are, Marc," said a third. "Join us."

"Hush, you fools," muttered someone else. "Who
knows who may be listening?"

"The Archangel Michael's Sword of Vengeance will cut
down the blood-soaked rulers, the soiled priests, and the
Jewish sorcerers," said a voice from the darkness. "Just as
on his day in our grandfather's time, he saved us from the
French invaders."

But when they turned to see who spoke, there was no
one.

Romeu, his eyes bright, his first cup of wine still only
half-drunk in his hand, smiled. He set down his cup, ex-
changed a word or two with the landlord, paid for yet more
wine, and slipped out into the warm night. His work was
only just begun.

Halfway through the night, the moon had slipped below the
hills and heat still lay like a blanket over the velvet darkness of Girona. The smell of mud and dead fish oozed up

from the river, combining unhappily with the more domestic perfumes of the city: old cooking smells, rotting garbage, privies, the dying smoke of kitchen fires.

The town was quietening down. Only a few determined revelers had not yet sought a bed for the night—a fragrant meadow, a pair of soft arms, or even their own lonely pallets. At the north gate to the city, Isaac the physician bade farewell to his escort, gave a word and a coin to the gatekeeper, and walked purposefully in the direction of the Jewish Quarter. The soft touch of his fine leather boots on the familiar cobbles echoed in the still June air. He paused. His echo continued for a moment and then stopped; someone else was lurking in the night. Isaac caught a whiff of fear and of lust drifting through the still air, and then the rank smell of evil. He took tight hold of his staff and quickened his pace.

The footsteps faded in the distance, and the physician turned his mind to the ailing child he had just left. This past week had seen a definite improvement in his condition; his appetite was good, and he was eager to play in the stables or by the river again. With no more physic, and no treatment but good air and food, he should be as strong and lively as any boy his age by summer's end. His father would be pleased.

The gate to the Quarter had been locked and barred long since. Isaac pounded on the heavy planks with his staff; nothing happened. He pounded harder. "Jacob," he called, in a deep and penetrating voice, "you lazy do-nothing. Wake up. Do you expect me to stand out here all night?"

"Coming, Master Isaac," grumbled Jacob. "Coming. Was I to hold the gate open all night in the hope that you might wander by?" By now his voice had retreated to a mutter, and could be ignored. Isaac set his basket on the ground, leaned on his staff, and waited. An infant breeze sprang up, carrying the heavy scent of roses down from the Bishop's garden; it flicked Isaac's hair off his face and then died. Somewhere a dog barked. In the Quarter, the thin wail of a baby pierced the night air. To judge by the sickly tone of the cry, it was likely the firstborn son of Reb Samuel, not yet three months old. Isaac shook his head. His heart grieved for the rabbi and his wife. Any minute now, their maidservant would be at his gate, begging him to don his robe and come to the child.

The heavy bar was shifted from its seat, a key creaked in a lock, and the small gate squeaked open. "It is a terrible late hour to be letting someone in, Master," said Jacob. "Even one as honored as yourself. And this is a worrisome night, filled with drunken louts with mischief on their minds. This being the second time I was dragged from my bed," he added meaningfully. "And the other I let in was seeking you as well."

"Ah, Jacob—if the rest of the world had untroubled nights, you and I could spend the hours of darkness in peaceful sleep, could we not?" He pressed a coin into the porter's hand. "But how would we earn our bread?" he added with a touch of malice, and headed in the direction of home.

He was greeted at his gate by a voice he didn't recognize. It sounded as if it belonged to a large youthful male, and its accent was that of the backcountry mountain-dwelling Catalans.

"Master Isaac," said the stranger, "I am sent from the convent of Sant Daniel. One of our ladies lies gravely ill. She screams in pain." He spoke as if his words had been painfully memorized, and were being offered up in snatches. "I am asked to fetch you, and your medicines."

"To the convent? Tonight? I have just come in."

"I was told I must fetch you," said the stranger, his voice rising in panic.

"Hush, lad," said Isaac softly. "I will come, but first I must collect what I need. Let us not wake the household." He unlocked the gate and entered. "Wait in the courtyard," he said, pointing ahead. "I have business in the house."

The gardener's boy from the convent watched Isaac with curiosity bordering on awe. It was true what they said in the town. Master Isaac could ascend a flight of stone stairs without a sound. They also whispered that you only knew Isaac had passed you in the dark if you felt the breeze as he flew by. The boy strained his eyes to see whether the Master climbed or was carried by his attendant demons to the upper stories of the house.

Something soft and formless and menacing pressed against his leg, interrupting his speculations. He leapt in the air, heroically suppressing a yell of pure terror. His strangled cry was answered by an interrogatory meow. A cat. Ashamed, he bent down to scratch its ears and settled himself to wait.

When Isaac reached the head of the stairs he listened briefly at his wife's door, and went to the room across the hall. He knocked delicately. "Raquel," he whispered. "Are you awake? I have need of you."

The soft voice of his sixteen-year-old daughter answered him. He leaned against the wall to wait.

"Isaac!" The word pierced the night air like Joshua's trumpet; he steeled himself to prevent his walls from crumbling. When he least expected it, Judith's concern could reach out and encompass him like a suffocating cloth, sapping his strength and vigor. "What is wrong?"

He heard her climb from her bed and move quickly across the room. The door creaked open, allowing a cool breeze from the hills to sweep into the airless hall.

"Nothing, my love," said Isaac. "All is well. I am sent for from the convent, and Raquel must assist me."

"Where have you been?" asked Judith. "All night you've been out alone, without even a servant to accompany you. It isn't safe."

He reached out a hand to touch her face, and still her complaints. "The rabbi's son is near death, my dear. His wife is distraught. After waiting more than three years for a son, she finds it a bitter blow. If they send for me, say that we will go straight there from the convent."

Judith was silent, trapped by her own elaborate and rigid code of behavior. One did not grumble aloud over assisting the rabbi. But Judith herself had lost two sons in infancy before the twins were born and felt secretly that the rabbi and his wife did not have a monopoly on grief. Indeed, her internal debate over what she should do now distracted her so that she failed to notice that Isaac had not answered her question. "I can't understand why the entire household should not sleep because a nun is ill," she said. "What have the nuns ever done for you, husband?"

"Hush," said Isaac. "The Bishop has been a good friend to us—"

Fortunately, Raquel slipped out of her room before her mother could express an opinion on the Bishop. She gave her mother a quick embrace and, in spite of the heat, wrapped herself securely in a cloak.

"Wait an instant," said Judith.

"For what?" said Isaac, with a hint of impatience. "This is a matter of some urgency."

"I will walk as far as the rabbi's house with you," she said. "Go. I will meet you in the courtyard."

Raquel followed her father down the stairs. He unfastened the door to a wide, low-ceilinged room that served him as herbarium, still-room, surgery, and, when he was expecting a summons in the night, bedchamber.

Isaac took down another basket from its place and began filling it with vials and cloth-wrapped packets of roots and herbs. "Lad," he called softly through the open door. "What do you know of the lady's malady?"

"Nothing, Master," he said. "I take messages and fetch necessaries from town. Otherwise I work in the garden. They tell me nothing." He paused for thought. "I heared her scream," he said, sounding pleased. "When the Abbess give me the message. The Abbess herself told me to fetch you."

"How does she scream? A loud scream?"

He thought for a moment. "A loud scream, Master. Like a stuck pig, or—or a woman brought to bed with child. And sobbing. Then she stops."

"Good lad. Come, Raquel. I hear your mother."

Extraordinarily, Abbess Elicsenda herself was waiting at the heavy portal, with the bursar, Sor Agnete, and the porter, Sor Marta, standing by. "Master Isaac," she said. "Thank you." She murmured hasty introductions to the two nuns in a voice taut and heavy with anxiety, and then abandoned any attempts at light conversation. ''I shall be brief. Lady Isabel is a ward of the convent. The illness has come on her quickly. She is aware of her surroundings only for short moments; the rest of the time she raves, under the influence of troubling visions. I fear she may not last the night. If nothing else, I pray you will be able to allay her suffering a little. I have also sent for the Bishop. Sor Marta will take you to her.''

Sor Marta gave Isaac no time to wonder why his friend the Bishop, rather than the convent's usual confessor, should be dragged from his bed to attend to a dying convent girl. She hurried them up narrow winding stone stairs and down long passages, her soft leather shoes moving rapidly and quietly through the corridors. The footsteps slowed. Isaac heard a loud scream, a sob, and the gasping heave of dry retching. Sor Marta knocked once on a heavy door and moved away, murmuring that Sor Benvenguda, the infirmary sister, would be with them shortly.

The door opened and closed again. A rustle of garments and the nearness of a warm body heralded the arrival of the infirmary sister. ''Master Isaac, we welcome your assistance,'' said her tongue, although her voice reverberated with anger and resentment. ''The Bishop himself has recommended that we send for you. You will want to know what troubles her.''

The door opened to allow someone else into the corridor from the sickroom. The smell of fever and dehydration, and a faint stench of rotted flesh was carried out with the newcomer.

''I can tell you what is troubling her,'' said Isaac sharply. ''She suffers from pustular sores, causing great pain and fever.''

One of the sisters in the corridor drew in a sharp breath of amazement.

''Before I can say more,'' he added, ''I must examine her to determine their cause, and judge whether my poor skills can aid her.''

Sor Benvenguda was not amazed; she was outraged. "That is not possible. Her modesty—"

"Will not be offended by a blind man's gaze."

The infirmary sister paused, at a loss for words. "I did not know, Master Isaac," she said at last. "I am new to this convent, from our house in Tarragona." Then she drew in a deep breath and returned to the battle. "Still, it is not fitting that even a blind man be allowed to uncover—"

"My daughter alone will touch her. She will tell me what she discovers."

"We cannot allow that. Not even our own sisters can do that."

"The case is not the same," said Isaac decisively. "Your sisters are bound to take particular care not to offend their own modesty. My daughter is discreet and virtuous, but she has taken no vows that she would have to break in helping this unfortunate lady."

"Impossible."

Two more sets of footsteps swept down the corridor and stopped near them. "What is impossible, Sister?"

"That I should permit this man and his daughter to examine Lady Isabel, Mother."

"Lady Isabel is the niece of our bishop," said the Abbess, sharply. "He has entrusted her to our care; we are responsible for her health and happiness. I ask you to remember that His Excellency condescended to advise us, Sister," she added, "that he wishes Master Isaac to examine his niece, and do whatever might be required to cure her. I think we cannot ignore his wishes." Her voice cut like steel through the heavy air.

"Yes, my lady," murmured Sor Benvenguda.

"Bring lights and whatever else they may need."

"Lights? But he doesn't need—"

"True enough, Sister. She does." Footsteps sped away along the corridor. "What is your name, daughter?"

"Raquel, madam." Isaac heard the sound of her light fustian gown brushing the stone floor as she curtsied.

"You have our gratitude and our prayers for your efforts, whatever the outcome, you and your father. It may help you to know that Lady Isabel is seventeen and, in the five years she has been at the convent, has been blessed with excellent health—until this illness. If there is anything lacking, send for me. Sor Agnete will stay to ensure that I receive your messages promptly.''

Raquel entered the infirmary with her father and led him to the narrow bed in the middle of the room where the sufferer lay. On the right wall was a large fireplace, with kettlehook and hob. In spite of the heat of the night, a fire burned on the hearth, and a charcoal brazier glowed not far from it. A very old nun sat on a stool between the fire and the brazier, stirring a porridgelike substance in a copper pan. Every once in a while, she reached into a basket that sat on the floor beside her, removed a handful of herbs, and threw them on the brazier. Their sweetness served a little to mask the smell of infection in the room. A lay sister with strong arms and a pugnacious expression stood between the room's two narrow windows, looking out of place, as if she had been sent for to wash the body, and had arrived too early. The large room was lit, dimly, by one candle and the flickering firelight. Two younger nuns, pale with fatigue and drenched with sweat, stood near the light with the infirmary sister, and the ferocious-looking Sor Agnete watched them all from the door.

''Here is the bed, Papa,'' said Raquel, ''and the table is at your left hand. There is another table at the foot of the bed, large enough for the basket. Shall I put it there?'' Without waiting for a response, she set the basket at the foot of the bed.

''Tell me something of my patient, my child.'' Isaac addressed her so softly that the waiting nuns were scarcely aware that he spoke.

Raquel fetched the candle and held it closer to the girl. She drew her breath in with surprise when the light fell on the delicate features. ''She looks—'' Raquel began, noticed the watching nuns, and started again. ''She looks ill, Papa. Her eyes are sunken, her lips dry and cracked, her skin pale—and—'' The door opened, bringing with it some

cooler air and two nuns with more candles. They set them
down on tables near the bed and lit them. "They have
brought more candles. In the light, I can see that her skin
is gray, with no yellow in it. She has feverish patches on
her cheeks. She tosses her head, Papa, as if she is in great
pain, but she lies on her back, rigid and straight in her
bed."

"Ask her, gently and carefully, where the pain is."

Raquel knelt beside the bed to bring her face close to the
patient's. "My lady," she murmured. "Do you hear me?"
The skull-like head moved. "Tell me—where is the pain?"

"Ask her to point, if she can, to where it is. And stand
between her and the prying nuns."

Lady Isabel heard, and reached out her hand. She pulled
Raquel close to her and whispered hoarsely in her ear.

Raquel stood up on tiptoes and whispered in her father's
ear. "She says the swelling is on her thigh, Papa."

Isaac turned, moving his head back and forth until he
thought he located the infirmary sister. "There are too
many people in this room, Sister," he said with authority.
"They foul the air and destroy the peace. Send them
away."

Sor Benvenguda looked at Sor Agnete, who nodded,
grimly.

"As you say, Master," said the infirmary sister. "But
surely not Sor Tecla? She was our skilled and respected
infirmary sister, and can be of great help." Her voice
dropped to a murmur. "She worked here alone after all her
assistants were taken by the Death. She will be distressed
if she is sent away." She raised her voice again. "Sor Tecla
is preparing a poultice of bran and oats, should it be
needed."

"I, too, lost a valued assistant to the plague," said Isaac.
"But the Lord in His wisdom has given me a clever daughter with deft fingers to take his place. Certainly Sor Tecla
may stay. She will not be in the way."

"I shall stay as well," said Sor Agnete. "No one else is
necessary. I shall stand here by the door, and deliver any
messages that must be delivered. Sister, you may wait out-

side until you are needed." Sor Benvenguda favored her with a vicious glance and headed for the door.

"Thank you, Sister," said Isaac. He waited for the rush of footsteps to subside, and for the door to close, before he turned again to his patient.

With great delicacy, Raquel lifted the bedclothes and then the fine linen shift to expose a huge, shiny, red swelling high up on Lady Isabel's thigh, close to the groin. As she worked, Raquel's soft voice carried on a steady description of what she saw and did.

Isaac paused to consider. "What kind of swelling?"

"It is a pustular swelling, I am sure, not a plague sore," said Raquel. She bent down. "How long has it been there?" she asked her.

Lady Isabel blinked, trying hard to focus. "Friday," she whispered. Her eyes closed again; she tossed her head and muttered incomprehensibly.

"Has it spread?" he asked.

"Not yet, Papa. At least I do not think so."

"I must touch it, my brave Lady Isabel, so that I will know what to do. But I am blind, and cannot see you. My fingers see for me."

The young woman moaned, opened her eyes wide, and reached out to catch Raquel's hand. She tried to pull it toward her face. "Mama," she whispered.

"Try not to scream," said Isaac, "or the good sisters will think I am murdering you."

"She is past understanding you, Papa," said Raquel.

"Perhaps. But perhaps not. First we will ease the pain."

Raquel took a flask of wine from the basket, half filled a cup, and added water and a vial of dark liquid to it. She propped up Lady Isabel and held the cup to her lips.

"You must drink it, Lady Isabel," said Isaac firmly.

From somewhere in her delirium she heard, and swallowed half the mixture. Isaac waited, counting the moments, stooped over the bed, and Raquel led his fingers to the edge of the swelling. He felt it and nodded.

• • •

Raquel's steady hands lanced the abscess, and cleaned up the rush of infected matter. She swabbed the wound with wine, added some leaves and dried herbs to the old nun's poultice, and bound it in place.

"How are you feeling now, my lady?" asked Isaac.

Lady Isabel, drunk with exhaustion, cessation of pain, and a combination of strong wine and powerful opiates, did not answer. For the first time in days, she slept soundly.

Isaac picked up his staff and made his way across the sick chamber. Before he reached the unfamiliar door, Sor Agnete opened it for him, and bid him a friendly good night. In the corridor, a large hand gripped his own firmly, and a familiar voice hailed him. "Master Isaac, old friend. I am grateful for your attention to my niece. How is she?"

"She is sleeping, my lord Berenguer. Raquel will stay to tend her. I will not tempt heaven by saying that she is out of danger, but I don't feel the Lord is ready to take her yet. I'll return in the morning to mark how she progresses. Raquel will send for me if I am needed before that."

"Come," said the Bishop of Girona. "That is good news. We will walk together a little way."

As they descended the staircase a bell-like soprano voice soared, echoing, through the still corridors. It was joined by two or three more, whose rich lower tones supported the mournful chant. Isaac stopped.

"It is the sisters," said Berenguer, "out of their beds and singing laud. A penance paid by a few," he murmured with a hint of laughter, "for having better voices than the many."

"A small price for such beauty. Lady Isabel is your niece, Your Excellency? I have not heard you speak of her, I think."

"There are reasons for that, my friend. And just to be clear, she *is* my niece, my sister's child, not an error of my youth," said the Bishop as they waited for Sor Marta to open the convent door. "Born in a most fortunate hour, seventeen years ago. A modest girl, but courageous, with a clever mind and a witty tongue. I am fond of her." He paused so that they might descend the steps together. "Since the death of her mother, I have been her guardian. I keep her here where I can oversee her education."

A figure slipped past them on Isaac's side, leaving behind the heavy scent of musk and jasmine, overlaid with animal fear. Hurried, nervous, female footsteps lost themselves in the hubbub in the courtyard, where the Bishop's retinue waited, their horses stamping and rattling their harness. The smell of the woman's perfume was swallowed up in the odors of the night: horses, torches burning, sweating men. A jesting remark rose to Isaac's lips and died. It was none of his affair if a nun chose to keep a midnight rendezvous. "The night is dark?" he asked the Bishop.

"As the pits of hell," answered Berenguer, clapping his friend on the shoulder in high good humor. "The moon is down and the stars appear to have left with her. You shall have to lead me through the streets." The Bishop waved at his followers to keep their distance behind him, and the two men headed on foot onto the road that followed the River Galligants, and would take them to the north gate into the city.

The frightened nun slipped out through the crowd at the front gate of the convent. She adjusted her veil to hide her pale face and white linen wimple, and faded at once into the wall beside her. She felt her way with trembling fingers along the walls, peering into the blackness, until she reached the point where she was in the open, between meadow and river. The distance from the convent to the bridge that would take her to the Baths seemed endless; she felt as visible as a black cat on a snowy field. She stumbled at last down the path leading to the door, straight into Romeu's arms. He clapped a hand across her mouth to stifle her cry, and pulled her into the building.

"Where is she?" he whispered fiercely.

"I couldn't get near her. She is sick—dying. They say there is no hope for her. I could not possibly—" She burst into a flood of weeping.

"You and your friend could have carried her."

"She lies in the infirmary, with the physician and a whole flock of nuns in attendance. Did you get the child?"

"His nursemaid is bringing him. To the east gate."

"How did you convince her to do that?" she asked in astonishment.

"She's been told it was an order from His Majesty. We need her. We don't want a wailing baby on our hands, do we?"

"Please. Let's forget the whole plan," she said, with urgency in her voice. "It's too dangerous. We can't succeed."

"Too late. The nursemaid will be at the gate at sunrise. And there are others involved. It would be dangerous for everyone if we tried to go back now." He dismissed the issue with a vague wave of the hand. "Did you not know Lady Isabel was dying before this?" he added vehemently.

There was a silence. A long silence. He shook her, and she spoke again. "I will take the child, and I will go to Her Majesty and tell her that I heard rumors of a plot, and that I feared for the Prince's life, and so I took him from where he was to bring him to her. She will forgive me. She has a hasty temper, but a forgiving disposition."

"Not only are you incompetent, but you are stupid as well," he said. "And when they ask who helped you, what will you say then?"

"I would never betray you. Never."

"Fortunately for me," he said coldly, "you won't have the chance."

"How dare you speak to me like that?" said the woman, pulling the shreds of her rank and dignity around her.

"I dare because I must, if we are both to survive. Be sensible, my lady. Wait here for me. There are things I must do. If I have not returned by first light, then meet us outside the eastern gate. I brought your clothing. Change before I return."

"What can you say of the cause of my niece's malady?" asked Bishop Berenguer, all too casually, as they strolled slowly through the darkness. The flickering torches behind them cast enough light for Berenguer to see his way. The street was too familiar for Isaac to need guidance.

"There are many possible causes, Your Excellency," replied Isaac, very cautiously. "It could have been the bite of an insect whose poison rankled and festered. Had Lady Isabel been a soldier or a brawling lad, I would have said it was from a small wound that festered through neglect."

"It could not have been induced by a malicious hand?"

Isaac stopped. "I would not think so. It would be difficult—" He considered the possibility. "Raquel will discover the circumstances when Lady Isabel awakes. Do you have reason to fear malice?"

"No—and yes. She is the only child of my sister—my half sister, to be precise. Doña Constancia d'Empuries. But, Isaac, my friend, if you could see, you would know what everyone who looks at her knows. Her paternity is written across her face." The Bishop stopped and looked about. A sudden chill breeze sprang up from somewhere and he wrapped his cloak around him.

"And her father is well known?"

"If you concede that Pedro of Aragon is well known," he said, in his mildly ironic tone. "There is a look to her eyes that speaks of my dead sister, but every other feature is her father's. If his wife's children look one tenth as much like him as Isabel does, that lady will be well pleased," said Berenguer. He stopped and laid his hand on Isaac's sleeve to stop him as well. "Do you hear something, friend?" he murmured.

"A disturbance," said Isaac. "Somewhere in the town."

"Louts, celebrating the Eve of Sant Johan with a skin of wine apiece. In the old days, they'd be safe in a corner of a field with a woman by now, instead of disturbing the peace of honest folk." Berenguer laughed and returned to his own concerns. "As it is, I suspect my niece is a thorn in our young queen's flesh. She has troubles enough already. The chief of them being fear that the Infant Johan, our new Duke of Girona, will die."

"But surely she will have more sons."

"They say that she fears that she will become barren, or

like her predecessor, the mother of girls only. A rich marriage for the daughter of Doña Constancia might remind her how fickle Dame Fortune can be.''

"And is that likely, Your Excellency?" said Isaac. "The marriage?"

"It is. Don Pedro is delighted by her beauty and learning. He has an important marriage in mind for her." He stopped and laughed. "Spoken aloud like that, my fears seem foolish. And Her Majesty is the least bloodthirsty of ladies," he added. "But some of her followers would do anything to give her a few moments ease."

"Like bringing her news that Lady Isabel had perished from—an insect bite?" said Isaac.

"The nuns are loyal, and careful. And I know that you will look after my niece as if she were your own child. If Isabel survives this, we shall be very grateful." The Bishop paused. "Now that we are far from prying ears, how is Johan, our young prince? Like to confirm his mother's fears?"

"Not this evening, or any evening very soon. He has not the smell of death on him. When I left him, his little fever was gone, he had eaten well and was sleeping quietly, like any other child of three. Of course," said Isaac, "in time, death comes to us all."

The breeze strengthened and caught at the skirts of their robes. The Bishop tightened his hold on his cloak. "Thank the good Lord for the cool wind. We are in need of it this summer to keep away the pestilence. But to return to the young Prince, it will suffice for His Majesty and Doña Eleanor if death will wait until he can be crowned King of Aragon and have sons of his own."

"A day or two of rest and he will be himself again," said Isaac. "His constitution becomes stronger, I think, and where he lies, the air is sweet and good. Her Majesty may rest easy."

The Bishop stopped. "I am afraid that, in my selfish enjoyment of our conversation, I have carried you out of your way. We are almost at the palace. I will leave you here, my friend."

A distant murmur of human voices had been teasing the edges of their consciousness while they were climbing the steps toward the cathedral and the Bishop's palace. Then it suddenly erupted in a barrage of shouts and curses. Behind them, across the plaza, Isaac heard the sharp crack of a stone hitting the cobbles, or perhaps a wall, followed by the thud of an angry fist or a stick hitting soft human flesh. He winced. "This is more than drunken revelry, Your Excellency. There are rioters abroad."

"There are," said the Bishop, angrily. "On the night of Sant Johan, the streets attract drunken fools. And some of the fools, if I am not mistaken, live entirely too close to the palace. Those sweet voices over there come from my students, I think." He looked behind him. "Hola, officer," he called.

The closest of the Bishop's retinue put spurs to his horse. "Your Excellency."

The Bishop laid his hand on the horse's withers. "Stay on your mount, my friend. I would have you ride at once and rouse the captain of the guard. Tell him to see to it that the rabble are kept away from the palace. Then ask the canon whose charge it is what is happening in the seminarians' sleeping quarters." He looked around him. "Well, Master Isaac, I don't like the look of things. But we'll soon have the students off the plaza and into their beds. If you go straight across the square and down, you'll avoid the streets where the rabble from the town seem to be congregating. I'll send an escort with you."

"How goes the night?" asked Isaac.

"The first light of dawn is just edging the roofs."

"This cold wind and the light of day will bring the revelers to their senses," said Isaac. "I beg you not to disturb yourself. I know the city and, in the dark, see as well as any man sent to lead me."

"You are no doubt right, Master Isaac. The rising sun will chase them home in an hour or two. But I would be easier in my heart if I sent one or two with you."

"Your Excellency, it's time we were in our beds, and I fear I may have one more patient to visit before I sleep," said Isaac. "Let your long-suffering followers go to their beds as well. The Lord and my other senses will guide my footsteps. I shall be safe in the narrow alleys."

Isaac strode confidently across the square toward the stairs leading down to the Quarter, his staff in front of him, his feet on the cobbles telling him exactly where he was. When he reached the center, he paused. The noise was growing louder. His ears—sharper than the Bishop's—had located the two sources of sound—the drunken seminarians on the cathedral grounds and the townspeople congregating near the river—long before his friend had noticed a disturbance. Now he heard feet on the stone stairs that led up toward the cathedral. He heard doors and shutters opening, more footfalls, angry cries for quiet answered by loud curses. The situation had changed drastically in the last few minutes. If he continued on his path, he would walk right into a crowd of drunken revelers of uncertain disposition. He shifted direction, and headed on a diagonal toward the quietest corner of the plaza. When he was perhaps halfway along his new path, a stone landed close, bounced, rose, and hit him a painful blow on the arm. Automatically, he swerved from his path. Another stone landed on the other side of him with a sharp crack.

"It's a Jew," cried a drunken voice, and another stone whistled past his ear. "Kill him!" Then a volley of stones was let loose in his direction. Some landed on his back, and another on his arm. A fast-moving missile grazed his temple and sped harmlessly on. But when he raised his hand to his face, it came away warm and sticky with blood. He put his head down and quickened his pace.

Suddenly he was in the midst of a swirling crowd of angry stick-wielding men. He raised his staff, and a hand grabbed his cloak. He whirled around, jerking it free. Someone—his attacker?—stumbled. A voice near him cried out. "Marc, you drunken swine, get your hands off me."

He heard the sound of cloth tearing as a knife struck his cloak and he swung his staff angrily. It landed with a solid thud on something soft. There was a cry of pain. "I got him," said a triumphant voice, thickly.

"No, you haven't, you fool," said another. "That was me. You broke my arm."

A scuffle broke out somewhere close by.

"Over here," yelled a voice. Someone fell to the cobblestones with a crack. A hand grasped Isaac's upper arm. Once more he whirled around, lashing out with his staff. Suddenly there were hands grabbing at him from all directions. Gambling that his attackers were by and large shorter than he was, Isaac chopped down hard with his staff. It landed on target and was caught. He wrenched it loose, and swung it again with all his considerable strength. He jerked it free once more and smashed it down again. From across the plaza came the sound of hooves on the cobbles and shouts. The crowd began to move, dragging him inexorably across the plaza with them. Isaac tried to raise his staff and beat his way clear, but the press of stampeding panic-stricken bodies held his arms to his side like a set of iron bands.

He stumbled, recovered his footing again, and felt the stones under his feet change to an unfamiliar pattern. The crowd around him thinned momentarily. He reached out and touched a wall that was not the wall on the other side of the plaza. He paused, uncertain. The crowd began to press in on him once more. Then a small firm hand grasped his and pulled.

"This way, lord," said a voice close to his ear. "Quickly, before they tear you apart."

TWO

The insistent pressure of the small hand dragged Isaac, stumbling, bumping into people and things, scrambling down the stairs, next to walls that felt alien to his fingers, turning and twisting with no idea where he could be, and praying that the hand led him for good, and not for some evil purpose.

"Stand there, lord," said the voice, and pushed him into a doorway.

He stood a moment, and realized that he was alone, except for the owner of the hand. "To whom do I owe my poor life?" he asked.

"My name is Yusuf, lord."

"You bear a noble name, Yusuf, but you pronounce it, I think, in a Moorish fashion. Are you a Moor?"

"From Valencia, lord."

"And what is a Moorish lad named Yusuf doing in the middle of a riot, helping a Jew, on the eve of a Christian holy day? It is as dangerous for you to be here as it is for me."

"I am passing through, lord."

"From where to where, Yusuf? Where is your master?"

"I am my own master, lord."

"And for that you travel by night, do you? Then you had best spend the rest of this night safely behind my gates."

"Oh, no, lord. I can't do that." The voice was shrill with panic.

"Nonsense. Since you have lost my way for me, it is your duty to find it again. It is a grave offense to set a blind man out of his way."

"I did not know you were blind, lord," said Yusuf, his voice trembling. "I swear I will set you in your path."

"Don't worry. You shall take me to my gates and be free to fly away again when you will." He reached out his hand, and it was grasped once more by the smaller one.

"You are indeed blind, lord?" asked Yusuf, as soon as they were on their way down a quiet lane. "I thought you, too, were a stranger to the town, and it seemed cruel that the crowd should treat you like that." He stopped, and let go of Isaac's hand. "Where do we go?"

Isaac, mistrusting him still, reached out and touched a small, bare shoulder. It was painfully thin, and trembling with fear. "Can you find the gate to the Jewish Quarter? From there, I can lead you, and we shall break our fast together, with bread and fruit and soft cheeses, and rest for a while. Then you may leave on your journey."

"Yes, lord. I can take you through the alleys, where no one will see us, or care who we are."

Yusuf had been as good as his word, and now he stood, safe behind locked gates, in the courtyard of Isaac's domestic establishment. Against the south-facing wall was an arbor, with vines trailing over it, and a table beneath it, just visible in the light of early dawn. A fountain splashed softly in the center, making Yusuf faint with thirst.

"It is light, is it not?" asked Isaac.

"It is still night, lord," said the boy. "But in the east is the glow of dawn. The sun is an hour from rising. It is dark here."

"Are you frightened to wait here alone?"

"No, lord. It is safe in here."

"Good. Wait under the arbor. I shall return at once."

Isaac moved tirelessly up the stairs again, just as the cook descended from her chamber under the eaves with shuffling footsteps. "Naomi," he called softly.

There was a sharp intake of breath. "Lord in heaven, it's the master," she replied. "And hurt. The mistress will be—"

"The mistress is watching with the rabbi's wife. She will return soon, I expect. Can you bind my wound, and then send some bread and cheese and fruit down to a hungry pair? And a warm garment for a small person—about elbow-high," he added with a gesture, "would not go amiss."

"Certainly, Master," said the cook, reassured. "I—"

A burst of laughter, wild and undisciplined, interrupted whatever she had been planning to say. Isaac went to the window, unfastened the shutters, and leaned out. There was a sharp, echoing crack, and the rattling of broken tiles down to a cobbled yard. Naomi edged in beside him, almost thrusting him out of the way to look.

"Stones?" asked Isaac.

"Nay. Broken tiles," said Naomi. "A few stones." She brought her head in. "They're trying to kill us, Master," she added soberly.

All around them came the sound of breaking tiles. More laughter cascaded down from above. "It will take more than that," said Isaac. "Although I wouldn't like to be outside." He drew his head in.

That shower of unlikely rain was coming from the cathedral close. The Bishop or the canons were unlikely to be pelting the Quarter with stones and broken tiles. That left the seminarians, even worse for wine than they had been earlier. He pulled the shutters to. "Come. Bind up my wounds. My small friend and I are ready for our breakfast."

Yusuf sat under the colonnade that ran in a semicircle around the courtyard, listening to the attack on the Quarter.

The stout roof above him seemed well designed to cope with such puny weapons of war, and when the attackers gave up, he would move out under the arbor once again. He stared at the bunches of tiny, hard green grapes that dangled sourly from the vine, taunting him with his hunger, and rubbed his arms. His dark tunic had been cut out of warm cloth for the child he had been five years ago. Now the tattered fabric scarcely covered his thin arms, and his legs not at all. He was tired, and hungry, and very cold.

He couldn't believe what a fool he had been. Only a fool would allow himself to be lured inside a locked house by a blind man. He had watched the two men climbing up to the cathedral plaza, with their escort keeping watch on them from a discreet distance. Their sober dress and manner, and the armed guard that protected them, shouted wealth and importance. When the attack came, he had taken the hand of the tall man with the kind face because he had hoped for a coin or two in reward. He had meant to flee just before he was trapped, and his constant vigilance had slept for a moment. He wondered whether the blind man would keep him as a slave, or sell him, or give him over to the authorities. He had learned long ago that, kind faces or not, people offered to help him only if it was for their pleasure or convenience. He drew his bare legs and feet up under the tattered remains of his robe and wrapped his arms around them for warmth. He heard a thud beside him on the bench and turned his head. A small brown tabby cat with large golden eyes regarded him solemnly. Then the cat rubbed against his leg, and settled down with its warm head and paws stretched out on Yusuf's cold, cold feet.

The blind man returned, accompanied by a manservant holding up a tray of soft, flat bread, three kinds of cheese, dried dates and raisins, and a plate of almonds, fresh apricots, and other small fruit. Behind him, Naomi carried a steaming pitcher of a mint-scented herbal drink. Isaac had a pile of brown cloth over his arm. "Yusuf?" he said.

"I am here, lord," said Yusuf, uncurling himself and

standing up. He caught the avid look on the manservant's face and began to tremble.

"I believe we are safe from further attack from the heavens, or the top of the hill at any rate," said Isaac. "Shall we sit beneath the arbor and eat? I, at least, have been up most of the night, and have a hearty appetite." He shook out the cloth draped over his arm, and it turned into a loose-fitting mantle, generously cut in the sleeves and body. "Can you make use of this?" he asked. "I thought your own garments seemed small and worse for wear." He held it out. "Put it on. The dawn is chilly. And eat."

Don Tomas de Bellmunt, at three and twenty years of age secretary to Her Majesty, Eleanor of Sicily, Queen of Aragon, and Countess of Barcelona, rode up to a large oak in the meadowlands to the south of Girona, and dismounted, frowning. He was feeling definitely irritable. He had ridden more than six miles on an empty stomach that morning, prepared at every moment to meet death or disaster, and found—nothing. The rendezvous point outside the south gate to the city was deserted. He glanced at the sky. It was bright to the east, and the first rays of the rising sun touched the hills behind the city. Girona looked to be asleep still.

A clatter of hoofbeats behind him startled him and he whirled around, his hand on his half-drawn sword. His manservant slid rapidly from his saddle. "Señor. My apologies. I was delayed."

"Where is Doña Sanxia?"

"That is the reason for the delay. She was not at our meeting place, nor could I discover any sign of her. Then I thought that she might have come directly here to meet Your Lordship."

"Where were you to have met her?"

"Outside the city walls. At a deserted hovel." He waved his hand in a vaguely northeast direction. "I've been waiting for her there since first light. She may have come to some harm—there were riots in the town last night. Shall I go back, señor, and inquire for her?"

"No, you fool," snapped Tomas. "She's not supposed to be anywhere near Girona this morning."

Romeu bowed and remained silent.

"For a full hour after sunrise," said Bellmunt, "we wait, rest our horses, and try not to attract attention. Then we return to Barcelona."

"Without her?" said Romeu, shocked.

"Without her." Bellmunt's jaw tightened stubbornly.

"Her Majesty will surely wonder——"

Bellmunt stared off into the forested land beyond the town, as if hoping that some solution to his dilemma would come riding out of the dark woodlands. Her Majesty surely would wonder why he had left Doña Sanxia in Girona and ridden off without even a token attempt to find her. Or would she be even angrier if he compromised the secrecy of their enterprise by trying to find the missing lady? He turned to look at the sunrise. Romeu was probably right. He usually was. "Then go into town, if you like," said Bellmunt, "and look around, but for God's sake, man, be discreet. And be quick about it. I will stay here with the horses."

Sunlight stabbing directly in his eyes forced Big Johan into consciousness of a sort. With consciousness came feeling; and with feeling, misery. Johan's head throbbed to the point of explosion; his mouth was as dry as the deserts of Arabia.

Then fragments of memory detached themselves from the confusion. Last night when he had gone out, his purse had been heavy with coins. And last night he drank prodigious amounts of cheap, raw wine. He felt for his purse, hanging inside his loose tunic, with terror in his heart.

The purse was still there and full. That was odd. He remembered, uneasily, a gentleman buying wine for him, but surely the tavern keepers had not been giving their wares away all night. He had disjointed memories of a crowd of hell-raisers rampaging through the city, and dragging him along. His last memory was of stretching out in a quiet corner by the Baths. How did he come to be in his own bed? With the sun in his eyes?

"Holy Virgin," he cried aloud. "The Baths."

The Arab Baths had been Big Johan's life since the day he first stepped inside them, twenty years ago—the year of the Great Hunger. His parents had either died or thrown him on the streets, and Old Pedro, the Keeper of the Baths, had found him on the feast day of Sant Johan, crying with hunger. He had taken him in, named him Johan after the day, given him bread and cheese and a thick pallet of straw to sleep on, and set him to work with him at the Baths. He had been so small that he had to climb on a stool to see over the edge of the baths. The patrons had laughed, and dubbed him Big Johan, and given him coins to spend or to save, as he liked. For the first time in his life he had decent clothes on his back and enough food to fill his belly. Ten years later, Big Johan had grown into his name, and towered over his master. When Old Pedro died, the respected physician who enjoyed the privileges and responsibilities of managing the Baths granted the hovel and the position of keeper to the young Johan. For ten years, he had been at his post before the bell for prime sounded at the convent. He unlocked the building, swept the floors and cleaned the baths, and then watched over them until vespers—and occasionally, by very special arrangement, even later—when he closed and locked the building for the night. It was a position of importance and responsibility. God had dropped it in his lap twenty years ago, in his hour of need; now Johan had tossed it aside like an old cabbage leaf. He moaned.

He staggered up from his bed. Despair gripped his soul, and sickness his belly. He stepped outside and got rid of the remains of last night's excesses. His belly felt considerably better, and despair lost a little ground. If he hurried, perhaps no one would notice how late he was. After all, most of the town had been up half the night, swimming in wine.

He stumbled down the path, lurching between trees and bushes, tripping over roots, mouth dry and stomach uneasy still. He reached for his key, which for ten years had hung on the ring that dangled from his waist.

The ring was empty.

He sat down by the door, staring at the ring. It was still empty. Perhaps he dropped the key last night. He fell to his knees and searched. No sign of it. Maybe it was inside. He opened the door and began to search. It took some time, in his pitiable state, for Johan to realize that without the key he should not be inside the Baths.

Johan pulled himself up from his knees and sat down heavily on a wooden bench at the foot of the steps leading down from the door. He looked around, bewildered. Soft green light filtered in through the apertures high up in the domed ceiling, bounced off the blue-and-white tiles, and shimmered on the white pillars that encircled the main bath, rising up to the dome. Even as it had done on that day twenty years ago, when he had first seen it, the light bathed his troubled soul in peace. Here, surrounded by beauty, he was safe. Automatically, he stood and picked up his broom. He moved over to the far side of the room, and began to sweep conscientiously toward the door. When he reached the bath in the center of the room, he stepped up to its edge, gripping a cool pillar, and leaned over. The feel of the stone under his hand, and the sight of the clear water on the brilliant tiles, were to him more beautiful than the high arches, rich tapestry, and brightly colored windows of the cathedral.

Then he widened his eyes and blinked, twice. The cool, clear water of the bath was black and no longer translucent.

In it, half floating and half resting on the bottom, was a Benedictine nun, lying facedown, her black robes spread out like a thundercloud about her.

THREE

Big Johan plunged his brawny arms into the water, grasped the nun, and pulled. As he hauled up the dripping bundle a cry of pure joy burst out of him. He draped the creature unceremoniously over the edge, reached down again, and fished a key off the bottom. His nightmare was over. The key to the Baths was restored.

On the other hand, the water in the bath was ominously pink in color. He stepped back and looked at the sister, flopped on the edge of the bath. There were signs around the head and shoulders that her body had begun to stiffen. She was definitely a corpse from which the soul had fled some time ago. He picked her up and laid her on her back on the floor. Her wimple, horribly stained, was torn and put aside, revealing a gaping wound in her throat. Big Johan shook his head. He pulled the wet cloth across her throat, arranged her limbs and habit in a seemly manner, and after thinking the matter over for a while, set out to ask the Bishop what he should do.

Isaac spent the last hours of the long night at Reb Samuel's house. He sent his yawning wife home as soon as he arrived, and did what he could for the baby with the help of the maidservant.

It was not enough. The infant's struggles for breath grew weaker and weaker. The distraught mother clung to Isaac's arm, begging him to lay his hands on the child and pray, to bring it back to life and health.

"Oh, Mistress," said Isaac, in deep distress. "I have no prayers that will rescue a soul from death."

"We will pay," she said, desperately. "Gold. All we have. Anything."

"If I had such power, I would use it gladly, and not accept a dish of lentils in payment. But I do not."

"It's not true," she whispered. "Everyone knows you are the successor, the incarnation of the great Master Isaac of the Kaballah, and have his powers. That is why your sight was taken. As a sign. Please—try."

Isaac shuddered in alarm. These whispers had come to his ears before, from the lips of the credulous, but to hear them from the rabbi's wife was another matter. "Do not say such foolish things, woman. They are dangerous. I am just a man, and do what I can do. No more. And do not let your husband hear you utter such blasphemies."

"It was he who told me," said the woman. "But I have no power to force you. I can only ask and pray," she said bitterly.

Isaac laid the dead child in his cradle. "There is nothing more that I or any man can do," he said. "He is dead, Mistress. Someday soon you will have another son to bring you joy, I promise you."

Her cries brought comforters crowding into the room. Amid the turmoil, Isaac put on his cloak, feeling guilty of some great betrayal, and left.

Judith should be back in her bed, and Yusuf, fed and warm, asleep in the small chamber off his study. With luck, Isaac would be able to slip into his study and snatch an hour or two of rest before returning to the convent. Very quietly, he unlocked the gate.

The courtyard seemed empty of human occupants. The songbirds in their hanging cage were competing with their

wild cousins to fill the space with sound. The flowers
opened in the sun, and filled the air with scent. Feliz, the
cat, jumped down from somewhere, landing on the ground
with a thud and a cry of welcome. From the top of the
house came the high-pitched shrieks of the twins quarreling, and Leah, their nursemaid, trying vainly to quiet them.
Savory odors and the sound of clanging pots and women's
laughter drifted down from the kitchen. Judith, resilient as
ever, apparently recovered from the rigors of the night, was
working and gossiping with Naomi. For the moment, they
lived their safe, and happy, and prosperous lives behind the
illusion of security that the protection of powerful men
offered them. But even so had the Jews of Barcelona, and
the Moors of Valencia lived, and now . . . Isaac considered
the events of the night and shook his head grimly. Then he
walked silently under the fruit trees and into his sanctuary.
Wrapping his cloak about him, for the morning was still
cool, he lay down on his narrow couch and fell at once to
sleep.

"Your Excellency," said the voice. "Your Excellency," it
persisted.

Bishop Berenguer de Cruilles opened an eye and repressed the irritable response that rose to his lips. Not for
the first time did he wish that his canons could handle small
emergencies without seeking his approval for every action.
"Yes, Francesc, my son. What is it now?"

Francesc Monterranes repressed his own twinge of irritation. He, too, had been up most of the night, dealing with
a pack of overgrown, drunken irresponsible fifteen-year-
olds, dignified by the name of seminarians. But as Canon
Vicar, he was not supposed to be affected by such transitory
discomforts as the loss of a few hours of sleep. "My apologies for disturbing you, Your Excellency. But there is a
person outside who wishes to speak to you most urgently."

"A person? What kind of person?"

"One known as Big Johan, who is—"

"I know who he is, Francesc. What brings him here?"

A lay brother had entered the Bishop's chamber, and was

stumbling awkwardly about, opening shutters and officiously moving things from place to place. Francesc Monterranes glanced briefly in his direction, and then leaned over to whisper Big Johan's grim news.

Berenguer gave it a few seconds' consideration. "Who else knows this?" he asked in a murmur, and pointed to the carved wooden peg on which his sober black robe was hanging.

"No one, Your Excellency," said the canon, very softly. He fetched the Bishop's robe and helped him into it. "The Keeper of the Baths is a silent and prudent man."

"And one whose head is the worse for wine this morning, I suspect," said Berenguer, his fingers automatically doing up the long row of buttons that stretched from chin to knees. "I distinctly remember seeing his delicate form stumbling about the plaza, singing bawdy songs, when we were dragged from our beds to deal with the seminarians."

"Do you think he—"

"No. I think he was too drunk to formulate the intention to piss, much less to murder a nun in his baths." Berenguer de Cruilles and Francesc Monterranes had long been friends. The Bishop turned to the jug of water and towel laid out for him. "I must wash a little wakefulness into me, and then we will see this keeper before breaking our fast."

Berenguer's private study was bare and fortresslike. Only a rudely fashioned crucifix—carved for him when he was a boy, by a gardener on his family's estate—adorned its plastered walls. The room contained a writing table, three chairs, and a shelf for his private collection of books. At one end of the shelf was a set of sermons and *exempla,* those lively moral tales without which a sermon would seem dull and unadorned, and at the other, a volume of the works of the Angelic Doctor, Thomas Aquinas. Nestled between them lay further witnesses to the Bishop's mind and heart: tales of chivalry, love lyrics, philosophical and scientific works, in Catalan and Castilian, Provençal, Latin, and Greek. The documents on the writing table were

weighted down with a bleached, aged skull, inherited from
Arnau Montrodo, his predecessor. "He felt his successor
would need reminding that he was mortal man first, then
priest, and last of all, bishop," he would say, wryly, to
those few who ever saw the room.

These walls were solid; the doors were oak, and firmly
fastened shut. One led to a main corridor; the other was
locked and barred, never opened, and led to an unused
chamber next to the study. Conversations in this room were
not likely to be overheard.

Berenguer de Cruilles sat down by the window; Francesc
Monterranes locked the door, removed the key, and handed
it to the Bishop. He gestured at Big Johan to sit, and then
seated himself on the remaining chair. Big Johan clutched
his hands; the Bishop yawned; the canon leaned forward
encouragingly. "Tell His Excellency what happened. What
you told me."

Johan plunged into his narrative with desperate haste. "I
was late in opening the Baths this morning. The first time
in twenty years, Excellency," he added, with a tentative
glance at his interrogators.

"Indeed," said Berenguer.

"I come there late, well after prime, and unlock the door
as usual," he went on, the sweat beading on his forehead
and pouring down his back from the effort of lying to these
two grave men. "I start my sweeping, and as I go near the
central bath I notice something black, like. I go closer and
see the poor soul. I fetch her out and lay her on the floor
as neat as I can. I come here to report it. Her being a nun."

"Rather than going to the convent?" asked the Canon
Vicar.

The Keeper of the Baths gave him a look of alarm. "To
Lady Elicsenda?" he asked. "Oh, no. I wouldn't disturb
Lady Elicsenda."

"Coward," said the Bishop cheerfully. "Did you recognize this nun?"

"I never seen her before," said Johan promptly.

"Then we should see who she is—or was," said the
Bishop. "Come along, and let us look at your dead lady."

• • •

"Do you know her?" asked Berenguer.

The Canon Vicar shook his head.

"Nor I," said the Bishop. "Odd. There are only twelve of them right now. I would have thought that between the two of us, we had seen all of the sisters at one time or another. Tell the men to come in. We will have her remains taken to the convent."

The morning chill was disappearing. The June sun rose into a cloudless sky. The countryside was alive with birdsong and the scent of lavender in bloom. Tomas de Bellmunt, still outside the walls of Girona, sat under a tree and tried to think of nothing. The horses—his own and Romeu's—cropped the grass and drifted in and out of equine semi-consciousness. Somewhere bells rang for tierce.

He was in the worst of all possible positions. He was as bold and courageous a man as any, but what monumental stupidity had dragged him to Girona at risk of both life and honor? The simple answer was Doña Sanxia de Baltier. Her thick red tresses and angelic countenance had snared him like a rabbit. She had confided to Tomas Her Majesty's plan to move the Prince to a place of greater safety, and had begged him to lend her Romeu to help. Then she asked him to abandon his post without leave and come to Girona. He must have been mad. So here he sat uselessly under a tree in a meadow, in charge of the horses, not daring to go near the town in case someone recognized him.

And where was Romeu? Tomas stirred uneasily in the hot sun, and swatted ineffectually at the persistent, biting flies the horses had attracted. How well did he know his manservant? When Bellmunt had first come to the Queen's service, his uncle had recommended the man, saying he was clever, quick, and trustworthy, and would keep him out of trouble among the intrigues of the court. But what if someone offered Romeu a well-filled purse and a better post to betray his new master and the mad enterprise he was embarked on? Gloom settled over him.

Then he noticed a figure in azure hose and a black-and-

azure tunic, fitting with fashionable tightness and belted
low around the hips, moving smartly along the road from
the south gate. "You have been an infernally long time,
Romeu," he called out. "You could have collected the life
histories of all the good citizens of Girona by now."

"News was difficult to smell out, señor," said Romeu,
rather breathlessly. "The riots have stilled the gossips'
tongues. But there are a few things being said in the
streets."

"Well? What are they?"

"Everyone is convinced that our young prince, the Duke
of Girona, is here in the city, but very ill, close to death."

"That isn't news," said Bellmunt impatiently. "Every-
one knows he was moved to Girona for his health. That he
is near death is a malicious rumor being spread by Don
Pedro's brother, Prince Fernando. Not that it would help
Fernando get nearer the throne if the Prince should die.
Doña Eleanor will bear many sons."

Romeu listened to this rousing declaration with a look
of supreme boredom. "Do you want the other news? It was
more difficult to collect."

"Of course."

"The body of a Benedictine nun was discovered in the
Arab Baths. Opinion in the market is that she took her own
life."

"Holy Mother of God," said Tomas, with sinking heart.
"Is it Doña Sanxia?"

Romeu shrugged his shoulders. "The person who told
me didn't know who she was."

"It is Doña Sanxia," said Tomas. "Nothing else would
have kept her from our appointment."

"Shall I go back to Girona, señor, and see what can be
discovered?"

"No, you fool. We must return to Barcelona at once, and
tell Her Majesty," said Bellmunt. "Wait—I have a better
idea. I'll ride to Barcelona. You stay in Girona and find out
what you can. I'll return the day after tomorrow. Wait for
me under this tree, say—at sundown."

"Earlier would be better, señor," said Romeu. "After

sunset, our movements in and out of the city will be more closely remarked upon.''

"It will be a hard ride,'' said Tomas, patting his muscular stallion.

"Not for Arcont, señor,'' said Romeu. "Over a distance, there is no speedier animal in all Cataluña. If you leave Barcelona at sunrise, he will have you here long before vespers. I will wait for you until sundown.''

"Otherwise, return to the palace as quickly as possible.''

"Yes, señor,'' said Romeu.

"What do you mean, the child is not here? Where is he?'' The wife of the castellan stared in alarm at the woman in front of her. "It is time to send the pony cart for the physician.''

"I don't know, madam. We thought he was out with his nursemaid, and the groom. Jaume spends a lot of time with the boy.'' The servant girl clutched her apron in panic.

"Out? Out where?''

"I don't know. I went to the stables, but I didn't see Jaume or Maria. They weren't down by the river either.''

"Is he with the friar?''

"Oh, no, madam. The friar is still in his bed. I believe he was out late last night celebrating the saint. With his fellow priests, no doubt,'' she added maliciously.

"Well, get him out of his bed, you fool!'' She stopped to think. "He must be with Maria. When did she go out?''

"I don't know,'' she said again. Tears poured down her cheeks. "I went to their rooms, madam, to tidy and sweep, and they were gone.''

The chatelaine of the small castle grabbed her by the arm and shook her. "How long have you known he was missing?''

She was answered by a wail. "Since breakfast, madam.''

"Breakfast!''

"But he likes to eat his breakfast outside. They sit by the river—him and Maria—and feed the birds and the fish.''

"Fetch your master, and the groom, at once. And the friar. Run, you stupid creature!"

The small noises of daily life in the courtyard broke through Isaac's dreams and dragged him from the velvety blackness of unconsciousness slashed with remembered colors to the blackness of daily life. And to judge by the temperature inside his study, the sun was high in the heavens. He rose stiffly, painfully aware of his bruised back and arms, and began simple preparations for his morning prayers. The murmur of his own voice speaking the ancient phrases comforted him in his darkness and gave a momentary sense of order to the chaos threatening from every side. Then, as he reached for a towel, his hand brushed against a misplaced cup. He could feel it tip. In trying to grasp it, he sent it hurtling to its doom. The illusion was over. A curse, hastily suppressed, sprang to his lips.

The noise evoked a panicked cry from the small chamber next to him. "Yusuf?" he called.

There was a muffled sound in reply.

"In here you will find water for washing," he said with his usual calm. "I shall be in the courtyard." And he went out.

Judith's voice stabbed at him out of the darkness. "Why is your head bandaged, husband?"

"I have a small cut. It is nothing."

"I heard you speaking to someone," she said, and paused for an answer. "It is true, then."

"The morning seems pleasant, my love," said Isaac, and made his way to the bench under the arbor. "Would you fetch me a cup of water?" He paused long enough for the request to distract her a little. "And what is true?" he asked innocently.

Her soft leather shoes slapped on the paving stones, and her skirts swished angrily around her as she fetched water from the fountain and brought it to him. "That you have brought home a beggar, a Moorish beggar, who will steal all we have and murder us in our beds. And that you have given him a very good mantle, and food, and Ibrahim's old bed. And how we are to afford it, I don't know, with taxation on us going up again, they say—''

"Ibrahim used to spend every night walking back and forth between his chamber and my study to make sure I was alive and well and still at home. If he had continued to sleep there, I might have murdered him, and brought evil on the house," said Isaac mildly. "The child, Yusuf, is quiet."

"Quiet, indeed. Sly and thieving. Waiting until we are not watching him, and then—''

"We owed him the food and a bed for saving my life. On my way home, I stumbled into a mob in the cathedral square."

"The Lord save us all," said Judith, with a gasp. "A mob? In Girona? They'll murder us, and burn our houses, like Barcelona. Oh, husband, we must gather up the twins and all we can carry— But what happened?"

"Calm yourself. It was naught but a drunken rabble. In it were a few stone throwers. The boy, Yusuf, came out and took my hand, and led me to safety. He proved you right, wife. You have always wished I would take a trusted guide with me when I am outside the Quarter."

"Why didn't you wake me? Were you hurt? Did a stone hit your brow?"

"You were away from home, with the rabbi's wife. And several stones hit me, but they were thrown by poor marksmen, much confused by drink." He smiled and gently touched Judith's cheek. "Yusuf had no desire to accompany me here, but he led me through so many passages that I became confused, and I forced him, with high moral arguments, to take me to the Quarter. I perceived how hungry and tired and cold he was, and how young, and brought him in, reluctant as he was."

"He is a runaway slave, then. We shall be dragged before the Albedín and lose all we have for—''

"Hush, love. I think it more likely that he is an orphan who lost his parents in the time of the pestilence. It hit Valencia very hard. As hard as it hit us. I would guess that he has been living on his wits since then. He seemed to be bare-limbed, in rags, and although I did not ask, I surmise he was near bare-bottomed as well. What clothing he had was doubtless made for a much younger child. A master would surely have supplied him with garments that would cover his nakedness decently.''

"He is a Moor," said Judith, stubbornly.

"He is," said Isaac. "But perhaps not a thief or a murderer."

The door opened, and Yusuf emerged. Standing in front of Judith was a boy of ten or twelve years, painfully thin, with ragged long hair and a face that had just been scrubbed. His eyes were large and filled with fear, but he held his head high, and stood erect. In spite of the unkempt hair, and dirty limbs, and a mantle much too large for him, he was a beautiful child.

"Who are you?" asked Judith. "And where are you from?"

"I am Yusuf," said the boy. "And I have traveled from Valencia."

"That far? Alone? I don't believe it."

"Yes. Alone."

"Who is your master?"

"I am my own master."

"How have you stayed free, if indeed you are free?" asked Judith, in her prosecutor's voice.

"I am free," said Yusuf. "Three times I was taken by thieves and slave traders, and each time I escaped. The first time was easy; the man was drunk, but after that it was more difficult. It is to my shame that I was taken at last by a blind man because he has a kind face."

"Hush, child," said Judith quickly. "You are free to go whenever you wish. You need not stay here, looking for what you may steal."

Yusuf's eyes strayed to the remains of the loaf and a few dates that sat on the table under the arbor. "I do not steal," he said, offended. "Except sometimes scraps of food for hunger's sake. Nothing else."

"Not very likely," said Judith. "Remember—I will harbor no thieves in this household."

The two combatants glared wordlessly at each other, Yusuf with his chin high, Judith bending toward him.

Isaac broke into the momentary stillness. "If you wish to pause in your travels for a day or more, and work for your keep and the clothing you wear," he said, "I have need of a quick, careful messenger who can take me through the town and keep me from trouble." He turned toward his wife. "Is that not true?"

"Someone, yes," said Judith. "But—"

"Until you are ready to continue on your journey," said Isaac. "A boy like you in this household is clothed decently and shod, and gets his keep. And at year's end, another suit of clothes and a silver groat."

"Isaac!"

"But you do not wish to stay until year's end. So you must make do with food and clothing."

Judith continued to glare at Yusuf, but spoke to her husband. "If he is to stay another night, Ibrahim must take him to the Baths. He is in no fit state to be seen with my husband."

"But first," said Isaac, "clean or dirty, I wish him to go with me to the convent this morning. We will stop at the Baths on our way back."

The door closed behind Isaac and the boy. "I know the quickest way to the convent, lord," said Yusuf, taking the physician by the hand.

"Patience, Yusuf. The convent is not our only destination. We have other errands this morning," said Isaac. "First the market, and then I would pay a visit to a scribe."

"I know a scribe in the *alcaicería,* lord. Shall I take you to him?"

"This is a particular scribe, Yusuf, whose business keeps him at the Bishop's palace and the courts of law. To visit his house, we must go to Sant Feliu. If you are to be my trusted guide," he added, "you must, of necessity, be the guardian of my secrets at times. Are you to be my guide?"

he asked. "Will you postpone your journey for a time?"

Yusuf paused. "How long is a time? For I have a solemn promise to keep, lord."

"Long enough for you to rest and eat and grow a little. Shall we say at the third full moon from the one that shines four days from now?"

"And then you will release me?"

"I do not hold you now, Yusuf. But then I will hasten you on your journey if that is what you wish. That is my promise. Now—will you be my trusted guide and keeper of my secrets?"

Yusuf looked at the blind man's slightly ironic smile and shook his head. "I do not know, lord," he said, in a troubled voice. "Men do not usually entrust their secrets to me. Not since—" His voice died. "Will you be taken before the judge, like a thief or a slave, if I say where you go and what you do?"

"No," said Isaac, with a laugh. "Only before that most terrible of judges, my wife."

"I can surely keep a secret from her, lord," said Yusuf. "It is easy to keep secrets from your enemies."

"She is your mistress for the time being, Yusuf, not your enemy. She will soon grow to appreciate you. She is not quick to trust people." They went out the south end of the Quarter into the working heart of the city, with its jostling, noisy crowds of buyers and sellers, Jews and Christians, laughing, arguing, and bargaining at the tops of their voices for exotic imported merchandise and finely crafted local wares. The heady scents of dyed woolen cloth and fine worked leather drifted past Isaac like a map, telling him precisely whose shop they were passing. He let his hand rest very lightly on Yusuf's shoulder as they made their way through the market vendors' stalls, until they reached the seller of spices. Isaac stopped to buy fresh ginger and cinnamon to strengthen Lady Isabel's appetite and hurried Yusuf on until they were through the north gate. "Now we stop at the house of the scribe, Nicholau, on our way to the convent. Turn up the road by the cobbler's shop. There lives my daughter Rebecca."

They moved in silence for a while. "This is my secret, boy," Isaac continued at last. "My daughter has married a Christian, and has become a *conversa*. You understand what that is?"

"Yes, lord. We have them, too."

"Her small son, too, is a Christian. My wife has never seen him. Your mistress is a very religious, virtuous woman, Yusuf. Many times more religious and virtuous than I am. She may speak sharp and unkind words, but she will not maltreat you, because you are a child, and at least temporarily in her service, and it is her duty to treat you with kindness. But she is as hard as stone where she believes herself to be right. I, myself," he added thoughtfully, "who have studied much, and—when I could still see— read the words of great philosophers, and studied the secrets of the great mystics, have never achieved that much certainty concerning what is truth, and what is righteousness. We turn here."

Isaac walked a short distance and paused. From the house in front of them came the sounds of a quarrel reaching its apex. "Then leave, you drunken sot," shrieked a woman's voice. A baby cried. A pale, disheveled young man stumbled out the door and into the street. Without a glance around him, he turned in the direction of the north gate and the cathedral.

"You will wait outside, I think," said Isaac, and walked up to the door. It opened.

"Papa. It's you," said the pretty woman on the doorstep, and burst into tears. The door closed.

Yusuf settled himself on the stoop to wait.

Abbess Elicsenda shook her head in dismay. "She is indeed of our order. Look at her habit. But I have not seen her before."

"Could she have traveled from Tarragona? Had you word of anyone?"

"Traveling alone? Remember that our sisters do not wander the highways and footpaths like mendicant friars, Your Excellency." She stood aside to let the light fall on

the face. "She has a familiar air, but I don't recognize her.
I know many of our sisters in Tarragona, and she is not
one of them."

"I would sooner believe her not to be a nun," said Berenguer de Cruilles, "than to believe that you wouldn't recognize one of your flock."

The Abbess gave him a searching look. "Nun or not,"
she said quietly, "how did she get inside the Baths?
They're locked at night, are they not?"

"I am afraid their honest watchdog was celebrating the
festival of his namesake, good Sant Johan, and was betrayed by Brother Grape last night. Along with a good
many other people," said the Bishop. "But how *did* she
come to be in the Baths?" he asked suddenly. "How many
keys are there?" He turned to Johan, who was huddling
miserably near the doorway.

"Only mine, Your Excellency," said Johan, swallowing
hard. "And my master's, but he's off in the country somewhere."

"We know about that. And you locked the Baths last
night?"

"Yes, Your Excellency."

"And gave no one the key?"

"Yes, Your Excellency. I mean, no. I gave the key to
no man."

"Or woman? And how would you know, Johan? When
I saw you last night, you didn't know your own name,
much less where your keys were. How do you know someone didn't steal them from you, and return them while you
slept?"

"I don't know, Your Excellency." The sweat poured
from his brow.

The Abbess intervened swiftly. "Thank you, Johan, for
your assistance and your honest testimony. Sor Marta will
see that you are refreshed. You may go now." She waited
until he had been handed over and the door closed before
turning back to the Bishop. "I cannot imagine a desperate
woman searching that man for his keys in order to get into
the Baths just to do away with herself."

"You are assuming that she cut her own throat, Lady Elicsenda?" asked Berenguer.

"And then threw herself into the bath? I think not. But the alternative is difficult to contemplate."

"Was she a nun?" asked the Bishop.

"We shall see," said Elicsenda. She moved aside the stained and torn wimple with one finger, pushed back the veil, and pulled out a long, thick lock of red hair. "No," she said coolly, holding it up for the Bishop's inspection. "Not with this hair. Or perhaps I should say it's unlikely."

"Then why did she dress herself as a nun in order to meet her death?"

"That I cannot say," said the Abbess. "Unless it was to pass more easily through the streets unnoticed."

But the Bishop was concentrating on the sodden pallid face of the dead woman, and scarcely noticed the Abbess's response. "There is something familiar about her," said Berenguer. "Can you remove her wimple and veil?"

"I shall do it, Lady Elicsenda." Sor Agnete lifted the stiffened body enough to unfasten the strings and pins of her head coverings and, with great care, pulled veil and wimple away. She arranged the thick hair as neatly as she could, and straightened her habit.

The Bishop drew in his breath sharply and stepped back, as if to distance himself from the figure on the table. "I would prefer that this body had been found elsewhere," he said at last.

"Who is she, Your Excellency?" asked Sor Agnete.

"This puts us in a very troubling situation," murmured the Abbess.

"One that could hardly be worse," said Berenguer. "The manner of her death has somewhat distorted it, but there is only one woman in this country with that face—and that hair," he said. "I was blinded by the trappings of a nun."

"As no doubt she intended you to be," said the Abbess.

"But why should the Doña Eleanor's chief lady-in-waiting come to Girona dressed as a nun?"

"To seek concealment in my convent," said Elicsenda. Angry patches of scarlet bloomed in her cheeks. "When the bloody intrigues of the court reach into the cloister and affect my nuns, something must be done.''

Berenguer de Cruilles looked at the two women. ''And will be done, at the proper time,'' he said. ''It would be unwise, I think, to mention her name or the manner of her death to anyone as yet, until we can find out more about it,'' said the Bishop. ''How long has she been dead?''

''Her body is stiff,'' said Sor Agnete. ''But the physician is here to see to the Lady Isabel. Perhaps he can say more.''

''He is no gossip,'' said the Abbess. ''Let him be summoned. When he has examined the body, it is to be prepared and conveyed decently to the chapel. We shall pray for her soul with the same fervor and ceremony that we would use for one of our own sisters in Christ.''

''Very commendable,'' said Berenguer. ''And prudent, too, of course.'' He looked down at the dead woman again. ''I would like to speak to the physician. Then I will bring him to look at the body.''

Isaac felt the head and jaw of the dead woman and stepped back. He brought his fingers to his nose and sniffed. ''I can tell you that she was killed between laud and prime, as you name the hours.''

''You are very precise, Master Isaac. Can you be sure of that?'' asked the Abbess.

''Very sure. The sisters were singing laud when we left the convent last night. At almost that same moment, this lady rushed by us. She was alive then. Johan said he found her soon after prime. She was dead then.''

''I didn't see her,'' said Berenguer.

''I'm sure she took care that you would not. But either she knew of my blindness, or took you to be the more dangerous witness. When Sor Marta opened the convent door for us, this lady ran out, brushing between me and the doorway, and leaving a strong scent behind her of musk, and jasmine, and fear. All that is left now is the musk and jasmine in her hair. The fear has died with her.''

''She *was* in the convent, then, disguised as one of our sisters,'' said the Abbess.

"Surely one of us would have seen her," said Sor Agnete.

"It could be done if she had a friend who was shielding her," said the Abbess. "There are rooms in the new section where the workmen are finished. No one enters them except with the architect to inspect them. She could have been hidden there."

"But to what end?" asked Sor Agnete. "Why hide in the convent? A lady requiring sanctuary must have known it would be granted."

"For no good purpose, Agnete," said the Abbess impatiently. "But who is to discover the reason, Berenguer? My nuns cannot go about the town, seeking out those who would take advantage of our refuge."

"Very true," said the Bishop. "I will send my officers—"

"Forgive me for intruding on your deliberations," said Isaac, "but the Bishop's officers are as well known as you, yourself, madam, or His Excellency. If they inquire after nuns and strangers, the town will talk of nothing else. But I go everywhere, and ask anyone anything. I will take on the task of finding out what I can, and report to you."

"That is kind of you, Master Isaac," said the Abbess, doubtfully.

"May I have a word with you, my lady?" said Berenguer. He stepped out into the corridor, and the Abbess followed. "The physician's offer is a very interesting one. You might be well advised to consider it."

"But, Your Excellency, consider who he is. Surely a matter pertaining to the reputation of the Church should be in the hands of one of us."

"Not if we are unable to carry it out, Lady Elicsenda."

"Very well, Lord Berenguer," said the Abbess, with an on-your-head-be-it look, and swept back into the room. "Tell me, Master Isaac," she said, "how you could look into a matter so centered in the convent. I fear you would have no opportunity to make inquiries."

"All manner of people are my patients, and few have

the wit to fear a blind man's scrutiny. But, as you know, my ears are very acute.''

"All alone?'' she asked. "Without the gift of sight to aid you?''

"Raquel is my eyes, my lady, and while she is looking after Lady Isabel I have a small helper, with sharp eyes and quick feet. Between us, there is nowhere we cannot go, and nothing we cannot observe, except within your doors. When I hear why the great lady behaved so strangely, and by whose hand she met her death, I will let you know.''

"Then we accept your offer of assistance most thankfully, Master Isaac,'' said Elicsenda gracefully.

"I'm afraid your inquiries might lead you into perilous territories, friend Isaac,'' said the Bishop. "Should you need my officers, send your quick-footed helper for them. Give them this.'' And Berenguer handed Isaac a ring.

The physician traced the pattern on the gold with his fingertips. "Are you sure you wish to trust me with this?''

"I have already trusted you with more than a mere symbol of family wealth, my friend. I have trusted you with my life and with the life of my beloved niece. That ring is a toy in comparison.''

FOUR

On the grounds belonging to the small castle, a group of men and several dogs fanned out near the river, searching through grass and undergrowth. Don Aymeric, the castellan, stood back on a rise, scanning the heavens.

"By blessed Saint Anthony, do something. Don't just stand there, gawking at nothing," said his wife, Urraca, desperately. Ahead of her, she could see nothing but ruin for them, and panic made her shrewish. "You will never find the Prince by looking at the sky."

"No, but he will find birds, Doña Urraca."

Don Aymeric's wife gasped in fear, and then turned and dropped a hasty curtsy to a tall man, wearing the habit of a Franciscan, who had appeared on the rise as if by magic. "Birds, my lord Count?"

"Certainly, madam. Always look for birds during a hunt. Your quarry will be found where they are rising. Is that not so, Don Aymeric?"

"Indeed, my lord. And if we listen," he added impatiently, "we might hear the child. Or Petronella. She'll bark when she picks up the scent."

"The Prince does not cry easily," said his wife, shaking her head.

"My temporary charge is courageous," said the Franciscan politely, and turned to the castellan. "I think perhaps we should coordinate the hunt," he murmured. "This is my fault, not yours. I heard people abroad in the night, and kept watch outside his tower, but when all seemed quiet, I confess I, too, sought my bed. It was a mistake." He looked down at his friar's habit. "These garments are awkward for hunting, whether game or man, but I think I will keep to my disguise for the moment."

"Certainly, my lord."

"Have you found his nursemaid?"

"The lazy slut has disappeared," said Doña Urraca. "And Jaume, the groom. I don't trust him. Whenever you turn a corner, there he is, listening at doors and spying."

"Miquel has gone toward town to look for him," murmured Don Aymeric.

"Miquel has trouble finding his dinner on the plate," said Doña Urraca bitterly.

"Then I shall help him as soon as my horse is saddled." And Count Hug de Castellbo strode off to the stables, looking very unlike a friar, in spite of his habit.

"And we will continue the search from here." Don Aymeric turned his eyes to the sky again, but they were as bleak and hopeless as his wife's earthbound gaze.

"How is Lady Isabel?" asked Isaac, closing the door to the sick chamber behind him and walking softly over to the bed.

"Sleeping," his daughter replied. "She awakened once, and drank the infusion of fever-purging herbs and bark. Then she fell into a deep sleep." There was worry in her muted voice.

Isaac stopped by the side of the bed, listened, and shook his head. "Once the pain and fever abate, you must expect her to sleep soundly."

Raquel lowered her voice to a whisper. "Papa, she seems a very copy of our lord the King as she lies there. As if she had a woman's body and the head of a man. The old nun says it is the devil working in her to steal her soul before she dies." Raquel grasped her father's hand tightly. "Do you think it could be true?"

"And since when did the devil walk the earth in the shape of our good king?" said Isaac, his voice troubled. "Don Pedro is our earthly lord and protector. We owe him much. He has saved us many times already from the ignorant rabble, and I suspect we will need his help again soon." He paused, and smiled at his daughter. "Lady Isabel has a much better reason than devilish mischief for looking like the King, my child. But it is not discreet to talk about it here. Let us examine that wound."

The room still smelled of burning herbs and the bubbling mess on the hob, but the stench of infection and putrefaction had almost dissipated itself. A voice from the hearth began to mutter hoarsely in a jumble of Latin and Catalan, intermixed with snatches of song. "How long has the old nun been like that?" he asked sharply.

"For hours and hours, Papa," said Raquel. There were tears in her voice as she automatically straightened the bed linen with a rustling of cloth. "I think she has a jug of wine under her skirts," she whispered.

"We will deal with her later. Place my hand upon Lady Isabel's forehead," he murmured. His hand rested very lightly on her skin. "Her brow is moist and somewhat cooler. Good. Have you changed the dressings?"

"Twice, Papa. Each time I bathed the wound with wine and placed a fresh poultice on it."

"Let me touch the skin around it," said her father.

She guided his hand and watched as he probed delicately all around the wound. He straightened up, apparently satisfied with what he had found. "Are you awake, my lady?" he asked.

"Yes, Master Isaac." The girl's voice was thick with sleep.

"You recognize your physician. That is a good sign. How came you by that wound?" he continued, in the same noncommittal voice.

Isabel opened her eyes and blinked.

Raquel bent over to hold a cup of water to Lady Isabel's

lips. "Drink, my lady, before you try to speak."

She drank most of the cupful, and dropped her head back. "Thank you, Raquel. You see I know your name as well," she added. "But my wound. How it happened," she said. "It was nothing, a trifle, I thought."

"Tell me of the trifle," said Isaac as his fingers searched busily through the basket.

"We were at our needles," she began. "I was searching in my workbox for a brown silk to work a fleeing stag, in a hunting scene—"

"And?"

"Someone dropped her workbox and knocked over my frame, and when I reached for it she fell on top of me, and I was stabbed with a needle."

"Whose?"

She shook her head weakly. "In the confusion, I thought it was mine," she said slowly. "But now I am not sure. It could have been her needle. But I believe it was innocently done." She spoke with great dignity. "Whoever injured me was doubtless afraid she would be punished."

"Let us hope that, with the help of the Lord, the consequences of this innocent act will soon be over," said Isaac. "You have exerted yourself enough. Rest, and do as Raquel tells you, my lady, and all will be well. Your uncle will be pleased."

A knock cut short any further colloquy. Isaac turned in the direction of the door. "Who knocks?"

"It is Sor Agnete, Master Isaac. May I have a word with you?"

"Stay here with your patient, Raquel," murmured Isaac. "I shall see what troubles Sor Agnete."

Raquel watched her father leave the room, closing the door firmly behind him. She took a step back from the bed, stretching her tired back and shoulders. She was desperately weary. Since she had been awakened in the night to come to the convent, she had not slept, except to doze lightly for a few minutes at a time as she sat by her sleeping patient. The scene around her, painted in the colors of exhaustion, had developed a nightmarish quality. Daylight filtered in through the narrow arched windows, dimly illuminating the room. A single beam of sun fell on the dying fire and the coals from the burning brazier, sucking away their red-and-orange hues and leaving pale tongues of flame flickering against the stone wall; the smoke cast a blue haze over all. The room was oppressively hot. She felt as if she had stepped into a painting of hell from one of her father's books. In the corner by the hearth, the old nun muttered and cackled to herself like some demonic spirit, and then splashed liquid from the jug between her feet into her wooden cup and drank. "Hola, pretty daughter of Israel," she called. "Leave the usurper's dying bastard where she is, and come and drink with me. I know who you are, and what you are, and who and what she is. We're a pretty trio to find in the convent." Her voice rose in a shriek of laughter, trailed off, and then her head drooped down on her chest. She began to snore.

Raquel shivered and kept silent.

Isaac shut the door behind him. "Yes, Sister?" he murmured.

"The Abbess instructed me to tell you directly, Master, as soon as she heard of it," said Sor Agnete. Her words tumbled out of her, scrambling in their haste.

"Tell me what?"

"Of the vial. Here. I have it in my hand."

"What vial, Sor Agnete?"

"I discovered it in Doña Sanxia's clothes. As I prepared the body. You had spoken of perfume, and so I uncorked it, but it doesn't smell at all like perfume."

Isaac reached out his hand for the vial. He rolled it about on his palm, sniffed it, and then removed the cork. He sniffed that, touched the wet end, and frowned. He rubbed the liquid between his thumb and middle finger, and then very delicately touched the end of his tongue to his fingertip. It was bitter to the taste. "Not something I would recommend drinking," he remarked dryly, extracting a cloth from his robe and vigorously cleaning off his hand.

"What is it?" asked Sor Agnete.

"Does it have any color?"

"Not precisely color," said Sor Agnete doubtfully. "It is a dark, muddy-looking liquor."

"A strange thing to be carrying on a visit to a convent." He paused for a moment. "I believe I should speak to Lady Elicsenda on this matter."

They retraced their steps down the winding staircase. Sor Agnete opened the door to a cool, airy chamber and bade Isaac wait.

Isaac walked up and down the room, taking its measure, all the while touching the tip of his tongue to the roof of his mouth, and considering the problems raised by the presence of the vial. Rapid footsteps and a soft whisper of cloth heralded the return of Sor Agnete with the Abbess.

"Master Isaac," said Elicsenda firmly. "I am at your disposition."

"Lady Elicsenda. I thank you for your haste. I have examined the vial Sor Agnete brought me. I placed no more than a hundredth part of a drop on the tip of my tongue, and from its effects, I would say it contains a powerful opiate. Two or three drops would put a man to sleep. Ten or twenty, and he wouldn't wake up again. It was destined for Lady Isabel, I would guess." He paused. "Even in this refuge, I fear for her safety."

"But surely, with the death of Doña Sanxia, the danger is past," said Sor Agnete.

"No doubt," said Isaac. "Nonetheless . . ."

"I agree with the physician," said the Abbess. "She is in our care, Sor Agnete. She is our spiritual daughter, and must be guarded as such."

"Raquel is a most careful guardian," said Isaac, "but she is alone. At sixteen, one must sleep from time to time."

"Sor Benvenguda, our infirmary sister—"

"I think not, Lady Elicsenda. How well do you know her?"

The Abbess paused. "Not well. She is highly skilled," she said at last. "But she came to us only three months ago from Tarragona. The pestilence had taken all our sisters who cared for the sick, except Sor Tecla, who has become too old and infirm to carry on.''

"Someone whom you trust absolutely should be with Raquel at all times. And Sor Tecla must be removed. She is drunk with wine—''

"Drunk? Who has given her wine?'' asked the Abbess.

"I don't know,'' said Sor Agnete. "But I will find out soon enough. She has a weakness—''

"And her weakness is well known?''

"It is,'' said the Abbess impatiently. "She has wrestled with it for many years. But if someone gave her wine . . .'' She stopped. "Sor Agnete will be relieved of her usual duties to help your daughter.''

"Very good, madam,'' said Sor Agnete.

"Let no one near them but one of us,'' said Isaac. "The strange vial in the false nun's clothes troubles me.''

Yusuf sat in the shade of a wall near the convent gate, drawing pictures in the dust and wondering why he had agreed to stay with the physician. Why not get to his feet and leave at once? The small portal used for common business was open; the fat nun who guarded the gate was unlikely to run after him. And yet he stayed, drawing pictures, caught by a strange lassitude that bound his limbs and made his head heavy. He had slept and eaten more these last twelve hours than he had for many days past, and still his body seemed to cry out for more. He thought of the wooden table under the vine in Master Isaac's courtyard, laden with delicacies—dates and figs and apricots, and soft cheese beaten with honey and chopped nuts. It dissolved and became a great festive table, groaning with food: thin spiced cakes, dripping with honey, jellies flavored with the heady aroma of roses, sweetmeats, rich and sticky, rice, piled high, bright yellow and saffron-scented, and small fried cakes of meat, with ginger and cardamom and other spices he could not remember the names of. . . .

"Yusuf!'' said a voice above him. "It is time to take you to the Baths and clean you up, or we will be home too late to dine.''

The boy woke with a start, and scrambled, frightened, to his feet. It took him a moment to decide where he was. "Yes, lord," he said.

The torpor of the afternoon was beginning to empty the streets of the town. The rattle of wheels over cobbles and cries of the peddlers of trinkets died down. Merchants covered their wares and closed their shops. From every side came the smell of food boiling, baking and grilling over fires. Big Johan had ceased emptying and cleaning the central bath, and was preparing to cut open his loaf and piece of cheese for dinner when Isaac and Yusuf arrived.

"Hola! Johan!" called Isaac from the top of the stairs that led down to the Baths. His voice echoed in the cool, softly lit hall. "I have a boy here in need of a scrubbing."

"Good day, Master Isaac," said Johan, looming out of the darkness of his private corner. "The large bath is closed—"

"The Bishop told me," said Isaac. "Can we not wash him anyway?"

"There is the small bath. And hot water. Is this boy named Yusuf?"

Yusuf looked up at the giant of a man towering over him. "It is, sir. I am Yusuf."

"I have fresh clothing here that was sent by your mistress."

"Good. Take him away and wash him," said Isaac cheerfully. "And dress him in clean clothes. I shall rest if you will find me a bench."

Isaac's peaceful meditation was interrupted by a scream of protest. "I won't take it off!" The words resounded shrilly from the vaulted ceiling, and bounced off the tiles. They were accompanied by a deep bass rumble.

Isaac felt his way along the wall with his hand and staff, and headed through an arch in the direction of the voices. When he thought he had a chance of being heard, he broke in. "Yusuf? Johan? What is happening? You must take your clothes off to bathe, Yusuf. There is no shame in it."

"It is not that," said Yusuf, his voice close to tears.

"It's this purse around his neck, Master," said Johan. "It's leather, and will get soaked in the water. He won't give it to me to keep for him."

"Will you give it to me until you are bathed and dry?" asked Isaac gently. "I will guard it very carefully." He moved closer to the voices, feeling his way along the wall.

There was a pause. "Do you swear solemnly by the One Lord whom we both worship, although in different ways, and by the truth and honor of your forefathers, that you will return it to me without opening it as soon as I ask?"

"It is a somewhat complicated oath, but I swear it," said Isaac, trying very hard to keep the amusement from his voice. "I shall return it as soon as you ask for it without opening it, by that same Lord. And my forefathers. May I ask what I will be holding that is so valuable?"

"Not valuable to anyone but me, lord," said Yusuf, in a small voice. "Just some writing in my own tongue that I would not lose."

As soon as the boy grasped the leather bag that hung about his neck from a stout leather thong, Big Johan could see that it contained no material wealth—no round gold coins, no bumpy, sparkling gems—and his curiosity evaporated like the summer dew. Isaac bent over and allowed Yusuf to place the bag around his neck; the boy turned and walked back to Johan.

"Stand here while I rinse the mud off you," said the keeper. "Then we'll scrub you clean." He poured tepid water scooped from the bath over Yusuf, before fetching two large ewers from the fire in the far corner. He set them down beside a small fountain that ran a steady stream of pure cold water. He hitched up his tunic, and sat on the ledge of the small bath.

Yusuf stepped into the bath, and stood, shivering, in front of Big Johan. The smell and touch of the water loosed another wave of memories of summer, and the sound of splashing water, and women's laughter; the warm sun caressed his skin, and tall palm trees rustling in the light wind spread sweet, cool shade over him. Tears rose in his eyes; he pushed the memories away fiercely.

Johan scrubbed Yusuf with a sponge and soft soap until his skin glowed and his hair was piled on his head with lather. "Wait there," he said, and went over to the ewers. He took a dipper, and added cold water to them with a judicious hand.

The hot water over his head hit Yusuf like a furnace blast, burning away soap and dirt. He looked down at his bare skin, cleaned of its surface grime, and saw thin limbs with their bones painfully evident, covered with scrapes and bruises, and alternating dark and pale patches where the sun had found its way through his tattered clothing. Never, not even in the darkest days of his journey, had he felt more impoverished and unclean.

"There, lad," said Big Johan. "You do me credit. Clean as can be, from hair to toes. I'd put you in the cold water to refresh you, but small and thin as you be, I fear it'd be too much for you. Now let's dry you off and see how the new clothes fit."

Johan wrapped him in a great linen sheet, and picked up a neatly folded bundle. "Your garments, young sir."

Yusuf's hand touched his bare neck, and he let the sheet fall. "But my—" He stopped. "My purse," he cried in a panic-stricken voice. "Lord. Do you still have my leather purse?"

Isaac stepped forward, reaching out a hand until it touched the boy's wet hair. Gravely, he took the leather bag from his own neck, and placed it over Yusuf's head. "You see," he said, "my vow is kept. Now dress yourself before you take a chill."

Yusuf picked up a linen shirt and pulled it over his head. He fastened the overlarge hose below his knees with ribbons and put on a loose tunic of fine brown cloth. He slipped on the shoes, binding their thongs tightly to compensate for their size, and shook his head. The mistress was a strange woman, to clothe so well someone she hated so much.

•   •   •

"This is a cool and pleasant place," said Isaac. "The Bishop tells me you keep it in a wondrous state of cleanliness and repair."

"The Bishop is a kind and generous man," said Johan. "To say that. That was why finding a dead sister in the bath took away my breath, like."

"They don't normally come here?" asked Isaac. "Nuns?"

"Never," said Big Johan quickly. Isaac could almost hear him sweat.

"When you pulled her out of the water—that was just after prime, was it?"

"A little later than that, Master."

"Perhaps an hour?"

"The sun was high and bright, Master."

"Was she stiff at all?"

Big Johan relaxed. He neither moved, nor uttered a word, but the keeper's relief was so palpable that Isaac felt it. "She were. Around the head like. That's where they start. I've helped carry the dead, and lay them out, and so I know."

"So at somewhere an hour or more after prime, she had begun to stiffen. She died after laud, and perhaps by an hour or two." And at that point, he reflected, the revels went from noisy to violent. And the Bishop had seen Big Johan too drunk to know his own name.

There was a gentle patter of feet on the hard floor. "My new clothes are very fine, lord," said Yusuf. "I wish you could see them."

"Here, give me them rags," said Big Johan. "I'll put them on the fire for you."

"I think I'll keep them," said Yusuf. "I may want them someday."

The Count Hug de Castellbo had searched the village—five or six dwellings huddling against the castle walls—and scoured the countryside between the castle and Girona, but it was Don Aymeric and his searchers, led by Petronella's keen nose, who found the nursemaid, Maria. She lay in a small hollow near the road, hidden by tall grass. Her throat had been slashed. Beside her lay a bundle wrapped in a bright kerchief. The castellan, Don Aymeric, picked it up and untied it. Out spilled clean clothing for a child, and some bread and fruit.

The castellan's huntsman gathered up the clothing. "It would look as if she had planned to leave and take the child with her."

"With Jaume?" asked Don Aymeric. "I can't believe that."

The huntsman shook his head. "If Jaume did this, he will have some fine marks on him from her nails and teeth," he said soberly. "Maria was no delicate maiden. Some of these lads here were marked by her when they tried to slip a hand into her skirts. They soon stopped."

"No sign of the child?" asked the castellan, his face expressionless. The longer the hunt had gone on, from the riverbank, to the woodlands and other rough ground on his estate, to the road into town, the more frozen into hopelessness his countenance had become.

"Señor," called a voice from behind them, on the road. "I have found something here." It was Miquel, the stable lad, returned from his fruitless pursuit of Jaume, the groom. He held out his hand.

"A carved horse?" asked Don Aymeric, looking at it.

"I carved it, on Sunday," he said. "And gave it to the Infant Johan."

The castellan turned to his huntsman. "Does *everyone* know who the child is?" he asked quietly.

"I'm afraid so, señor," said the huntsman. "Maria tried, but she was too accustomed to calling him Johan. We soon realized who he was."

The castellan turned back to the stable lad.

"He loves horses," said the lad. "I took him for rides on the gray pony, and carved him this when he was sick. It's supposed to be the pony."

"Thank you, Miquel. You have sharp eyes, and a kind

heart," said the castellan in despair. "Now I must ride to Barcelona and tell His Majesty."

"One of us will go for you, señor," said the huntsman.

"No," said the castellan. He shook his head. "He trusted me to keep the Prince safe."

FIVE

Pedro, King of Aragon and Count of Barcelona, sat in
a private chamber in his palace in that coastal city, in
consultation with one of his ministers. He was looking
down his finely sculptured, high-bridged nose—Charle-
magne's nose, the flatterers were fond of pointing out to
him—at the worried man perched on a chair at the far side
of the table.

"He is in the palace now, Sire. With a retinue of a dozen
men in the courtyard, and at least fifty more horse and
attached foot soldiers at the edge of the city."

"You worry too much, Arnau. Why wouldn't our brother
visit Barcelona to pay his respects?" asked Don Pedro, raising one eyebrow sardonically.

His minister groaned inwardly, and pursued his subject.
"Don Fernando has not always been a friend to Your Majesty," he said, sticking to the obvious. "In this visit there
could be some danger to your person."

"My dear Arnau, either you take me for a fool . . ." He
allowed his voice to drift off.

"Sire, I know you are no fool," said Arnau hastily, only
too aware of how true that was. He was beginning to sweat,
in spite of the late-afternoon breeze that cooled the room.

He prayed silently and fervently for the miraculous return from across the sea of Don Bernat de Cabrera. At least His stubborn Majesty would listen to Don Bernat.

"We have not lived this long to be unaware of Don Fernando's feelings, Arnau. The kingdom will not collapse because two brothers meet. We shall receive Don Fernando, inquire after the health of his mother, and wish him a prosperous journey back to hell or wherever else he may choose to go. Rest easy, my dear Arnau. You will not be exiled to your country fields for failing to protect us. You see, I know your orders." A smile flickered over his lips.

When his brother entered the inner or private hall in which Don Pedro received visitors of strategic importance, the King was seated comfortably on a heavy, carved chair that bore an unsettling resemblance to a throne. The room also contained a footstool, a carved *prie-dieu* with a cushion for the royal knees, and a heavy table. There were no other places to sit.

Don Fernando glanced around the room, and observed that he had been given a choice of kneeling, crouching at his brother's feet, or standing. He clenched his jaw and bowed. "How goes Your Majesty?" he asked.

"In excellent health and spirits, praise be to God," he replied. "And how goes our brother Fernando?"

"I am well, Sire."

"How delightful. And Doña Leonor, our revered stepmother?"

"She is in good health."

"Excellent," said Don Pedro. "Pray convey our wishes to her for a tranquil and happy old age."

Fernando winced. His mother, Doña Leonor of Castile, was not only far from elderly, but in her ambition and ruthlessness, the least tranquil woman in the kingdom. She would not thank the messenger who brought that greeting from the stepson she loathed. "I shall do so, Sire," he said. "May I be permitted to inquire after the health of the Infant Johan, my young nephew? News had reached my ears of a most disturbing illness suffered by the Duke of Girona."

"Talk, my dear brother, only talk. A trifling childish complaint, quickly cured by a change of air."

"I am glad. I beg you guard him well, Sire. And my dear sister, our queen? How is she? I had hoped to present my respects to her."

"She begs to be excused, but the preparations for her removal to Ripoll occupy her. In her present condition, she is advised to travel at a moderate pace. Should she delay her departure, even for such a pleasant reason, she would not arrive before the worst of the summer heat."

It took a moment for the import of Don Pedro's words to reach his brother. Then on either side of the bridge of his nose appeared small white angry patches. They were as palpable a proof of a weapon reaching its target as a spreading bloodstain on a linen shirt. Don Pedro smiled.

"My prayers and wishes for her safe delivery go to my sister," said his brother in a tight voice. "I hope she does not find the journey too burdensome. Or dangerous."

"We thank you for your prayers," said Don Pedro. "But the Queen is in excellent health and spirits."

"I wish them both well." Don Fernando contemplated the ceiling and smiled. "I understand Lady Isabel d'Empuries is to be married," he said.

"Women's gossip," said Don Pedro, with a dismissive wave.

"And has she not been promised in marriage? Rumors abound."

He hesitated. "We are not hastening to dispose of her in marriage."

"In this, as in all things, Your Majesty acts wisely," said Don Fernando, and smiled that thin-lipped, self-satisfied smile that had always driven his brother mad with irritation.

After Don Fernando had taken his farewells, Don Pedro remained in his place. He considered the thinly veiled threat to his heir, and wondered what interest his brother might have in Isabel's marriage. It was possible, or even likely, that Fernando was hoping that fear would spur his brother into unwise and hasty action. But why? A sound broke his train of thought; he raised his head in the empty room and said, "Come out from there."

The tapestry on the wall behind him was pushed aside, and Don Arnau emerged from a broad niche, followed by two armed guards.

"We have an urgent message to be delivered," said the King. "You had better go yourself, Arnau. By first light, you will ride north and present our compliments and a letter to the Bishop of Girona."

Fernando strode out of the palace, sprang on his horse, and rode at breakneck speed to the outskirts of Barcelona, where he dismounted at the door to a large house and stormed inside, followed by his panting retinue. Don Perico de Montbui and a rather flushed young woman were sitting cozily in the principal room over a jug of wine. They scrambled to their feet. The young woman took one look at Fernando's face, still white with rage, curtsied, and left the room hastily. Don Fernando turned to Montbui. "Why didn't you tell me that bitch was with child again?"

"I didn't know, Your Lordship."

"You didn't know. Every waiting woman and serving wench in the palace must know, and you couldn't find it out."

"Is it important?" asked Don Perico, incautiously.

"It is crucial, you fool. We must pry my brother loose from his guards, and act now. He must be dealt with before she has a chance to have another son."

Don Tomas de Bellmunt arrived at the palace in Barcelona hot, tired, and ill-tempered. Five or more hours along the road from Girona, the weary Arcont, lathered in sweat and breathing hard, had stumbled and pulled up lame. The two of them had finished the journey—another five or six hours—at a slow walk, side by side, like the old friends they were. After a long and complex discussion on the wisdom of one poultice as against another, and the value of special diets in this case, he commended his mount to the care of his groom, and headed inside to wash and change his clothes before presenting himself to the Queen.

Freed of the mud and dust of travel, his thirst and hunger both slightly assuaged, he set out resolutely for Doña Eleanor's apartments. His heart was heavy and his stomach fluttering; he would rather walk barefoot to Girona and back than tell Her Majesty that her principal lady-in-waiting had disappeared. Poor Tomas. His family name and a pleasant smile had secured him his magnificent post with Doña Eleanor, not a smooth tongue or the gift of a ready answer, and he had no idea how to break the news to her. What should he tell her? He, Tomas, did not *know* that Doña Sanxia was dead. He had not seen her body; he had received no reliable report of her death. In addition, he had no idea what excuse Doña Sanxia had given Her Majesty for absenting herself for a week.

It had occurred to Tomas on the long walk to Barcelona that Sanxia had been slipping rapidly from favor lately, and was not so privy to Her Majesty's thoughts as she had been. He should have realized weeks before that she was an odd choice for such a private and delicate mission. With only Arcont's sympathetic ear turned to listen to his arguments, he had faced the possibility that it had not been Her Majesty who had ordered Sanxia to abduct the Infant Johan.

If Doña Eleanor had wanted the Infant Johan taken to a safe refuge, why didn't she ask him herself? And why would Her Majesty tell Sanxia that he must not allude to the enterprise in front of her? For secrecy's sake, Doña Sanxia had said. At that moment, any child of eight would have suspected that the order had not come from Her Majesty. But not a besotted lover. Not Tomas de Bellmunt, the Witless One. Now that he had time to think, the worm of suspicion crawled into his breast, and gnawed away at his faith in fiery hair and emerald eyes. He was green and stupid and as gullible as a newborn baby. He had been duped. He broke into a cold sweat at the thought. Arcont had nodded in apparent agreement, and limped gamely on.

Standing in the cool, broad corridors of the palace, Tomas began to search for words in which to beg forgiveness—not for his part in the aborted abduction, not now—

but for absenting himself without notice or permission. If Doña Eleanor hadn't needed him, she wouldn't have noticed. If she had, all her sweetness would disappear in a well-deserved blast of Sicilian hot temper. He raised his chin and turned the corner.

"Don Tomas!" The voice through the open door was petulant, demanding. Its whispered command could not have reached much farther than his own ears, but it was impossible to ignore. Don Perico de Montbui stepped out into the corridor.

"Don Perico," said Tomas, bowing. "I am at your service."

"Come in here."

"But I must attend Her Majesty, my lord," said Tomas, with more deference than he felt. "She is expecting me." It irritated him that this pompous, self-important little man should be so rich, and that his uncle, his mother's brother, Don Hug de Castellbo, should take him seriously, and expect his nephew to do the same.

"I am instructed to tell you that Her Majesty has retired for the night. At dawn, she leaves for Ripoll. The heat increases daily, and she does not wish to travel any later in the summer."

"Oh," said Tomas, dismayed. "Then I must prepare for the journey. She will need me."

"No." He brought his face closer to Tomas. Waves of sour wine and foul-smelling breath enveloped the younger man and he stepped back until the wall stopped him. "She needs you elsewhere," whispered Montbui hoarsely. "Now listen. You are to leave for Girona before dawn. There you are to meet with a certain person who shall be named in the documents I give you. He will deliver up to you a—let us say, hostage, or prisoner of quality, who is to be taken to Doña Sanxia's *finca* and treated with the utmost care and courtesy. You will be expected. You know where that is?"

"Yes, my lord."

"The Count your uncle has requested me to draft your instructions. I will have them delivered to your chamber.

You will be awakened before the first cockcrow, and therefore you will need to rest.''

"There is no need for you to trouble yourself, Don Perico," said Tomas, stiffly. "I shall be waiting on my uncle this evening to take my leave. He can give me the instructions himself."

Montbui glared. His round jowls turned pink. "Count Hug de Castellbo is indisposed," he said stiffly. "He does not wish to be disturbed."

Tomas opened his mouth to protest, then turned on his heel and went back to his chamber.

"But where is Tomas?" Doña Eleanor, Queen of Aragon and Countess of Barcelona, frowned in annoyance.

"I don't know, madam," said her maid. "It's two days since I've seen him."

"There is so much to think of before we depart. I need him. And where is Doña Sanxia, Saurina?"

Saurina looked up from brushing Doña Eleanor's hair. "She has not returned from Figueres. Perhaps her husband is very ill."

"She wouldn't stop long because of that," said the Queen, with a touch of malice. "Except to say a prayer for his hasty end." She took an almond from a dish in front of her and nibbled on it. "She has no business absenting herself like this. It's outrageous. I must get rid of her." The Queen paused, reflectively. "Why did Don Pedro appoint her lady-in-waiting? You must know, Saurina. You hear everything. Was she his mistress?"

"Oh, no," said Saurina quickly. "Never. I heard it was because her husband is rich, and did him some service in Valencia during the uprising. He has had no mistress since Doña Constancia. Not that I know of."

"Don't speak to me of Doña Constancia, Saurina," said Her Majesty petulantly. "For two years that was all Doña Sanxia could talk about. His mistress, and how learned and beautiful and charming she was."

"Don't concern yourself over Doña Constancia, madam.

She's been dead these five years," said Saurina, who was
a practical young woman.

"I am weary, Saurina," said the Queen, yawning suddenly. "Come. Help me into my new shift, and bring me
hot spiced wine. I think His Majesty may have an hour or
two to spare for me from his talk of war." And with a
lightning shift of mood, she erupted in a most unregal burst
of laughter.

Tomas de Bellmunt set his candle on the table, and took
out a sheet of paper. He had wanted desperately to speak
to his uncle, so desperately that he had braved his possible
wrath and presented himself at his apartment. Unsuccess-
fully. His uncle's secretary, a wizened, shrewd, unmovable,
and unbribable man, had shaken his head, and said that his
master was not to be disturbed.

Tomas pulled the page toward him, mended his pen,
dipped it in the ink, and painfully composed a letter describing the failed mission to Girona, and his doubts and
fears regarding Doña Sanxia. *My dear uncle,* he ended,
*there is no one in this country in whose wisdom and dis-
cretion I have more confidence. I beg you to consider this
problem, and to be generous enough to offer me your wise
counsel. I fear I have been led into treachery. What should
I do? Your affectionate nephew, Tomas de Bellmunt.*

He stared at the letter for a long time, altering a word
here and there, sprinkled fine sand over the page to dry the
ink, shook it off, and then, folding the sheet carefully,
heated a stick of wax and sealed it firmly with his ring.

SIX

The eastern sky was tarnished silver and the road underfoot still invisible when Tomas de Bellmunt began his miserable journey. He was not happy. On his arrival at court the year before, his wealth had consisted of three generous presents from his uncle: an elegant suit of clothes, and two excellent horses, the magnificent Arcont, and Romeu's sturdy chestnut, Castanya. Carrying the rest of his possessions—not a heavy load—had been Blaveta, whose back he now straddled. Her gait, as always, was awkward, and her ears quivered with bitter resentment at the unaccustomed weight on her back. The journey to Girona was going to be long, and painful, and very slow.

A letter of instruction from his uncle, written by Montbui, had arrived the night before as he was preparing for bed. He had read it carefully, scribbled his acquiescence in a blank corner, and as requested, returned it to the waiting messenger. Its contents had done nothing to ease his mind. And ominously, it had made no reference, not even in a hastily written postscript, to Tomas's own letter. But perhaps his uncle wanted to conceal any hint of the botched abduction from Montbui, and would reply later. Of course. Tomas had paced the room, waiting for a message from his uncle, and then flung himself down on his bed, still waiting. He had slept fitfully, and awakened long before dawn. When a sleepy-eyed servant arrived to wake him with a note from his uncle's secretary, he had already breakfasted and was ready to leave. The note was brief, dry, and unhelpful. *The Count wishes you a good journey and success in your mission.*

Angrily, Tomas de Bellmunt had seized his small pack, and had left, tired, confused, and more uncertain of what he ought to do than ever.

When dawn began to creep over the horizon, the city lay far behind him; the birds stirred—a chirp here, a trill there; somewhere a cow complained and a dog barked. A lone rider, disheveled and pale with fatigue, appeared out of nowhere, spurring his sweating, foam-flecked horse past Tomas in a desperate hurry to reach Barcelona. Then he was gone and the road was dark and empty again. Tomas clapped spurs to the nag; she laid back her ears, shook her head, and launched into her well-remembered, you'll-be-sorry, bone-jouncing trot. It was going to be very long journey, indeed.

Twenty-four hours earlier, the groom, Jaume, had awakened suddenly from a deep sleep, with the conviction that he had heard something odd. He slipped out of bed, dressed, and ran to check on Maria and the Infant. He found only two empty beds. He headed for the stable. Still no Maria, but someone had planned a rapid exit. The gray pony, saddled and ready, was standing in the stable yard. Jaume unsaddled him and turned him out to pasture with an encouraging slap on the rump. The pony was fast and wary; catching him would slow the defector down.

A quick search of the castle turned up no one but a solitary kitchen maid, starting the fires. Before sunrise, Jaume was on his own mount, combing through the tiny village and nearby fields.

There was no trace of child or nursemaid. He dismounted when he reached the road that wound up through the hills in one direction, and down into the city in the other. There, in its dry, dusty surface, Jaume picked out the blurred traces of several carts, some donkeys, and at least one horse moving at a gallop. Here and there, in the direction leading to town, he made out footprints that could have belonged to Maria and the boy. Not a great deal of evidence, but it was enough to send him that way.

He had ridden slowly, searching from side to side for traces of the boy and his nursemaid, stopping at the top of each small rise to listen for them. It had taken two hours to cover the five or so miles to Girona. But within sight of the city, a noisy gathering of crows had led him directly to the muddy patch of long grass where Maria lay. He caught sight of her bright kerchief, wrapped around her bundle; it had fallen close to her outstretched hand. He had looked, murmured a brief prayer for her soul, and crossed himself before backing away and beginning to look for the boy. He had found the wooden horse, and come to his own conclusions. Leaving the toy horse and the body of the unfortunate nursemaid where they were, the Infant Johan's unhappy bodyguard set out at a gallop for Barcelona to report his disastrous failure to His Majesty.

Then, shortly after dawn the next day, having passed Tomas bouncing uncomfortably and inelegantly on his way to Girona, Jaume, pale, dirty from travel, his left arm bound tightly against his chest, knelt in front of his sovereign lord the King and delivered his news in as few words as possible.

Don Pedro's face was white and still as a rock. "You are sure of this?"

"No, Sire, I am not sure. I know only that I did not prevent the Infant from being taken from the estate during the night, and that his nursemaid is dead, and that I could not find him. The castellan is, as Your Majesty judged, shrewd and incorruptible. I have no doubt that he is continuing the search with all the resources at his command. I set out at once to inform Your Majesty. I should have been here yesterday but my horse collapsed under me, and I had some difficulty finding another." His face was now ashen, and he swayed perceptibly.

"And you are injured."

"That is not important, Sire, except that it slowed my progress." With those words, Jaume crumpled in a faint at his ruler's feet.

Don Pedro touched a bell at his left hand. "See to this man's injuries," he said. "Quickly. And summon Don Eleazar."

Isaac sat in the courtyard, apparently half-asleep in the morning sun. "The market, when the sun begins to be high in the heavens, don't you think, Yusuf?" he said suddenly. "That would be the best time to start. First we will visit the convent. We must give the rumors surrounding Doña Sanxia's death time to grow."

"Indeed, lord." Yusuf stopped playing with the cat, and scrambled guiltily to his feet. "I am ready when you need me."

"Good. Then fetch my basket. Spread a clean cloth in it, and two bundles of herbs from the middle shelf, at the end nearest the door. The ones that smell chiefly of sage."

"What are they for?"

"To make an infusion of sage, willow, and borage for an old woman with a stiff knee and the headache. That will also give us a reason to linger and gossip. What Caterina does not know of happenings in this town would fit into my wife's thimble."

"Has she sent for you, lord?"

"No. But her complaints will be blooming today. The air is heavy."

"Master Isaac!" said old Caterina with an expression of astonishment on her face. "Not a moment ago it was I said I must send for you, ask anyone—they'll tell you—and here you are. My knee is that stiff and swollen— They'll be carrying me to my bed tonight, and leaving me in it until they carry me out again if you don't help me." She paused to snatch a breath. "How did you know?"

"Because, Caterina, when my elbow aches, you cannot move your knee. Nothing magical." As he spoke his fingers gently manipulated the woman's leg. "Strange happenings at the Baths," he murmured. "And you must keep moving this leg gently, even when it's bad, Caterina."

"Yes, yes," she said impatiently. "Strange happenings indeed. They say the poor creature was a nun. Cut her own throat, they say. But there's some as wonder how she got to her feet and climbed into the water after it was done. Not easy, that. And Master Isaac, I heard that hers wasn't the only cut throat on the eve of the blessed saint."

"Oh?"

"Another woman outside the walls, found by the road to the hills. So they say. There's a butcher about, you'll see. No woman is safe."

"Who says?"

"I don't know. Some farm folk."

Yusuf danced impatiently from foot to foot, trying, by pure effort of will, to drag Master Isaac away from the seller of sweetmeats. Caterina had given him more than one sharp blow with her ready fingers or her long staff in the past, when she had judged him to be too close to her tempting display. The sight of her reminded him painfully of hunger and misery. "We knew all that," he observed with a touch of superiority as they finally moved on to the flower seller's stall.

"Perhaps," said Isaac. "But I believe we did learn something. Choose me some fresh lavender, lad."

Yusuf sorted through the bundles of lavender and picked out one. "What did we learn, lord?"

Isaac handed Yusuf his purse. The boy looked shrewdly at the woman and extracted a small coin from it.

"Trusts you with more gold than I would," said the flower seller.

"Yes, but then, *he's* not a fool, Mother."

Isaac ignored the exchange. "We discovered that even Caterina doesn't know as much as we do. What does that mean?"

Yusuf paused. "It means—I don't know, lord. That the assassin has not boasted of his deed?"

"Clearly," said Isaac dryly.

"But why should he?" said Yusuf, dissatisfied. "He must have taken care not to leave traces. There must have been a lot of blood."

"More than you can imagine, lad."

Yusuf froze. Into his head leapt the image of a blood-stained woman, not floating in the Baths, but lying on a floor whose colorful mosaic was drowned with even brighter blood. Then he saw an arm and a hand, both scarlet with evidence, clutching a bloody dagger. He shivered and forced himself to pay attention to the physician's thoughts.

"He must have taken great care," Isaac continued, "and he must have the means to change his garments and hide the bloody ones."

Yusuf dragged himself back to the market, and to the problem. "He must own two suits of clothes, and a room to keep them in, at least," he said. "That means he is not a poor man, or he has friends who will help him," said Yusuf.

"Just so." Isaac turned away from his acolyte and fell into a jesting quarrel with the flower seller over the price of medicinal blooms.

Yusuf felt, rather than heard, the rustle at his feet. Looking down, he saw an extremely grubby—even by standards at the market—rather frail-looking child of two or three years crawl out from under the flower seller's stall. The child righted himself and sat on the ground, adding another layer of dust and mud to his clothes and limbs. He rubbed his eyes, spreading the dirt around on his tearstained face, and then paused to observe his surroundings. Directly across from him sat a display of large baskets filled with rolls and breads of every kind imaginable. The child rose to his feet and, with the determination of a horse heading for water, went straight to the nearest basket and took a roll.

Bedlam broke loose.

A shrill voice broke though the general babble surround-

ing them. "Away with you! Dirty little thief." The bread
seller flapped her hands frantically in the air. "Look at
him!" she screamed. "I've had enough of children stealing
my wares. You come near my stall again and I'll box your
ears." She swooped down on the unfortunate child,
snatched away his prize, and rather in advance of her promise, boxed his ears.

He responded to the loss and the blow with a startled
look and a loud wail, followed by heartbroken sobbing. He
ran from the unexpected hostility as fast as his legs would
carry him, straight into a basket of walnuts that tipped over
and spilled out onto the cobbles. The nut seller's roar, the
screeching of the baker's wife, and the laughter of the passersby combined to create pandemonium. The child stepped
back and looked around desperately. Then he saw a familiar
face, and cried out, "Nunc Isa! Nunc Isa!"

Isaac turned, astonished. "Where is that child, Yusuf?
Do you see him? Fetch him quickly. Run."

"He's coming toward us, lord. Do you know him?"

"Only one child calls me that," said Isaac softly. "Bring
him to me at once, Yusuf."

Isaac heard a scuffle and some exclamations. Then a pair
of small hands clutched at his tunic. He bent down, picked
up the heartbroken Crown Prince of Aragon, and patted him
soothingly on the shoulder.

"Do you know that child?" said the woman in pursuit.
"Two of my rolls he's stolen—ate one and muddied the
other with his filthy hands so no decent folk will touch it."

"Little Samuel?" said Isaac, nodding at the child who
clung fiercely to his neck. "He's my niece's lad. She'll be
grateful for your generosity. Yusuf, pay her for two rolls
and buy Samuel another. A large one."

A stocky, prosperous-looking man, dressed for travel,
leaned against the flower seller's stall and observed the
small drama playing out in the market. In his hand, he held
a bloodred carnation that he had plucked from a bundle of
flowers fresh in from the country. Abruptly, he threw it to
the ground, tossed a coin at the flower seller, and walked
away.

"How come you to be in the market, my little friend?" murmured Isaac. The Prince, much comforted by the combination of a familiar face and a large fresh roll, was walking along between his two rescuers.

"I in a cart," he said vaguely, being occupied with cramming as much bread as he could into his mouth. "I sat on a big sack. And a gray horse."

"Where is your nursemaid?" asked Isaac. "Maria, is it?"

His voice became troubled. "The man looked for me." He paused to attack his bread again. "I rode on a cart," he added, on a happier note.

"Did the man find you?"

He shook his head vehemently, and tears appeared in his eyes again.

"He shakes his head, lord," said Yusuf quietly.

"I lost my horse," said the Prince, his lip quivering. Then the memory of another grievance rose up. "He hit me and called me bad things."

"Who hit you, Johan?" asked Yusuf.

The Infant Johan stared at the boy, and shook his head again.

"He won't say, lord," said Yusuf.

"Perhaps he doesn't know," said Isaac. "Why did the man hit you, Johan?"

"I never say my name. Maria says I mustn't." His grip on Isaac's hand tightened. "Maria was hurt," said the Infant Johan. "She wouldn't answer. She said, 'Hide, Johan,' and I hid. I lost my horse." And he cried bitterly at his loss.

Isaac's daughter Rebecca looked at the trio on her doorstep in amazement. "What gutter did you find that in, Father? What a poor miserable little creature."

"May we come in?"

There was a moment's hesitation, and then Rebecca stood back to let them pass. Isaac waited until the door was firmly closed. He paused for a moment to consider what he would say, and then shook his head. "I know—I think—

that I can trust my Rebecca,'' he said. "And Yusuf, I need to be able to trust you. If you fail me, the consequences for me, for everyone, will be disastrous.''

"You can trust me, I think,'' said Yusuf, in a troubled voice.

"I cannot ask more than that,'' said Isaac gravely. He bent down over the child, who was clinging desperately to his hand. "Your Highness, may I present my daughter, Rebecca? She will care for you until we can take you to your mother. Rebecca, the Infant Johan of Aragon.''

Rebecca stepped back in amazement, and then bent down to the child's level. "You're very welcome, sweetheart. Your Highness,'' she said, gently. "Poor little thing.''

"He is hungry,'' said Isaac, "tired, and Yusuf tells me, very dirty. I beg you to feed him, wash him, clothe him, and put him to bed. But first, you must write a note for me to the Bishop. He will know what to do. But do not, at all costs, let anyone else know who the child is. I think he is in great danger.''

"Certainly, Papa. Not even Nicholau. It will make him nervous,'' said Rebecca, as calmly as if she sheltered desperate members of the ruling family every day. She fingered the torn and mud-soaked clothes. "I'll try to rescue these,'' she said. "If I can. You are well disguised, Your Highness.''

"Fortunately for him,'' said Isaac.

The Crown Prince, not surprisingly, was distressed when Isaac, the only firm rock in his currently shaky world, showed clear signs of leaving him with Rebecca.

"Papa,'' said Rebecca. "Stay and dine with us. I will make a little bed for Johan in here, where he can see and hear you, and then perhaps he will sleep. Just for a while.''

And so Yusuf delivered Isaac's letter, securely folded and sealed with the Bishop's own ring, to a lazy and suspicious-looking porter at the Bishop's palace. "The Bishop is not to be disturbed,'' said the porter, "on the word of some boy who thinks he bears an important message.''

"It carries the Bishop's seal,'' said Yusuf with cheerful insolence. "Or so they told me. They said the Bishop would want to see a letter at once that was sealed with his own ring.''

"Impertinent imp of the devil,'' muttered the porter, snatching the letter and slamming the door in Yusuf's face.

And having delivered the letter, Yusuf found himself back at the market, with a small store of coins and instructions to discover, if he could, why the Prince had been wandering around as lost and miserable as a beggar-woman's unwanted brat.

The bustle of the day's trade, which started at dawn and built through the morning, was quietening down. The thrifty housewives had been and gone again, finished with their bargaining and gossip. It was time for the hawkers and stall holders to pause, and devote themselves to their midday meals before the lazy afternoon unfolded itself.

"What do you want, then?'' The sour-faced seller of breads paused in her task of covering her wares. "To finish robbing me blind?''

"You got well paid for the ill-baked and miserable loaves the child took, Mother,'' said Yusuf.

"I'm no mother of yours, you heathen bastard,'' she retorted.

"How would you know?'' he asked airily. "I will take a big loaf. And it's for my master, so make sure it's well baked.'' He pulled the leather purse out from under his tunic and took out a penny. "When did little—uh—Samuel get to the market?'' he asked. "He's a rascal, running off like that. His mother was out of her mind with worry.''

"Dunno,'' said the woman, snatching the coin and handing him a loaf. "Caterina! When did that miserable thieving little brat turn up?''

"He was here when I came, sleeping in with Bartolomeo's fish,'' said Caterina. "Do you begrudge a penny-worth of bread for a hungry baby? He's naught but a baby.''

"Baby indeed. His mother sent him down here to steal, thinking no one would mind, that's what. I know women like that. And I didn't notice you offering him honey cakes. Still, Bartolomeo shouldn't encourage them.''

"What did he do?" asked Yusuf.

"Bought him milk to drink, and a little cake, because he cried and said he was hungry. Stupid fool!"

Bartolomeo was a small, quick, dark man, with eyes that darted back and forth and a reputation for selling excellent fish at high prices. Housewives grumbled and bargained and cursed at him, and bought and bought again. He grinned at Yusuf. "I see you found yourself a soft berth," he said. "Not so long since you were begging for food in the market yourself. Well, Master Isaac's a good man, and he's not so soft as he looks, so mind yourself, lad."

"Don't worry about me. Where did that little boy come from?"

"Master Isaac's nephew?" asked Bartolomeo, with a snigger. "My aunt, just as likely. He's not from the Quarter. He came in with the fruit and vegetables. From the country."

"Son of his wife's niece, he is," said Yusuf. "The one who ran off to the country and married a farmer. She'll be mad with worry. How did he get here? Who brought him in?"

Bartolomeo grinned. "Felip, it was. It seems the lad crept into a big basket of greens old Mother Violant set out, all neat and covered, for Felip to bring to market. He fell asleep until they got here. Felip was in a rare temper about it, too. Half of it was crushed and ruined."

Yusuf took Isaac's purse out from his tunic again. He scooped up two coins and held them out for Bartolomeo. "My master asked me to repay those who had helped his little nephew. He is very grateful. Tell Felip he will be paid as well."

The bread under his nose reminded Yusuf that he was famished, and he turned in the direction of Rebecca's house. There had been something in her kitchen that had given off a heavenly odor of spice and garlic and meat, and he was at least hopeful that some of it might come his way. He ran, lightly and quickly, turned a corner, and bumped directly into a well-dressed, stocky, red-faced man who grasped him firmly by the arm and would not let him go.

"I've been looking for you, boy," he said, smiling and tightening his grip. "I want to talk to you. And I've something for you."

"What have you to do with me?" asked Yusuf.

"Nothing, and a great deal," he said. The answer seemed to amuse him, and he smiled broadly. "You serve Isaac the Jew, do you not?"

Yusuf considered the wisdom of answering truthfully, and could not at the moment see why he shouldn't. Everyone in the market knew that Isaac had employed him. "I do," he said.

"Is he a good master to you?"

He paused again.

"Come now. That's a simple question, even for a heathen to answer. Is he a good master?"

"He is fair enough," said Yusuf finally. His arm was beginning to ache from the pressure of the stranger's grip.

The stranger held up a coin in front of Yusuf's face. He blinked. It was a silver groat, an enormous sum in his eyes, and Yusuf's suspicion changed to real fear. "Tell me, boy, whose is that child he found? The one he called his nephew. If I like your answer, this coin is yours."

"What kind of answer will please you, sir?" he said, in his best begging tones. "I can give many answers."

"A truthful one. If it tells me something I want to hear, so much the better. But I shall know if you lie," he said, shaking him, "for I know more than you think I do."

But Yusuf had now moved onto familiar ground. He had heard such threats before. "The child is certainly no nephew of my master's," he said knowingly.

"Even though he called him uncle?"

"They all call him uncle. You must know that. That is some beggarwoman's brat."

"And why is he looking after some beggarwoman's brat?" The grip tightened on his arm. "Is the child his?"

"Did the child look like he'd been fathered by my master? No. My master once had a feeling for the mother of the child." He shrugged, as if such emotions were beyond his range of belief. "But she disappeared some little while ago, and he wants to find her. I was sent to nose around in the market to see what news I could get. Myself, I think she's probably dead in a ditch somewhere."

"Is that true?"

"I only know what I'm told, and what I hear. But my ears are sharp."

"What you have told me is worth no more than a penny, unless you can tell me where to find the child." He held up the coin again.

"Alas," said Yusuf, staring hungrily at the silver groat, "I do not know. He paid some countrywoman a penny to get rid of the brat—to return him to wherever he came from. He's not interested in the child—only in its mother."

"You're lying," said the stranger, abruptly. "I can smell it. And when I find out what you're lying about, I'll have your hide off."

"You promised me a penny," said Yusuf boldly, his heart now pounding so hard he was sure the stranger could hear it.

"Get out of here, you heathen scum." He let go of Yusuf's arm and raised his fist.

Yusuf darted out of the way and raced by a long and roundabout road to Rebecca's house.

Rebecca set down the fresh loaf and a savory dish of shin of beef cooked with onions, garlic, apricot, and ginger. She looked from her husband to her father and frowned. "Tell Papa, Nicholau," she said abruptly. "He ought to know about it."

Nicholau cleared his throat unhappily and shook his head. "It was nothing, Rebecca. Malcontents with a skinful of wine apiece in them. Sober, they'd never say that."

"Tell him, Nicholau," said his wife, slowly and emphatically. She held the ladle in her hand, poised above the empty plates.

"Yes," said Isaac. "If it is something I should know, then please, tell me."

Nicholau looked from wife to father-in-law to dish of stew and crumbled. He was hungry, and tired, and had been through two days of domestic hell. He could stand it no longer. He began hesitantly. "At Sant Johan I was in Rodrigue's tavern by the river." He glanced at his wife, but she had elected to grant immunity on that subject for now. "It was a hot night, you'll remember, and the mood was—well, sour. Pere tried to get people going by lifting his cup and drinking to a good harvest and a prosperous year. Someone asked him why he bothered and that didn't cheer anyone. Around then a stranger walked in. His name was Romeu, he said, and he was from Vic. He started throwing money around like a bridegroom who's just married a sackful of gold, buying jug after jug of wine. Then Martin, the bookbinder, started complaining that the Bishop and the Canon Vicar were giving all his work to Jews."

"That was because Martin got drunk and let his apprentice ruin a fine presentation copy of the Bible," observed Rebecca, ladling stewed beef into a plate by way of encouragement, and setting it in front of her father.

"I was getting uncomfortable with the turn of the conversation," said Nicholau, "because you know that Raimunt at the seminary has petitioned the Canon Vicar to keep lay scribes from having any cathedral work, and since almost all of my work is in the diocesan courts, I'm the person he means."

"Because of me, Papa," said Rebecca quietly.

"I don't understand it," said Nicholau. "There's a shortage of scribes. There is enough work for all."

"It is not just scribes, or bookbinders," said Isaac. "It is in every trade. The clumsy, half-trained journeyman expects that because the master carpenter is dead, he will have the master's work, and the master's fee. When he ruins a piece of fine wood and another master carpenter is called in, he burns with resentment. But if this is what you wanted to tell me, I knew it already, my son."

"No, there is more, Papa Isaac. While Martin was complaining, someone—and I think it was Josep the paper maker—said that if the Sword of the Archangel Michael went too hot after the Canon Vicar and the Jews, it might find itself melted down. That really stirred everyone up, and someone said the Sword was right, and several spoke against the Canon Vicar, and the Bishop, and the Jews, and even against the King. Those last were the words that started the riot, and I think they were spoken deliberately by the Fellowship of the Archangel's Sword in hopes of creating trouble.''

''And is this Romeu a member of the Fellowship? In your opinion?''

''I believe so. I think he was manipulating the talk—not very subtly, either—so that the Fellowship could be brought into it.''

''But why, Nicholau?'' asked Rebecca. ''What good could they hope for from a night of brawling?''

''I don't know,'' said her husband. ''And I don't know where the Fellowship comes from, but in the last ten days, I have heard it whispered about here and there. I would guess that Martin, and Sanch, and maybe even Raimunt belong to it. I don't like the sound of it.''

''And did you run with the rioters?''

''He was too drunk to run with anyone,'' said Rebecca coldly. ''He slept in a stable and crawled home at dawn, not fit to be seen.''

''Good,'' said Isaac. ''Drunkenness can have its uses. I am glad he was not abroad that night.''

''But there is something else very important,'' said Rebecca. As a sign of forgiveness, she heaped a generous serving of stew into her husband's plate, and set it in front of him. ''Remember?''

''Ah, yes,'' said her young husband, much more cheerfully, ''the cathedral. At Mass, last Sunday, I saw that same Romeu, dressed like a fashionable rich man, in company with a lady.''

''And did he appear to be a rich man at the tavern?'' asked Isaac.

''No, not at all,'' he said, attacking his dinner with bread and a wide spoon. ''His hose fit badly, and his tunic was threadbare in places, and of an old cut.''

"And the lady wore a fortune on her back," interrupted Rebecca. "Silk and jewels."

"Dressed like a harlot?" asked Isaac.

"Oh, no, Papa. Dressed like a lady of the court. Rich, and fine, but not immodest. You couldn't help but notice her. It was her hair. Red, a deep, bright red, and dressed low, in the French fashion, in twists over her ears, with emeralds and gold wire bound into it to fasten on her veil."

Isaac rose to his feet. "I must go to the Bishop," he said. "He will want to hear this. Where is Yusuf?"

"In the kitchen, with Johan. They are both eating again, and Yusuf is teaching him how to draw horses with a piece of burned wood. But, Papa, you have scarcely touched your meal. Stay and dine, and then you can go to the Bishop."

"We have lost too much time already," said Isaac.

"Master Isaac!" said the Bishop, rising to greet him. "You come in a good hour. I have just sent a man to fetch you. How is the child?"

"He was frightened but unharmed by his experience, I think," said Isaac. "He has eaten well and is now sleeping peacefully."

"Your letter did not say where he is hidden—"

"I thought it unwise. A letter can fall into many hands," said Isaac.

"Very prudent. And I would urge you not to shout the information aloud in this room," he said, very quietly. "Come to my private study, where we can speak without undesirable witnesses." Berenguer took Isaac's elbow and directed him toward the stairs.

"I received a letter today from His Majesty, brought by Don Arnau," said Berenguer, once they were settled in the Bishop's private quarters. "It forewarns us of a new attack on his peace, in the most veiled and diplomatic language. He believes that it could well start here in Girona."

"As indeed it has," said Isaac.

"Of course, the half-witted porter who took your letter gave it to Francesc, saying that it was not important. Until an hour ago I knew nothing about the Prince's abduction, and assumed that His Majesty meant an attempt on Lady Isabel. But as soon as I read your letter, my friend, I realized he was warning me against an attack on the Infant.'' He paused for a moment. ''Did you know that the child's nursemaid was found by the side of the road with her throat cut?''

''I knew only that the child had seen something terrible happen to her,'' said Isaac. ''But what were they doing out alone?''

''No one seems to know,'' said Berenguer. ''I wrote to His Majesty as soon as I received your letter, describing what I knew of the situation, requesting further instructions. I advised placing the Prince with the nuns, where we know he will be safe, unless His Majesty would like Arnau and his men to return him to the palace at Barcelona.''

''He is much distressed at the loss of his nursemaid,'' said Isaac. ''He found her body, I believe—from what he says. His own escape, you will agree, was miraculous,'' he added. ''He is safe for now, and I suggest that he be allowed to stay where he is until tomorrow. He needs to rest.''

The Bishop stirred uneasily. ''It is in the Quarter?''

''No,'' said Isaac, skirting on the edges of the truth. ''It is with an honest, charitable Christian man and his wife. He does not realize who the child is. He believes him to be recently orphaned, and in need of temporary safekeeping from greedy relatives. I assure you that the Crown Prince will disappear from view among the couple's own children.''

''I would bring him here,'' said the Bishop. ''This is a safe refuge from the stranger outside the gate, but I fear that even in the Bishop's palace the King has enemies. They would quickly realize who the child is. Let him rest where he is. Tomorrow we shall transfer him to the convent until we receive further instructions. Once my niece is a little recovered, she can play with her small brother. How is Lady Isabel, Master Isaac?''

''She continues to grow stronger. This morning she was

able to eat a little. I am almost confident now of her quick recovery.''

"I am much relieved to hear that.'' Berenguer pushed back his chair and started to rise, but Isaac raised his hand to stop him.

"One moment more, I pray you, my lord Bishop. I learned something else today.''

Berenguer sat down again. "To do with the Prince?''

"I don't know.'' And Isaac gave him a succinct account of the observations made by his daughter and son-in-law.

"The Archangel's Sword. A curious coincidence,'' said Berenguer. "Today I received a letter from the man himself.''

"It is a man?'' said Isaac. "I thought it was a fellowship.''

"It may be both.'' Berenguer picked up a folded paper. "After the usual salutations, he says, 'The Incarnation of the Flaming Sword of Michael the Archangel addresses His Excellency, the Bishop of the Diocese of Girona. The Archangel wishes me to warn you that Girona, the City of God of which the saints speak, lies under his special protection. On this day, sixty-eight years ago, which was also the day of my father's birth, Saint Michael drove the French from its gates. As only son of my father, I am appointed to cleanse it of corruption and wickedness. The evil ones within its gates must perish. They are the wealthy clergy, especially the Bishop and his canons, and the Abbess and her nuns; corrupt rulers, that is, the King, and his heirs; and the Jews, who are agents of both.

" 'The Archangel has visited me, and instructed me to cut the throats of the ungodly. I have begun. Renounce sin and depart this place forever, or you will join the ranks of the dead souls in hell.' '' Berenguer paused. "He has a fine style, but I don't think the man likes me.''

"Nor me, my friend.''

"But Doña Sanxia might have died because she was wearing the habit,'' said Berenguer.

"And the nursemaid?''

"Perhaps because she was protecting His Majesty's heir, the Infant Johan."

"There are still many questions—"

"To which I don't know the answers. But the attempt to murder the Crown Prince has failed and he will be hidden or closely guarded until this madman can be taken. His Majesty has no other sons to be threatened, and I would judge that his brother, Don Fernando, can look after himself. I feel no particular sense of responsibility for his safety even if he can't," added Berenguer dryly. "Our problem has been simplified. We must shield the convent from scandal by discovering what Doña Sanxia de Baltier was doing there. We can leave the Archangel's Sword to others."

"I wonder who the Archangel's Sword is?"

"A madman. Perhaps this Romeu, whoever he is. My officers will search him out. It is unlawful to utter death threats against a bishop. Or anyone else, in fact," he added, yawning. "Isaac, I am weary and in need of relaxation. This day has had more than its full complement of crisis and agony. It is already too late for vespers, and still too early for supper. Do you have time for a game of chess, my friend?"

"I am sadly out of practice," said Isaac. "If Your Excellency will condescend to tell me where the pieces are when I forget, I shall try my poor skills."

"Hypocrite!" said Berenguer, and took a board and set of chessmen from a small table in the corner.

But the pieces were scarcely set in their places when the hammering on the door started.

"My lord Bishop!"

"What is it, Francesc?" Berenguer rose impatiently and unlocked the door.

"Your Excellency," said the Canon Vicar, "your niece Lady Isabel and Master Isaac's daughter have disappeared from the convent and cannot be found."

SEVEN

Raquel squirmed and shifted position in her hard chair, and thought longingly of the soft cushions and comfortable beds of home. A bed in the room had been prepared for her, but she was uneasy lying down unless Sor Agnete was there and awake. She straightened up and tried to think of something to pass the time. Nuns—about whom she was learning a great deal, she thought—seemed to have a remarkable tolerance for discomfort. Sor Agnete had been sleeping sitting bolt upright in a narrow chair until a few moments before, when she had excused herself, murmuring that she would return soon, and bring them both a little early supper when she did. Raquel stretched surreptitiously, and then turned to check her patient.

Lady Isabel's eyes were open, and fixed on her. Raquel stood up, grateful for something to do, and moved closer to the bed.

"What crime have you committed that you are condemned to stay with me night and day, Raquel?"

"It is no punishment, Lady Isabel," said Raquel.

"Nonetheless, it cannot be very amusing."

"Every minute I stay here, I learn something new about life in the convent. It is very interesting. What is commonplace to you, my lady, is a different world to me.''

"Then you must pray for my speedy recovery," said Lady Isabel, and laughed. "The nuns are kind, but once the novelty is over, you'll find them as boring as I do. Hush!'' she added. ''I think I hear one in the corridor.''

Sor Agnete swept into the room and placed a tray down on the table. "You look improved, Lady Isabel," she said. "I coaxed some special fare from the kitchen. I hope it is to your liking." She turned to Raquel. "If your patient seems well enough, Raquel, I would like to join my sisters for a while before vespers. The Abbess has asked to see me.''

"Please, Sister," said the invalid, "do not stay on my account. I feel almost well.''

Sor Agnete hesitated for a moment, then left.

"Now," said Lady Isabel, "let us see what the good sisters consider delicacies.''

Raquel carried the tray over, and lifted the napkin away from a tureen of soup, soft bread, a custard with fruit, and a pitcher filled with an infusion of ginger and other aromatic herbs. "The soup doesn't look very hot," said Raquel.

"Sor Agnete must have stopped to chatter on her way up here. It doesn't matter. Shall we have some? I'm hungry. You must be, too.''

The Abbess Elicsenda waited, standing erect and composed looking, in the small reception room near the entrance to the Bishop's palace. Only the heightened color in her cheeks betrayed her agitation. Sor Marta stood behind her, managing to blend into her surroundings as if she had no more substance that the flickering shadows around them. "Your Excellency, Master Isaac," said Elicsenda, in an uncertain voice. She stopped and began again. "I can only say that I am unworthy of my high office. I did not believe that someone could enter my convent in the light of day with evil intent, and carry out such a deed. I was not prepared, and I hold myself responsible for the disappearance of your niece and your daughter. That said, I have come to consult on what is best to be done now.''

"What has been done?" asked Isaac, his voice taut.

"Tell us on the way to the convent," said Berenguer, "lest more time be lost." He turned to the Canon Vicar. "Send the captain of the guard to me, but first have him dispatch officers to Sant Daniel and Sant Feliu to find if any strange, or suspicious-looking groups have been seen. Hurry.''

"In what way 'strange,' Your Excellency?"

"In any way imaginable, Francesc. We do not know how they have managed to smuggle two young women, one of them still gravely ill, out of the convent and away from the area. But it is likely that they have.''

"Yes, Your Excellency.''

"And now, Lady Elicsenda, what has already been done?" The group moved out, walking swiftly down to the convent.

"The convent has been searched except for the cellars and the unfinished rooms above the cloister. Four sisters are searching the cellars, and the architect and the builder have been summoned to help search the new wing. I do not expect much," she said. "A door near the kitchens, which is always locked and barred, was open. It seems certain that someone entered that way. I fear that Lady Isabel has been abducted, and Raquel with her.''

"And what does the nun who was guarding her say?" asked Berenguer.

"Sor Agnete?"

The Bishop nodded, grimly.

"She can say nothing. She was not there. Lady Isabel appeared stronger this afternoon, and I summoned Sor Agnete to help me with the accounts. She took some supper to Lady Isabel and Raquel, and left them, meaning to stay away only a short time. We were longer than expected, and she joined her sisters at vespers. When she returned, they had gone.''

"Another messenger must ride at once to His Majesty," said Berenguer. "But first we must examine the convent.''

"You think that someone in the convent—" Isaac was unable to complete the thought.

"I do," said Elicsenda. "That door was opened this morning to receive provisions, and then locked again by a lay sister. The lay sister returned the key to Sor Marta, who checked herself that the door was locked and barred, did you not?"

Sor Marta nodded. "I am responsible for making sure that the doors are kept secure," she said unhappily. "I cannot say how—"

"Someone," interrupted the Abbess, "almost surely one of our sisters, took a copy of Sor Marta's key, opened the door, and admitted their abductors. She must then have led them to the sick chamber, and assisted them." The door to the convent opened, the Abbess swept in. "Difficult as it is for me to believe, it is the only rational explanation."

"This must be suggested, at least once," said the Bishop, "and I will be the one to say it. If my niece had decided to run away—to elope—could Raquel have been convinced to help her?"

The Abbess stopped and looked over at Berenguer. "That is two questions. I can only answer for Lady Isabel. I can't believe she would consent to such a scheme. She is keenly aware of her position, and one of the least likely of our charges to make a misstep. Master Isaac?"

"Would Raquel have helped Lady Isabel to elope? Perhaps, if she had been well. They are both young, and the young can be foolish. But in her present state of health, Raquel would not have allowed her to walk to the garden, much less run away. She takes her responsibilities very seriously. They were, in my opinion, taken by force."

"And that is also my opinion. When did it happen?" asked Berenguer.

"During vespers. It is the only time someone could have reached them."

"And is the entire convent left unattended during vespers?" asked Berenguer. "Except for two helpless young women?"

"This is no time for anger," said Isaac.

The Abbess shook her head. "Anger is a luxury none of us can afford." She led them into her study and guided Master Isaac to a chair. The Bishop sat as well, and the Abbess paced slowly about the room as she talked. Sor Agnete slipped in, followed by Sor Marta. "How did they leave? Lady Isabel must have been carried on a litter; she is too ill to ride."

"We will soon know," said Berenguer, with more conviction than he felt. "Someone will have noticed whether a litter passed down the road after vespers. Unless they are hidden in the city."

"Impossible," snapped the Abbess. "Once word spreads that Lady Isabel has disappeared, they will not be safe anywhere in Girona. They will be betrayed. Therefore they are somewhere outside the city, at the distance a pair of horses carrying a litter could move in an hour at a moderate pace. But in which direction, I do not know."

"And what do you have to say, Master Isaac?" asked Berenguer gently. "You have been very silent. Is it from sorrow, or from thought?"

Isaac breathed deeply and turned in the direction of his friend's voice. "Can one hear screams from that room in the chapel? Is the room in disarray? Lady Isabel is too weak, but Raquel would not submit without screaming and struggling. If nothing was heard, and there are no signs of struggle, what did they eat? Who prepared it? Was it left unguarded at any time? The answers to these questions would tell us something about who planned the act, and how much help he required."

Sor Marta looked over at the Abbess, who nodded. She slipped out of the room as quietly as she had entered and eased the door shut behind her.

"And," said Isaac in a low voice, "how am I to tell my wife that her beloved daughter has disappeared, apparently without a trace?"

"Isaac, friend Isaac," said Berenguer, "your questions shall be answered, all but the last. That, I cannot say."

The room fell silent. The Bishop moved over to the Abbess's desk and began to draft a letter. Elicsenda walked to the window and looked out, as if she hoped to see the two young women come, laughing and chattering, from a prolonged evening walk. She turned back to the company. "Forgive me," she said. "I have been thinking what is to be done next. Sor Agnete, ask the searchers if they have found any traces of them."

Sor Agnete bowed her head, and left. Silence fell once more over the company, except for the scratching of the Bishop's quill over his paper.

At last Isaac raised his head. "I can do no good here," he said. "It would be better if I left."

As he rose to his feet Sor Marta entered the study again.

"Please stay a moment, Master Isaac," said the Abbess. "Sor Marta, what were you able to discover?"

"They are not in the building, madam. And if you scream very loudly in that chamber, while the door is open, it can be heard in the chapel, although possibly not during a hymn. The room was not in disarray. Lady Isabel's gown, the one that was hanging there, is gone, along with both young ladies' cloaks. The repast was a soup made of mutton and barley—"

"Does it have a strong flavor?" asked Isaac.

"It is a very savory soup, with spices to whet the appetite," said Sor Marta. "It was specially prepared by Sor Felicia and the cook for Lady Isabel. There was also bread, a *tisane* of ginger and herbs and a custard. They had soup, bread, and the *tisane,* but no custard. Sor Agnete took it, leaving it on a table unguarded while she talked to Sor Benvenguda."

"Thank you," said Isaac.

"You may leave now, Sister," said the Abbess. "And I would not be disturbed." She waited for the closing of the door. "They were drugged, and clothed, and carried out of here. It must have been with the help of one of my sisters. I am ashamed."

"The events of the last few days whirl in my brain like leaves in the wind," said Isaac. "It is possible that, like leaves, they make no pattern except that they have touched each of us. That may be their only connection with each other. . . ." His voice trailed off. "Where is Yusuf?"

"You sent him home," said Berenguer.

"So I did. Why did I expect him to return? No matter. I have walked the path between here and there many times alone."

EIGHT

Lost in silence and uncertainty, Isaac reached out a hand to feel his way out of the convent. His foot trembled as it searched awkwardly for the step. Then his staff caught on something and he stumbled.

"Pardon, lord," said a familiar voice. "A thousand pardons. I fell asleep and did not hear you coming." Yusuf caught his master's hand and steadied him.

Judith said nothing for a full minute. Then, turning on her husband, she hit him on the chest with her fists, again and again and again. "You took her there!" she shrieked. "To her death."

Isaac caught Yusuf by the shoulder and pushed him behind him. He made no other move. The storm of blows weakened and stopped. Judith gasped for breath. "I told you to keep away from the nuns. Now look what has happened. My Raquel! My beautiful Raquel!" She broke into a storm of weeping that subsided in a wrenching sigh. "She could have married a rich man, and been happy, and you took her to that place," she said in a curiously detached voice, and then fell to sobbing again.

Isaac waited impassively until she quietened a little.

"You cannot blame me more than I blame myself, Judith. But it is not certain, not even probable, that she is dead."

"After they are through with her, she might as well be dead," said Judith bitterly. "How will she be able to return here in her shame and disgrace?"

Without a further word Isaac pushed past his wife and walked across the courtyard. Yusuf looked at the stern back of his master disappearing into his study, and then at his mistress, collapsed on Naomi's soft breast, and raced after Isaac. He knocked softly. "Lord, it is I. Yusuf."

"Come in," said Isaac, wearily. He was standing in the middle of the room, with his arms hanging at his sides, and holding his head like someone listening, or a hunted animal searching for pursuers. "Bring me water to wash in, and water to drink," he said at last, and sat down heavily. "And then leave me. If I need you, I will call. You may go to bed when you have eaten."

"Shall I bring you supper, lord?"

Disgust and loathing flashed across his face. "I cannot eat. Just water."

With great deliberation, Isaac concentrated solely on his immediate actions. He washed himself with care, put on a clean tunic, and sat down, straight of back, head balanced, and hands resting on his knees—the perfect simulacrum of a man in repose. Only his breath, coming in ragged gasps, and his muscles, taut as drawn bowstrings, betrayed the turbulence of his spirit.

It was essential for him to find a rational and purposeful meaning in the disconnected events of the past few days. Essential but impossible. Fragmented memories, distorted by rage, poured into his head until they infected his heart and he could feel them—Raquel's fear, Lady Isabel's pain, the scent of evil stalking him, and his dependents and protectors. Then his old enemy darkness, unformed, uncontrolled and uncontrollable, pressed in. He could taste it, thick, hot, and dry, in his mouth; he could feel it, like a heavy blanket, wrapped tightly around his limbs. Having already deprived him of sight, darkness snatched away movement and reason.

Nor could he pray. He had no words to offer to the Lord, only the incoherent babbling of all-consuming rage. And so he sat, motionless, silent, and helpless.

Out in the courtyard, the noises of daily life gradually subsided. Judith ceased her weeping, or took it elsewhere. The twins' penetrating voices faded into the distance. Only the occasional footsteps betrayed any human presence but his own. Feliz meowed interrogatively at his door, and went away again. Judith knocked, and summoned him to supper. But the world outside his room was as far away as the underwater kingdoms of the fables. Voices came to him with a hollow, distant ring, and he could not force himself to reply.

Then nothing. It must be night, he thought. The world is silent.

That thought crystallized suddenly out of the seething chaos in his brain. It is night because the world is silent, he repeated cautiously to himself. Or is the world silent because, in my pride and arrogance, I have been struck deaf as well as blind? Terror replaced rage in his heart.

Then, from outside the door, he heard a faint bump, and a small cat noise. I am not deaf, he thought with relief, and it is night. He repeated the words, clinging to their simplicity and coherence, and gradually his breathing slowed, and his aching muscles relaxed.

Isaac considered those two things. He could hear with unusual acuteness, and in the dark, he was a match for any man. His body, aching and weary though it was, was powerful and adept. He could not think beyond that. When he tried, doubt, recrimination, and fear overwhelmed him again, and he returned to those simple words as to a raft in a raging torrent. It is night; I can still hear.

The city slept. The moon had set sometime before, and a scattering of black clouds obscured the stars. Here and there, a candle burned, unnaturally bright in the darkness.

In the chapel at the convent of Sant Daniel, the nuns sang laud, and Abbess Elicsenda knelt in prayer. She prayed for the physical safety of the two young women, and she prayed for the safety of the soul of the unknown nun who had helped to abduct them, and pondered, uneasily, the question of who she might be. The voices died away; the nuns left, to snatch the remainder of a night's sleep. The Abbess remained, in prayer and speculation.

In his study, Bishop Berenguer trimmed his candle, mended his pen, and continued writing a coherent account of all that had happened, making what sense of it he could. Like his friend Master Isaac, he knew that Lady Isabel d'Empuries was worth too much in lands and gold to be harmed by an abductor with any sense of self-preservation. And while Isabel lived no harm would come to the girl, Raquel, who was needed to safeguard her companion's health and honor. But Isabel had been near death, and if she were to die—Berenguer shook his head and returned to his writing. It held thoughts such as those at bay.

In a room off his bedchamber, Don Pedro of Aragon sat with his secretary, and three slightly disheveled ministers of state, recently called from their beds; on the table were two letters that had arrived in rapid succession from Berenguer of Girona. The first had come at sundown, with joyful news. His Majesty had spent a turbulent evening, caught between profound relief at the recovery of his son, whom he had given up for dead, and cold rage at those who had abducted him. He was asleep when the second letter arrived; the messenger had traveled through the dusk and the dark from Girona, moving like the wind over the hills, taking advantage of the lingering daylight and the brightness of the moon. Then the moon set, and horse and rider had stumbled exhausted through the darkness for the last hour of their journey. The messenger had insisted firmly that His Majesty be summoned from his bed. He was.

The king sat in grim silence. Eleazar ben Solomon, as secretary, read the Bishop's letters, and gave a brief summary of the situation.

"Where is Castellbo?" asked the treasurer, looking around.

"Peacefully asleep, no doubt, in the castle near Girona, where he was supposed to be protecting the Infant," said the King, in a savage tone.

When his voice died, a heavy silence filled the room. While the four men ordered their thoughts Don Pedro thought long and hard about his brother, and contemplated his opening move.

I have become like Samson, thought Isaac, patching the words together with difficulty. Blind and helpless. In my pride I thought I could deal with the Philistines. I have given over my strength to them, and it has destroyed me. And then the absurdity of the analogy occurred to him. And who is my Delilah? The Abbess of Sant Daniel, of the cold voice and hand? He began to laugh, helplessly, until he was close to tears.

Then, sometime later in the night, when his body throbbed with exhaustion and sleeplessness, he became unable to hold his incoherent, panic-stricken thoughts at bay any longer. They crowded back, jostling for expression, and with them came a voice, strange and echoing, murmuring inside his skull—a demonic voice, mocking him. I have destroyed Raquel, he thought, and the exultant voice repeated, *Destroyed Raquel, Raquel, Raquel . . .*

I must stop this, he thought desperately.

Stop, stop, stop . . . echoed the voice.

"O Lord," he said aloud, "save me from madness and teach me how to find truth."

The voice in his head whispered, *Truth,* and faded. Then out of the swirling in his brain came another voice, dry and faint. *Do not forget that truth springs up from the earth, my child. It is everywhere.* It was the voice of his long-dead master, surfacing out of memory, or perhaps sent by the Lord to comfort him.

"I will not forget again, Master," he said aloud. "Nor will I forget whence justice comes."

Peace returned to his soul, and with it a profound and irrational conviction that Raquel was still alive.

For the first time in hours, Isaac stirred in his chair. Suddenly he felt trapped in that enclosed and airless room. He made a tentative effort to raise a hand. It responded, and he wiggled his fingers. They moved. Heartened, he stood, dizzy, swaying, and walked unsteadily to the door. He pulled it open and let in a rush of cool, damp air. The weather had changed. Then Feliz pounced joyfully on his foot, and rubbed against his ankle. He reached down to scratch the cat's ears, and his hand encountered a warm, soft body. "Yusuf?" he asked, in surprise.

"Mmm," said a sleepy voice. "Lord? It is you? Are you well?"

"Indeed. Why are you lying on the doorstep? You should be in bed."

But Yusuf refused to leave the courtyard.

"I welcome your company, my little friend," said Isaac. "I forget that you have become an owl in your travels. How goes the night?"

"Still dark, lord. The skies are filled with clouds, but the dawn shows over the rooftops in the east. It is like the morning we two met."

"Not so many days ago," said Isaac. "You have become useful to me in these short days."

"I do not deserve such praise, lord," said Yusuf, with the modesty of one who clearly thought he did.

"Perhaps not. But as useful as you are, I cannot do without Raquel, lad," said Isaac, his voice shaken with pain. "Who will read to me? Your mistress never learned her letters, and the twins are still too young."

"We will find Raquel, lord," said Yusuf confidently. "And until then, I shall read to you."

"You can read?" said Isaac, astonished. "How did you learn?"

"My father taught me to read in my own tongue, and the letters of the Latin speech were taught me by an old

thief and *jongleur,* who used to go from town to town singing, and telling tales, and stealing purses. I traveled with
him until he was taken by the officers. I will soon learn to
make out the words,'' he added, with a touch of boyish
arrogance.

"Soon," repeated Isaac, despairing. "I cannot wait until
'soon,' lad. I am losing the power to order my own
thoughts. I must return to the words of the masters or I will
go mad.''

Isaac raised his face to the heavens, as if some miracle
might fall on him, allowing him to see into the realm of
his troubled spirit, and understand. A rumble like the voice
of the Lord rolled in from the east, and the first gentle drops
of rain fell on his eyes and lips.

"Come, Yusuf. You must not get wet,'' said Isaac, with
weary courtesy. "We will sleep for a time. Wake me before
the sun is high.''

Raquel shook herself free from a dream of falling into a
deep and brilliantly colored pit. Her heart was pounding in
fright. Her head ached unpleasantly, and her mouth was dry
and evil tasting. For a moment, she thought she was at
home, in her bed, and then remembered that she was at the
convent. She opened her eyes. It was very dark, and she
was lying on something uncomfortable that jabbed into her
back. She sat up, and her stomach lurched queasily. Something was wrong.

She felt the surface she was lying on. It seemed to be a
coarse pallet filled with straw. Her hands moved farther out
until her fingers touched rough boards beyond it. The floor.
From below, she heard the stamp of a hoof, and the soft
nickering of a horse. Either she had gone mad, or she was
lying on a rough floor in a loft above a stable.

Then she realized that the darkness was not uniform. The
square of less intense black must be a window opening,
and the darker darkness an arm's length away, another pallet or other furnishing. She listened hard. Over the stable
noises from below, she could hear the sound of faint, shallow breathing. Dear Lord, she said to herself. Lady Isabel.

She and Lady Isabel, in some manner that she could not understand, had been transferred in their sleep to this unlikely chamber.

Cautiously, she stood up. Her hair brushed against the rafters and cobwebs pasted themselves over her face. She wiped them away with an impatient hand and headed for the square of gray, moving soundlessly in her soft leather boots. When she reached the rough opening in the wall, she leaned her head out. The air was cool and moist; dawn lightened the sky in the east. There were shapes—hills or clouds—on the horizon. She sniffed curiously; the smells were all wrong. They were somewhere in the country.

She crept back along the middle of the room, feeling for the limits of her space. Halfway along, her foot touched an irregularity in the floor, and she reached down. Her fingers traced the outline of a trapdoor; she found a hasp, and gave it a gentle tug. It shifted a hairsbreadth, and then stopped. Locked, or barred in some way. She continued on her silent progress. A board creaked and she froze. Below her, only the reassuring animal noises filtered up to her loft, and she continued on to the rough boards of the farther wall. She failed to find any sign of a door there. There was one way out and it was barred.

She moved to the other pallet and picked up Isabel's limp hand. It was hot, her pulse was faint, and her breathing rapid. She was clad in a heavy silk gown, and wrapped in a warm cloak; Raquel loosened her gown, and crouched by her side to await the dawn.

NINE

Raquel and Isabel were not the only travelers to wake up in a stable on that damp and cloudy Thursday morning. Long before the previous day's sun had reached noon, Tomas de Bellmunt had realized it would take a miracle for his tired mare to get to Girona before nightfall. The least promising mount from his father's modest stable, she had never shown a turn for speed, or much else of use, and for the past year she had been living well and in relative idleness. Poor Blaveta was cruelly out of condition.

As distant bells rang for tierce she slowed; well before noon, she began to stumble. At last, under the fierce sun of midday, she stopped, head down, a picture of dejection. After several useless attempts to revitalize her, Tomas gave in. He himself had no heart for this mission, and he suspected guiltily that his reluctance had communicated itself to the mare. He led her into the shade near a stream and the two of them rested under a tree, dozing until the sun moved into the west.

Somewhat revived, she managed a trot. Then the road turned toward the setting sun, and Blaveta decided she had had enough. The nearby river appeared more inviting; she slowed and veered sharply to the left. Tomas yanked the reins and spurred her on. She began to limp; he clapped the spurs into her sides again. At that, she laid back her ears, planted her forefeet into the dust and pebbles, and refused to budge. Tomas dismounted, acknowledging defeat. Surely the inn where he'd stayed Monday night was just over the next hill. Taking a firm grip on the reins, he led his reluctant beast forward.

He was wrong. The first dwelling he came to—alone in the midst of unpromising-looking fields—was a mean, ramshackle hovel of a farmhouse, with an appendage propped against its east wall that might be called a stable. Tomas looked at it doubtfully. But Blaveta's limp was worse, and his feet were sore. Any shelter would be better than moving on, or sleeping in the stony fields in the open. The sun still hung above the horizon, but the air was damp and heavy; he could feel a storm brewing.

The only sign of life was an occasional wisp of smoke from a brick oven in the yard. He called out, beat on the door, and waited. From inside came a scuffling noise, like the footsteps of hundreds of fleeing mice, and a dirty, dark-haired woman peered out through a crack in the door. She shrieked in alarm and retreated. "Fetch Papa," she cried, and the door opened again. A small child snaked through and pelted down the hill as if a thousand enemy warriors hot for his blood were on his tail.

"Good woman," called Tomas. "I mean no harm."

She answered with a faint shriek of alarm. A child began to cry; someone young and female yelled at it to be silent, and generalized bedlam broke loose.

"Who are you?" asked a voice behind him. "We don't want strangers here."

Tomas turned cautiously, his hand on his sword, and found himself eye to eye with a bear of a man, black-browed, dark from the sun, and powerfully built. At his side a big, rangy hound growled softly.

"I am on royal business, my good man," said Tomas, with more arrogance than he felt. "My horse and I have

need of harborage for the night. You will be well paid for
your hospitality.''

The battle between suspicion and greed was written
across his face for some time. At last greed won by a slender edge. ''What do you want from us?'' he said, in a
slightly less menacing voice.

''Stabling, and a bed for me, and food for both.''

''Let me see your coin.''

''Let me see my bed and stabling,'' said Tomas.

''You'll get nowhere near my wife and daughter,'' said
his genial host. ''You can sleep in the stable with your
horse, and I'll give you half a loaf. We can spare no more.''

The stable was empty, its usual inhabitants, if there were
any, being out to pasture somewhere. It was roofed over
with turf, and walled on two sides with rough boards and
stakes plastered over with mud. It was dirty, dark, and probably infested with every variety of vermin that plagues man
or beast. Tomas had slept in less comfortable quarters, however, and it was likely no dirtier than the house. The half
loaf was coarse and chewy, but large, and tasted like manna
from heaven after a day on the road. Once he had looked
after the mare, and eaten, he set himself to finding a corner
clean enough to bed down in for the night.

He was interrupted in this dispiriting task by the farmer,
who in a sudden fit of geniality brought out a jug of wine
and set it on the dirt floor. ''My woman thought you might
have a thirst.''

''Convey my thanks to her,'' said Don Tomas.

The farmer grunted and left.

Tomas hoisted up the heavy jug and took a cautious taste.
His host's wine was sour and rough, but cleared the dust
of travel from his throat. He headed for the fresher air of
the doorway, and sat down on an upended barrel, helped
himself to a longish draft, and stared thoughtfully at the
jug. There was several days' supply left in it, he would
guess. Giving it to a stranger seemed very openhanded for
such a grasping man. After a moment's reflection, he carried the jug into the stable and tipped it onto the dirt floor.

The wine ran in a small river toward the door, puddled, and sank back into the earth. Tomas spread straw over the wine-dampened ground, set the jug down by the entryway, wrapped himself in his cloak, and stretched out on a thin heap of straw in the corner behind the mare.

In spite of the early hour, exhaustion overtook him as soon as he closed his eyes, and he slept heavily for a time, dreaming of Doña Sanxia. She ran from him, laughing cruelly and tossing her magnificent red hair. When he reached out his arms to her, she melted into a puddle of sour wine, and he awoke. It took him a moment to realize that the voices he heard were not part of his dream, but on the other side of the wall.

"And if he wakes, husband?"

"He finished off that jug. He won't wake this side of judgment day."

Tomas sat up.

The farmer let himself out of his door, and crept quietly along the wall of the house and the lean-to. A small rush-light in his left hand lit up the ground around him, intensifying the darkness beyond. At the corner, he pulled his knife from his boot, and moved quietly toward the stable door. He held up the light and the mare moved restlessly.

"Evening, good man," said Tomas.

The farmer jumped, turned, and dropped his light on the dirt floor of the stable, where it continued to burn feebly.

"I'd stamp that out, if I were you," said Tomas pleasantly. He was seated on the barrel outside the door, and in his hand, his father's sword gleamed in the light of the burning oil on the ground.

The farmer stamped vigorously at the flames, continuing long after they were out. "I thought I heard a thief creeping about," he said at last.

"Ah," said Tomas. "You heard it, too."

"Yes. I come out to see what it were."

"I wonder your hound didn't hear it," observed Tomas.

"Off hunting," muttered the farmer. "Is Your Lordship spending a wakeful night?"

"Not at all. But my mare and I, we sleep with an ear open for trouble. Blaveta is a better watchdog than your hound, I think. I bid you good night, good man."

Tomas and his mare slept lightly until the first glimmer of dawn sent them on their slow, slow way.

The light strengthened outside the rough window in the stable loft. Rain had swept across the surrounding fields, but now a ray of watery sun crept in, lighting up their prison. Raquel's basket of herbs and remedies had been placed in a corner, along with a roughly tied bundle of clothing, but their captors, whether maliciously or not, had not left them water for drinking or washing. Isabel moaned, and tossed her head. Her lips were dry and cracked again, and her skin hot. She needed water, and cooling drafts, and her wound needed attention. However strange and terrifying the beings down below were, Raquel was going to have to beg them for assistance.

She called out nervously. "Is anyone there? Lady Isabel is ill."

There was no response.

Raquel looked at her patient desperately. She hit the rough boards with her fist, and called out the same thing again, a little louder.

There was still no response.

She went to the trapdoor and stamped a tattoo on it with her heels. A horse whinnied. Nothing else. They had been abandoned, locked in, without food, without water. Tears sprang to her eyes, and she almost missed the soft murmur of voices below. There were people down there, pretending not to be. Her fear evaporated. "Hola," she shouted. "You, down there. Are you going to leave the lady to die of thirst and fever?"

She waited for a response. None came, except from the disturbed beasts. "Assassins," she continued, louder. "Vicious sons of defiled mothers! Cowards, afraid of helpless women! Answer me!"

She stalked across the floor, examining her surroundings in the now bright light of day. Once again her feet hit the board that had creaked so menacingly earlier; she bent to look at it. It was old, dry, and cracked, and appeared to be held down with the flimsiest of nails. She grasped a loose end and pulled up with all her strength. It groaned, split, and pulled noisily away from the joist in a hail of rubble and insects. She could now see into the stable. The horse tethered below was pulling back in panic at the attack from above. Raquel picked up the board, rested one end on the floor, put her elegant small foot in the middle of it, and jumped. It broke in half.

Holding the broken board, Raquel looked down again through the space she had created. Below her the agitated horse reared and kicked and a frightened-looking man stared up at her. She knelt down beside the hole she had made, and shoved her piece of board through it. "Open the trap and fetch us water, louts, or I'll drop this on your heads," she said, with satisfaction. "And the next one will land on the beasts, and then—"

"She's destroying my stable," cried a voice, more concerned with property damage than imminent attack. "She's stronger'n a man, she is."

"And I'll go on destroying it," said Raquel, drunk with recklessness. "I'll rip it apart, and I'll put a curse on your cattle, peasant, and your hens. You'll look far before you have an egg or milk or a calf again. Bring us water, or you'll be sorry for this for the rest of your life."

"For God's sake, fool, do something." It was a new voice, sounding both cultured and irritated. Curious, Raquel bent forward until she saw an elegantly dressed man lounging in the open doorway. He smiled at her, an insolent, knowing smile. "Bring them water, and whatever else they need. We don't want the girl to die, do we?"

Raquel slowly pulled the rotten board up into the loft again.

"Can you really put a curse on them to stop their hens from laying?" asked Lady Isabel, after the arrival of water, fresh milk, and bread, and even a jug of boiling water, in which Raquel steeped herbs from her basket.

"No, my lady," said Raquel, soberly. It was one thing to frighten a couple of ignorant peasants, but the man in the doorway with his knowing smile had terrified her. "I wouldn't know how to start. But I was so angry I said the first things that came into my head."

"You're very clever."

"I don't know if it was very clever," said Raquel, "but it made them bring us food and drink. Who are they, my lady? Do you know?"

Lady Isabel shook her head weakly. "Enemies of my father," she whispered. "Or vassals of a lord after my lands. Or both. Probably both." She closed her eyes, and appeared to go to sleep. "If I have to marry an ugly old man who wants my estates," she murmured, "I'd rather he were one of my father's friends than my uncle's." She turned her face away from the light and fell into a doze.

At first light, Tomas led Blaveta back to the road. Two hills away from the miserable farm, a fast-moving rainstorm passed over, and soaked them both. The sun broke through; Tomas walked until the road began to dry, and then mounted his stiff, unhappy mare. They ambled at a gentle pace until the noise of the rain-swollen stream reminded Tomas that both of them were hot, dusty, and thirsty. Man and mare clambered down the slope to a small meadow on the edge of the river. Reflecting that—having missed his rendezvous by almost a day—another hour wasn't going to matter, Tomas rinsed his rain- and sweat-soaked shirt and hung it to dry on a branch, washed vigorously, stretched out on the soft grass, and finished the loaf from his supper.

It was understandable, and perhaps even forgivable, that Tomas should fall asleep. He had slept fitfully the night before, his sword in his hand, conscious of his host's avaricious disposition and sharp knife. A clump of small shrubs between the road and the stream hid them from passing strangers; the sun, although still low in the eastern sky, warmed his face. Blaveta grazed peacefully, and the river sang gently in his ear.

He awoke with the noonday sun full on his face and the

sound of horses in his ears. Blaveta was dozing under a tree. Tomas rolled over on his stomach to watch the passing parade.

In front was a churlish-looking fellow in coarse clothing, riding a horse too good for him, and leading a fine bay mare carrying a young lady of quality. At the end rode a gentleman on a magnificent chestnut. He was dressed splendidly in scarlet and black, the hilt of his sword glittering in the sun. In the middle was a litter slung between two sturdy grays, led by a young rustic in shabby boots and a grimy tunic. The gentleman in the litter, Tomas concluded, must be too ill to care about the appearance of his servants.

The procession drew closer, and Tomas swore. Castanya. He would have recognized that chestnut anywhere, just as he knew its rider. Romeu. Romeu, suited like a gentleman and bearing a sword.

His first impulse was to stand up and call out. Caution stilled his tongue. He looked again, and saw to his consternation that the young woman had her hands securely tied to each other, and then fastened to her saddle.

Her eyes flicked in his direction. "Stop! We need water," she called out.

"We'll stop when I decide to stop," said Romeu.

Tomas was outraged. This was what his uncle had meant by escorting prisoners of quality—commanding two slovenly rustics and his own servant, escorting a gentlewoman tied to her saddle and a gentleman confined to a litter. A shameful occupation for a knight. Tomas had imagined foreign hostages, or at worst, rebels of noble rank. Crouching down, he dressed hastily, unsheathed his sword, and began to work his way up the hill.

Raquel's eyes widened for an instant, and she turned to Romeu. "Lout," she said loudly. "My patient requires assistance. Whatever reason you have for abducting us, even you can see that it is not to your advantage to maltreat us. I assure you, we have friends—"

"Keep quiet," snapped Romeu.

Tomas dislodged a small rock that tumbled noisily down the hill.

"—who will make your lives a misery," Raquel continued as loudly as she could. "I insist that you allow me to dismount. If you wish to—"

"Quiet!" Romeu bellowed, dismounting. "I heard something."

"Nonsense," said Raquel, quickly.

"Romeu, my friend." Tomas spoke quietly. "Turn and justify yourself before I plant my steel in your back."

When Romeu turned to face him, his sword was at the ready. "It's the little master," he said contemptuously.

"Throw down your weapon and loose that woman," said Tomas steadily.

"Now, now, little master. Let me give you some advice. Don't risk your young life right now. Go home to your little *finca,* and we'll forget all about this. You're meddling in matters you don't understand."

"Throw down your weapon, Romeu," repeated Tomas in the same voice.

"Don't be foolish," said Romeu, and lunged.

But, although Romeu was just as quick and strong as Tomas, and much cleverer about political intrigues, he had not been packed off at seven years of age, like Tomas, to learn manners, morals, and the art of war from Tomas's uncle on his father's side. At thirteen, Tomas had sailed to Majorca beside his uncle to help capture the island for his king. At seventeen, he had gone on his own to fight against the *Uniones* at Valencia, and had been wounded in defense of Pedro's right to the throne. He had nursed his injuries at home until his uncle Castellbo found him his new post, where he floundered ineptly in the strange and hostile environment of the court. With a sword in his hand, however, he knew exactly what to do.

He attacked with all the cool cunning he had been taught by skillful masters, with all the rage and frustration building in him for the last four days, and with wild joy that he was, at last, facing an enemy he could see. Romeu's first deep thrust he parried easily, falling back a step. At his second thrust, Tomas went on the attack, feinting and striking, moving rapidly but easily along a carefully calculated line.

Romeu was skillful, but fatally hampered by a sense of his own brilliance, and the belief that his master was a helpless fool. Tomas drove him back to the edge of the road, and nicked his left arm. Romeu stepped back, and Tomas pursued him into the rocky fields. Tomas stumbled on the rough ground and took a minor hit on the forearm. He changed ground, feinted, and caught Romeu above the brow. With a look of amazement, Romeu lifted his hand to touch the bleeding wound, and Tomas lunged.

Romeu fell, with a mortal wound in his breast. Tomas pulled his sword out, slowly wiped it clean, and sheathed it again. "That's what comes from raising a sword against me, Romeu," he said, coolly. "And you were wrong to involve me in your treachery." The sound of hoofbeats deflected him for a moment. He turned his head in time to see the graceless lout on the well-bred horse disappearing in a panic. The lad on foot was nowhere to be seen. He turned his attention back to Romeu. "Did you kill Sanxia?"

"No, little master," said Romeu, gasping for breath. "And I don't know who did. She wasn't supposed to die. Not then." He coughed, a trickle of blood ran from his mouth, and he opened his eyes very wide. "And I don't know who killed Maria," he whispered. "She was on the other side of the city from our meeting place. She betrayed me and, for her pains, was killed by some passing thief." He began to laugh sardonically, coughed, and fell into his final silence.

Bellmunt placed Romeu's hands across his breast, crossed himself, murmured a prayer, and hurried over to the angry young lady. "Madam," he said, bowing, "Tomas de Bellmunt, at your service." He began to unknot the rope around her wrists. "I don't know why, but my manservant, who now lies in that field, seemed to be holding you prisoner—"

"We were abducted," said Raquel angrily. "Taken from the protection of the sisters at the convent of Sant Daniel while we were unconscious. Why?"

"I don't know," said Tomas hastily. "I swear it. I had taken Romeu for an honest man. I was wrong. But he has paid for his betrayal."

Raquel shook her wrists free from their restraints, rubbing them energetically. "Lady Isabel is very ill. She needs attention and rest, not being dragged about the countryside." She looked down at the ground uneasily, well aware that she was much more skilled in healing than in horsemanship. She glanced haughtily at her rescuer, turning pink with embarrassment, drew her right leg up under her skirt, and crossed it over the bay mare's back. With sudden decisiveness, she placed a hand on Tomas's shoulder, and jumped down from her well-schooled mount. She straightened her skirts with a rapid gesture and hurried over to Lady Isabel.

Then, remembering the request he had overheard, Tomas raced back to the river and filled his leather bottle with cold water. He followed the young woman over to the litter. "I overheard you ask for water. May I offer some? I will fetch as much as is required."

"Who is this, Raquel?" The voice from behind the curtained litter was low, and weak, and very sweet.

"Tomas de Bellmunt, my lady. It was his servant who kidnapped us."

"But not on my orders, I swear!" said Tomas. "I cannot imagine why anyone should want to abduct you. But whatever Romeu was attempting, he has paid dearly for it, my lady. I have killed him," he added soberly. "And whatever I can do to repay you for your sufferings, I will do gladly."

"I would like some water," said the voice from behind the curtain.

Raquel pushed back the curtain and took a cup from their bundle. She held it out to Tomas, who filled it expertly from the skin.

She pushed back the other side of the curtain, and Tomas looked down at a face pale as death, surrounded by thick hair that reminded him of honey, and ripe grain, and beech leaves in autumn. Her dark eyes were soft and luminous. She smiled, and Doña Sanxia scampered out of his memories forever. He felt he had known this beautiful lady, with her arching brows and finely drawn nose, all his life; she looked like a pictured saint, or a statue of marble, or—his sovereign majesty, the King. His heart sank.

She drank from the cup, and pushed it away. "Thank you, Don Tomas," she murmured. "For the water, and for rescuing us. I am Isabel d'Empuries, and my companion—" She coughed and reached for more water.

"And I am Raquel, daughter of Isaac the physician," she said as Tomas filled the cup. "We would like to go back to Girona."

"There is an inn close by," said Tomas. "I had hoped to reach it last night."

"We passed it less than an hour ago," said Raquel. She reached into her basket and took out a linen cloth. "If you will give me your arm, Don Tomas, I will bind up that wound."

Tomas held out his arm. Raquel undid his sleeve and neatly tied up the shallow cut on his forearm. "Thank you, mistress," he said. "If I may suggest—when you and Lady Isabel are ready to travel again—I will escort you to the inn and then ride to Girona to let your friends know of your safe recovery. I will return at first light to escort you back to the convent."

"Thank you, Don Tomas." Lady Isabel's voice was so soft he stepped forward and bent down to catch her words. "You are very kind."

Tomas reddened and backed away. "But first I must find my mare—down by the river—and catch Romeu's horse, which is my horse, because mine is in Barcelona, with a tender left rear leg, and so since Romeu had Castanya, I was forced to ride the other poor beast—"

Isabel smiled. Raquel began to laugh.

"Do I amuse you, madam?" said Tomas, hurt and somewhat offended.

"You do, Don Tomas," said Raquel. "And I am grateful. We have lived in such a strange nightmare world since yesterday that to hear you talk of horses so passionately

and so lucidly is a delight. You are not used to talking to
women, are you?''

"But I am secretary to Her Majesty, Doña Eleanor," said
Tomas, as if that answered the question.

"Please, catch Castanya, and rescue your mare, and let
us leave this dreadful place," said Raquel.

TEN

Isaac awakened to a light touch on his arm. "Lord," said Yusuf softly. "Lord, it is past midday, and the mistress is asking for you. I have brought you something to eat."

His master swung his legs over onto the floor and sat up. He was weary beyond belief, and his head swam with giddiness. "I will not eat. Not yet. Bring me a cup of water only."

"Here, lord," said the boy, and placed it in his hand.

"Now, lad. Listen to me. Go to your mistress and tell her—"

"Tell her what, lord?"

"Not the truth," said Isaac wearily. "The truth is that I cannot bear to speak to her. The truth is that, though I am surrounded by books full of wisdom, they are no use to me, because Raquel is gone. Tell her that I must have solitude in which to think, and that I am going out to the fields. Then get yourself food, and we will leave."

Isaac washed with cold water and put on fresh clothing. "We will cross the river," he said. "But slowly, for my limbs are stiff and sore this morning." And they set out at a leisurely pace for the bridge.

The river was still turbulent from the morning's storm,

but the sky was clear, and a breeze tempered the heat of the sun. "Where are we going, lord?" asked Yusuf. "We have crossed the bridge."

"To meet a man who has long wanted to speak to me," said Isaac.

"Yes, lord," said Yusuf, in a very doubtful voice.

"Somewhere not far from here," said Isaac, "is a large and leafy tree, under which a man may sit in peace, and be seen from every side."

"In that field," said Yusuf. "Beyond the church."

"Take me there, lad," said Isaac. "I shall sit under the tree and consider what needs to be considered."

Silently, Yusuf led his master across the field.

"You may leave me now." Isaac settled down with his back against the tree, and gestured at the boy to go. He laid his hands on his thighs and drew several deep, slow breaths.

"But, lord," said Yusuf, "what am I to do?"

"Go to the market and seek answers," said Isaac, in a drowsy voice.

"To what questions, lord?"

"If you cannot find answers, then you must first look for questions," said Isaac impatiently. "When you find them, return for me. If I have gone, seek me at home."

"Let me bring you food and drink, lord."

"No. Now leave me."

Yusuf started across the meadow. Before he had taken three steps, he stopped, and turned resolutely back. "There is one who has been following us." There was a panicked catch in his voice.

"A tall man, long of leg, in military garb?"

"Yes, lord."

"Watch for him, Yusuf. He smells of evil. And tell me when you see him again."

Tomas de Bellmunt looked over his troops—two gently raised ladies and five horses—and marshaled them with military precision. "I will lead the pair of grays," he said to Raquel. "Can you lead poor Blaveta as well as ride your own animal, madam?"

"Certainly," she said, and paused. "Or I think I can, Don Tomas," she admitted. "I've never ridden before today, as I'm sure you could see. But this morning's journey seemed easy enough."

"Excellent," said Tomas doubtfully as he helped her scramble onto the mare's back. She adjusted her skirts about her, grasped Blaveta's reins in one hand, the bay mare's in the other, and gave her mount a tentative kick. The procession lurched forward.

"If I'd known about this, I would have dressed for traveling before falling asleep," she remarked, looking down at her fine linen gown with a wry smile. But in spite of the discomforts she had endured so far, Raquel admitted to herself that this was the most exciting event of her generally tranquil life. With a certain sense of guilt—for surely her parents must be frantic with worry—she also realized that she was enjoying herself immensely. Boldly, she turned to Bellmunt. "How came you to be lurking down by the river as we went by, Don Tomas?" she asked slyly.

"Lurking, madam? I wasn't lurking," he protested. "It was that sad mare you're dragging along behind you."

"The mare was lurking?"

Something that sounded like a snort of laughter made him pause and look around. "Of course not," said Tomas. "The mare was limping, and I sought shade and water for her to rest. We had slept little the night before—"

"In short, Don Tomas, you went down there to sleep away the heat of the day, instead of carrying out your commission, whatever it was."

The knowledge of what his commission was to have been silenced him. He nodded, appalled at what he had almost done.

"And was this terrible, sleepless night at the inn where you propose to take us?" asked Raquel. "That isn't very kind of you."

"Oh no, madam. The inn is reasonably comfortable. Last night, Blaveta and I were accommodated in a stable, by a courteous, kindly farmer. He was eager to help the tired beast," he said wryly, "by lightening her load, of my purse, and of me as well.'' He thought of the incident with a curious sense of affection. If it hadn't been for the wretched mare and the dirty cutthroat, this whole adventure would not have happened. He laughed. A distinct ripple of answering laughter echoed back at him from behind the closely drawn curtains of the litter.

The inn was of the type travelers over a well-worn route have come to expect—providing rough wine poured with a heavy hand, unvarying but hearty food, uncomfortable beds, and dirt at exorbitant prices. But the accommodations were palatial compared with stables and haylofts.

It had a peaceful and welcoming air, slumbering by the road beneath a golden summer sun. At the moment, it was empty, for last night's travelers had left, and today's had not yet arrived. Few lingered more than a night by choice. Tomas went inside to reconnoiter. The innkeeper was snoring in his cubicle behind the common reception hall; the inn's watchdog opened an eye and closed it again. Tomas stepped over its recumbent body and banged his fist on a table. "Hola! Innkeeper,'' he called. The snoring stopped. He rattled a purse filled with coins in a meaningful way. A pair of boots hit the floor, and a tousled, sleepy-eyed man came into the room.

"What—" He blinked and looked at Tomas, from boots to hat. His voice took on an ingratiating tone. "My apologies, Your Lordship. Last night was busy, and I—''

"Yes, yes,'' said Tomas. "Never mind that. Can you accommodate two ladies in comfort and safety until morning? One is ill, and can travel no farther today.''

"Certainly, my lord,'' said the host, with his eye on Tomas's weighty purse. "I have a beautiful room, elegant, suitable for the noblest of ladies, with a room beside, where they may dine, and sit in comfort.''

"Let me see it,'' said Tomas suspiciously.

And so, Raquel and Isabel found themselves in a pair of rooms for the night, well apart from the common lofts and sleeping chambers that accommodated humbler travelers, where they were waited on by a wide-eyed servant girl who admitted, when pressed, to being all of eleven years old.

Isaac sat leaning against the tree trunk and waited. He bent his mind to mapping out sounds and scents—the perfume of meadow flowers, the humming and buzzing of insects, the many smells of grasses after a morning rain, and—so pervasive that it disappeared from consciousness—the rank smell of river mud in summer, and the ranker smell of people.

He felt, more than heard, the man's approach. It was as if the earth shivered at the touch of his feet. Then he picked out the faint swish of cloth, and the creak and smell of leather—not of ill-made boots, but of stiff harness. A sword belt. Last of all came the smell of sweat, horses, and fear.

Isaac waited.

The man's voice was harsh, but his speech was cultured. "You are Blind Isaac the physician of Girona," he said.

"I am," said Isaac.

"You are a Jew."

"I am."

"Do you know who I am?"

"I do not *know*," said Isaac. "But I believe you are the one who calls himself the Sword of the Archangel Michael. Am I right?"

"You are," said the Sword. "Why do you sit here on the ground, alone and unprotected, if you know you are pursued by the Archangel's Sword?"

"I wanted to talk to you," said Isaac, casually. "And I believed you wanted to talk to me. I decided to sit alone, in a quiet place, and see if you would come to me."

"There is nothing I wish to say to you, physician," said the Sword. "But I will hear you. What have you to say to me?"

"Only this," said Isaac. "Why do you pursue me and mine?"

"Only you," said the Sword. "I have no interest in those around you. I leave the less important ones to the others. You are my object."

"And why?"

"You're a clever man, physician. You know that answer."

"I am not sure what your reasons are."

"You are an evil man," said the Sword calmly. "A sorcerer. One who controls others. People like you must be crushed and cast away."

"Why have you waited seven days?"

"You have set spies on me," said the Sword. His voice sharpened.

"I had no need. For seven days a man—the same man—followed me whenever I left the Quarter. He had a very distinctive footfall, almost a limp—an old war wound?"

"From the campaign in Valencia," said the Sword.

"And he is mad. He stands before me now, the same man."

The leather harness creaked again. "By all that's holy, Isaac the Jew, you tempt me to draw my sword. Out here in the open, under the eyes of any who might pass by. I am not mad!"

"You are," said Isaac sadly. "I hear it in your voice; I smell it in the sweat that drenches every part of your body."

"Is that your diagnosis?"

"It is."

"I spit on your diagnosis, and on all your learning. You smell of useless fasting and worthless penitence, blind man. How dare you speak to the Sword like that?"

"I dare because I speak the truth. It is only lies that the lips find difficult to shape."

"That is true," said the Sword. "What you say—all of it—is true." His voice rose in amazement and exultation. "I have madness in me. But it is divine madness, God-given, and its purpose is to drive me to do what is right, and just, and pure, and good."

"In whose eyes?" asked Isaac.

"In the eyes of God," said the Sword. "No other eyes matter."

"Very interesting," said Isaac, as calmly as if he were

debating a point in logic. "Only one other person of my acquaintance knows what the Lord Himself considers righteousness, justice, purity, and virtue. How fortunate I am to meet two people who possess such divine certainty."

"And who is the other? Your friend the Bishop?"

"His Excellency? Certainly not. The Bishop is a humble man, a learned man, ready to admit that others may know the Lord's will more surely than he does. No. The other is my wife. An honest woman, chaste, true, and loyal, but unlettered, and perhaps a touch stubborn."

"You try to make a fool of me, Isaac. You are a strange and unsatisfactory enemy," the stranger added, and turned on his heel to go. "How can I fight a blind man, who is powerless to resist? Nonetheless, I will do so, and his throat shall be cut like the rest."

"But not here?"

"Not here, not now. It is not the time."

As the Sword strode quickly across the meadow again, Yusuf watched him carefully, from his hiding place behind a shrub, and trembled in fear.

Abbess Elicsenda stifled a yawn. This was no time to be thinking of sleep, no matter how long it had been since she had last seen her bed. She paced slowly back and forth in the small parlor, watched by Sor Marta, and concentrated on speaking as precisely as possible to the Bishop.

"I have spent my time since vespers yesterday in prayer and in speaking to every person in this house, one by one. I made interesting discoveries about my convent today. Some of them have nothing to do with Lady Isabel's disappearance. Others do." She paused to draw breath.

"And they are?" asked the Bishop, impatiently. The Abbess could wander on like a long-winded preacher, especially when she was worried. It irritated Berenguer intensely.

"Girlish high spirits—reprehensible, but innocent—caused Lady Isabel's injury. It seems that the children had been left unattended. Some embroidery frames were tipped over, and work baskets spilled—the first by accident, the rest—shall we say—in jesting retaliation. Lady Ana's work basket was knocked over, and when she moved to avenge herself, she tripped and fell, with an old, thick needle in hand, onto Lady Isabel. This morning Lady Ana discovered the cause of Lady Isabel's malady. She has spent the day in tears of fright and contrition.''

"There was no intent in her injury?"

"None whatsoever. Lady Ana is twelve, and high-spirited—even mischievous—but as innocent of political maneuvers as the convent's ancient hound. Her account has a ring of truth to it.''

"That's interesting, but it doesn't get us much further.''

"Well—Lady Ana told me something else, Your Excellency. It seems that early yesterday morning she filled a basket with figs from the tree in the garden, and ate most of them herself. She is growing like a stalk of wheat in spring, and is always hungry. By vespers she had developed the colic. She slipped out of the chapel, she says, out of dire necessity, and while she was speeding to the privy she was forced to hide while two very tall nuns—the tallest nuns she ever saw in her life—hurried by her.''

"How tall is she?"

"As high as my shoulder. She said they were much taller than I am, but beyond that she could not describe them.''

"Men," said Berenguer.

"I would judge so," said Elicsenda. "I am uncommonly tall for a woman, and to find two nuns walking together who were much taller than I would be extraordinary. One nun I could believe. Not two.''

"This brings us no closer to who they are," said Berenguer.

"Without a doubt the habits that they wore came from this convent. Lady Ana would have noticed if they had been oddly dressed. She didn't.''

"You asked her?"

"I did. And this afternoon, I ordered that all the habits in the convent be brought to me for inspection so that they may be cleaned and mended, and laid down in lavender against the moth. We will soon discover the missing ones.

That might tell me who had the opportunity to steal them, and from her we might discover who the impostors are. It does bring us closer." She sat down in sudden fatigue. "You had spoken of bringing the Infant Johan here for care and safekeeping."

"It troubles me," said Berenguer. "Until we know more, by moving him here, we may be bringing him into the den of the lion—"

"Lioness," corrected Elicsenda absently. "I agree. I wish it were not so, but it is. He is safe where he is?"

"I believe so. Apparently they do not know who they are sheltering, and their ignorance protects him."

Tomas stood in the dusty courtyard of the inn under the full heat of the sun and wondered what to do next. So far, he had invaded the kitchens and harassed the innkeeper's wife as she stood over her cooking pots, until she promised to create a meal of such unbelievable nourishment and delicacy that Lady Isabel would be able to eat it and become instantly recovered. He had sent the youthful chambermaid up to the rooms three times with wine, fruit, and tiny cakes. He was now considering saddling Castanya and riding out to seek a particular spring, of whose curative powers he had heard, and bringing some of its priceless water back for the invalid. His difficulty was that the physician's daughter had told him that Lady Isabel wished him to wait until she could speak to him. Then he would be free to ride to Girona and deliver the message that all was well. What if she should ask to see him when he was tearing about the countryside in search of a spring? He had better stay. Sweat dripped off his forehead. It might be wiser to wait in the shade.

Why had he come out here? he asked himself. The horses. He meant to check that the stable lad had taken proper care of the horses. He headed purposefully in the direction of the stables.

Tomas had not entirely recovered his wits since the moment when they all had realized that Lady Isabel would have to be carried up to her chamber. Raquel had looked

at her patient struggling to sit up in the litter, and then at
him. "She is too weak and giddy," she said. "Someone
will have to carry her."

And in a daze, Tomas had picked up Lady Isabel, and
carried her up the stairs and into the chamber. He had
placed her with great delicacy, as if she were the priceless
egg of some fabulous bird, on the bed prepared for her.
And as he bowed and left her, the imprint of her slender
body on his arms was burned into him forever.

He had been ready at that moment to ride to Girona for
her, or to Jerusalem, if that were wanted. What she asked
him to do, however, was much more difficult. Raquel had
floated down the stairs, smiling sweetly, and told him that
Lady Isabel was resting. Would he wait until she could
speak to him before he rode off to Girona? Would he wait?
He would wait until the walls of Barcelona crumbled into
dust, if need be.

And not long afterward, in the bedchamber, a considerably
restored Lady Isabel was engaged in a polite but determined
contest of wills. "But my lady," said Raquel, "an hour
ago you were too weak to sit up in the litter, and now you
mean to get up and receive Don Tomas?"

"I do," said Isabel. "Before I slept, my head ached and
I felt sick and giddy from that terrible potion they gave us.
Rest and a little wine and water has cured that. I was improved yesterday, you remember, and I am even better today. Please, Raquel, help me to get ready. Otherwise I shall
have to depend on our pathetic little waiting woman." She
giggled. "Do you think I could teach her to do my hair in
the French fashion?"

Raquel was not to be distracted. "The truth is that you
insist on talking to him, even if you die as a result."

"The truth is nothing of the kind," said Isabel with
spirit. "I have instructions to give him if he is to ride off
on my behalf. On our behalf," she amended tactfully.

"You could do that from your bed," said Raquel.

"If I were that weak," said Isabel, "I would. But I tell
you, I am not helpless anymore, and I prefer not to receive

any man in my bedchamber. Even in an inn, and under such strange circumstances.''

''And with your hair in disarray,'' said Raquel.

''Quarreling with you, Raquel, is more tiring than receiving ten visits from Don Tomas. You remind me of the nuns.''

Raquel gave up. ''I think it's foolish, but since I can't stop you,'' she said, ''I'd better help. But I'm no lady's maid, I warn you. I have trouble enough dressing my own hair without help.''

Isabel smiled sweetly, having won her point. ''We shall help each other,'' she said, ''like sisters.''

''Anyway, I admire your excellent taste,'' said Raquel. ''He is a very handsome man. Not the type I dream of, but very handsome. And sweet.''

''That means nothing to me,'' said Isabel airily. ''Ouch,'' she yelped as Raquel dragged a comb inexpertly through her hair.

By the time Raquel sent the little chambermaid off to find Don Tomas, both young women were as neat and elegantly attired as possible under the circumstances. Isabel rested on a carved wooden bench heaped with pillows, her leg with its freshly poulticed wound propped up comfortably and disguised under a froth of carefully arranged silk gown.

When he entered the room, Tomas saw nothing but the pale, lovely features of Lady Isabel. Stretched out on the makeshift couch, she looked as white as a ghost, or the marble statue on her own tomb. ''I was not expecting to find Your Ladyship up,'' he said. ''I'm afraid your strength is not equal to the effort. You must take care.''

''I'm not a weakling or an invalid, Don Tomas,'' said Isabel sharply, pulling herself upright on the couch. Faint color washed over her cheeks, and her eyes brightened. ''I suffered from a festering wound, but with the skillful help of my physician and his daughter Raquel, I am recovering.''

''Lady Isabel is much improved since this morning,'' said Raquel. ''Last evening someone must have drugged our supper with a soporific potion," she added. "It has taken a long time for us to shake off its effects."

"Do you know who it was?" asked Tomas abruptly.

"No," said Raquel. "We fell asleep while eating, and awoke in a loft. The three rough-looking men were in the stable below. But I can't believe they could have entered the convent, drugged us, and taken us away."

"You saw them?"

For the first time, Raquel blushed. "I took up a board from the floor and looked through."

Tomas stared at her in amazement.

"She tore it up," said Isabel with admiration, "with her hands. Then she threatened to hit them with it if they didn't bring us water and food."

"They were under the command of your servant, Romeu," said Raquel. "But whether he was the one who abducted us, I can't say. We were asleep."

"I saw only two men," said Tomas.

"The third stayed behind. It was his stable," said Raquel.

"I suspect Don Perico de Montbui organized it," said Lady Isabel. "He already has great wealth in ships and trade, but they say his heart is set on my lands. His first wife brought him fields and meadows next to mine, and before the poor creature was buried, he was after me."

"I don't doubt you, Lady Isabel, but why would Romeu abduct a lady for Montbui? He must have servants of his own he can trust."

"I don't know," said Isabel, with a puzzled frown. "They said very little when they were near us."

"How long has Romeu worked for you?" asked Raquel.

"Less than a year. My uncle recommended him to me. He said I needed someone who knew his way around the court—" He flushed scarlet at the admission of his ineptness. "I was a soldier," he said. "Not a courtier."

"That is very clear," said Lady Isabel softly. "Only an experienced soldier would be brave enough to attack three men and rout them all. We owe you a great deal, Don Tomas." She sank back on her pillows.

"We must ask Don Tomas to ride to Girona, my lady," said Raquel. "The afternoon is wearing on."

"What messages can I deliver for you in Girona, my lady? Madam? I must not linger here any longer. Your friends must be frantic with worry."

"That is very true," said Raquel. "My poor papa—he must be told that we are safe at once."

"Not your mother?" asked Lady Isabel.

"My mother has the twins, and her house and servants to occupy her hours. Papa has only me. He needs my help in almost all that he does."

"I apologize for keeping you here, Don Tomas," said Lady Isabel. "I forgot that we are the only ones who know we are safe. If you would go to my uncle the Bishop, and tell him all that we have told you—"

"He will inform my father," said Raquel.

"And mine, too, no doubt," said Isabel, with a hint of steel in her voice that boded ill for their abductors. "And the convent, of course."

Tomas took his leave and clattered down the stairs. Isabel drew a deep breath and looked guiltily at her nurse. "I am desperately weary, Raquel. Can you help me back to my bed?"

Raquel, who was as generous in spirit as she was fluent in arguments, refrained from comment.

ELEVEN

Isaac headed across the meadow in the direction of town, feeling his way over the rough ground with foot and staff, and calling up from his well-disciplined memory every word the Sword had spoken. He felt more puzzled than frightened. On that sunny afternoon in the meadow, the threat against his life seemed a remote and unreal possibility, even though Isaac was well aware that the man would annihilate him without a second thought. No, it was not fear of death that troubled him. Talking with a madman—particularly a madman who wanted to kill you—could be unsettling, but Isaac was accustomed to the wild fantasies of the disturbed mind. Perhaps it had been the lack of hostility in his voice that disturbed him. As if killing Isaac were a distasteful but necessary task he had agreed to take on, like clearing a barn or granary of rats. It was simple, he thought, with a grim smile. As far as the Sword was concerned, Isaac was not human.

But the Sword would not act yet. He had made that clear. There was something he was waiting for, some other action to be taken, before he would have the leisure to deal with the physician. Isaac had time to ready himself. But what did he intend to do?

A sense of profound helplessness attacked him, and he stumbled. He righted himself with the help of his staff and continued on. He saw, suddenly, that the unspoken conviction that had been his mainstay and support for the last five years—that he, Isaac, unlike other men, could control his own destiny, despite blindness and the ravages of pestilence all around him—was a mirage. What could he do about the Sword?

He could ignore the threat, taking care for the next few weeks not to walk the streets alone. Or he could go to the Bishop, or even the town council and raise a general alarm. The officers of the ecclesiastical and civil authorities together could deal with one demented soldier. He would tell them— Tell them what? That a man with long legs and a slight limp, wearing a sword, whose voice and smell only he, Isaac, would recognize, is a dangerous butcher? Of course, he could not describe him. He had no idea what the man looked like.

"Isaac," he said aloud, causing a bored cow to raise her head, "the great master was right. Thinking too much renders a man useless." The cow blinked and returned to her grazing. "I will set Yusuf to look closely at the Sword. The boy can describe him for those who depend on their eyes. Then I will go to the Bishop." Having reached that decision, he moved on at a brisk pace, lighter of heart.

As soon as Yusuf saw his master stir, he crept away from the shrubbery he was hiding behind. When he was far enough that his footsteps would not be distinguishable from the general noise, he broke into an easy run that ate up the short distance between the meadow and the Arab Baths. He had something to talk about with Big Johan.

In a few short days, Isaac had forgotten how much easier walking through the streets of the town had become if his hand were resting on Yusuf's shoulder for guidance. Alone, he stumbled on a cobblestone. An exclamation of impatience rose to his lips; he suppressed it with difficulty. Suddenly uncertain, he put out a hand to check that he had reached the turning toward the Quarter, and a shrill female voice cried out, "Watch where you go! Keep your hands off respectable women!"

"Master Isaac! Where is your quick-witted lad?" And then a new voice boomed reassuringly through the streets. "Master Isaac . . ."

"Ah, Your Excellency," said Isaac. "I sent him on an errand. Unfortunately, quick as he is, he cannot be in two places at once."

"I come from the convent," said Berenguer, in confidential tones. "The Abbess made some interesting discoveries. Let us walk and I will tell you."

"Men disguised as nuns?" said Isaac, when he heard. "A risky venture."

"Not during vespers, when they would meet very few people," said Berenguer. "And it sufficed as a disguise for the one ward who saw them. It was only later that she realized they looked odd. And she was completely unable to describe them, except as very tall nuns."

"Indeed," said Isaac. "Robes can indeed alter one's powers of observation. She could see them only as nuns, not as people."

"Interesting, perhaps," said Berenguer. "But not very helpful."

"I, too, spent an 'interesting' afternoon," said Isaac. "In the meadow conversing with a madman who calls himself the Archangel's Sword."

"Johan! Master Keeper! Are you in there?" called Yusuf. He stood hesitantly on the steps of the Arab Baths, peering down into the vaulted interior. His voice echoed eerily off the tiles and the water.

"Where else would Big Johan be, lad?" said the man himself, appearing suddenly from around a pillar. "What would you have from me? Another bath?" He erupted in an enormous laugh, and sat down on the bench near the door.

"Not today, thank you, Johan," said Yusuf, smiling nervously.

"You are well, young master? You look better fed,

like," said Johan. "Not so thin and starved."

"Cleaner, too," said Yusuf, and the keeper roared with laughter again. "Johan," the boy added, "do you remember—"

"Remember what, lad?" The alarm on Johan's face and in his voice was almost comical in its intensity.

"That bundle of rags you took from me. My clothes? My old clothes?"

Johan nodded. "You ask me to keep them, the Lord himself knows why, and keep them I do."

"Could I put them on here, and leave my new clothes in your safekeeping? Until sunset or before."

"And what would you be up to?"

"I only want to move around the market and the taverns without people noticing me, the way I used to. I can't do it in my new clothes."

"Thieving?" asked Johan promptly. "Because if you are, I won't do it. Master Isaac is a good man, and a good friend to me. When I was took so bad in the winter, he gave me potions and poultices for my throat and chest, and never a penny would he take. He said I got paid little enough for all my hard work. I won't have you getting Master Isaac into trouble."

"Johan," said Yusuf desperately. "Johan, I seek the Sword. He is after my master's blood. And how could I live with my master dead? In my rags, I can find him. I can crawl anywhere, and no one will see me."

"Not true, lad." Big Johan shook his head. "There ain't no Sword. That's just talk."

"Yes, there is," said Yusuf. "I know it. It's a group, and they—"

"I know it's a group," said Johan. "I been there. And I know, too, there ain't no Sword," he repeated emphatically. "One day, maybe, there'll be a Sword, but not now. You keep that quiet, mind. It's secret."

"Then who are the other members, Johan? Where can I find them?"

"Don't tell nobody I said." He looked around and dropped his voice to a whisper. "The Inner Council meets at Rodrigue's tavern, now. They asked me to join them, but I couldn't leave the Baths, could I?''

A few minutes later, Yusuf sped away, barefoot and in his rags, leaving behind him a puzzled and very troubled keeper of the Baths.

In the seven months before he met Isaac, Yusuf had come to know the layout of the city in minutest detail, especially the steeply raked streets down near the River Onyar. He knew what walls he could climb without being seen, which roofs led to interesting courtyards, and which small alleys gave access to them. He shared with the cats of Girona an entirely different map of the city than the one an honest and well-padded citizen might keep in his head. And for the same reason. His map led to places where he might find scraps of food, shelter from the rain and snow, and warmth on a cold night. One of these places was the unlovely courtyard behind Rodrigue's tavern. It was littered with broken barrels into which a boy could creep; it stank of rotting food, and cats, and urine, and human waste. A rudimentary staircase, leading to cramped living quarters above the tavern, ran across the back wall of the building; underneath the staircase was a low door that provided access to the kitchen.

Yusuf slithered quietly down the tiles of the nearby roof. He jumped into the courtyard, landing hard, caught his breath again, and crouched behind a broken barrel. Rodrigue's wife, square, solidly built, and as strong as her husband, was in the back room, making soup, and, no doubt, watering the already thin, sour wine.

He waited. The wife was shrewd and noticing, and never muddled her thoughts with tasting the wares she sold, unlike the husband. A mouse or a fly would have trouble getting past her, much less a boy. But Yusuf had learned patience on the road, and he waited. The potboy came and went, fetching and carrying. Once he slunk out into the courtyard, and Yusuf froze behind his frail shelter. Rodrigue's wife screamed out the door, and the potboy slunk back in again. Still, Yusuf didn't move. His legs grew stiff and ached with discomfort, and he didn't shift them. His nose itched, and he did not scratch. A cat came by, inquiring, and on receiving no sign of life from the boy, moved on. At last Rodrigue roared from the front of the tavern. "Woman! An extra jug for the gentlemen!"

She threw down her knife, cursed Rodrigue, the potboy, and the customers, filled a huge jug with wine from the barrel, and carried it out.

Yusuf darted into the kitchen, across the packed dirt floor, squeezed under the flap that separated the two rooms, and was underneath the bench that ran along the back wall before the jug hit the far table in front of Rodrigue. Yusuf landed with his eyes and nose inches away from a pair of dirty boots, worn over dirtier leggings fastened with leather thongs. A farmer, to judge by the smell of the dirt. He looked around the room. Some dozen men were grouped around the two trestle tables that lay between the kitchen and the stairs leading up from the street. There were no feet that he could see under the third table, off in the farthest, darkest corner of the room. He decided that he was not likely to see much more from where he was. He wriggled along the wall to the far side of the dirty boots, and then dove from under the bench to under the table. He worked his way, with due attention to the movement of feet, around the near end of a trestle and into a relatively empty space between the two rows of drinkers. It was not an easy way to travel. The floor under his knees and hands was fashioned of rough, dirty, and uneven wood planks. Every movement forward was paid for with scratches and bruises, but stopping anywhere invited discovery. He arrived at his first destination with throbbing knees and panting with the terror of the hunted.

Someone right above him began to sing. He jumped, startled by the sudden noise. Others joined in, beating time above his head with their fists. Trembling, unable to control his breathing or the pounding of his heart, he lay still until he realized that in all the noise and confusion he could join in the song himself and still no one would notice him.

From his vantage point he could observe most of the

lower half of the room. Anything less like a meeting of a murderous fellowship he could not imagine. The conversation, such as it was, was of cows, bullocks, and donkeys, and the criminally low—or high, depending on the speaker—price of grain. The songs degenerated in moral tone and performance. Then a tall, serious-looking man in a black cassock appeared on the stairs, glancing around as he climbed. A churchman, concluded Yusuf, to whom all degrees and conditions of Christian clergy were the same. The churchman rose slowly in Yusuf's field of sight until he, too, turned into a pair of boots, clean and black, which headed for the back far corner of the room. At that point he disappeared from Yusuf's field of observation. A little later, a second man did the same thing. When a third did it, Yusuf decided to follow.

He moved along until he reached an open space under the long table. He needed to be well away from old Rodrigue's sharp-eyed wife in the kitchen, and closer to the three newcomers. There was a spot free of feet, where he could slip from under the table, over the intervening floor space to under the bench, and then under the middle trestle table with a minimum of exposure. He had only to wait until there was enough distraction to keep anyone from noticing him.

At the start of a new song he moved, with the speed of a snake fleeing through the grass. His headlong progress was halted; stuck between two large pairs of boots, he found himself nose to nose with a shaggy brown dog. The dog growled and Yusuf backed up. A boot moved and caught him a sharp blow in the ribs. "Sorry, mate," mumbled a voice from above.

"Sorry for what?"

"For kicking you. How stupid can you be? Can't you tell when you've been kicked?"

"You didn't kick me."

Someone else joined in. "If it was my dog you kicked, you'd better watch yourself. He doesn't like it, and no more do I." The voice was truculent, loud, and slurred, and appeared to Yusuf to belong to a pair of stout legs and large feet. "Here, Caesar," said that new voice, and very slowly and carefully—for he had consumed more than his fair share of the wine on the table tonight—the owner of the stout legs bent over to check on his dog.

Yusuf watched the torso bend for a split second before he acted. Then, panicked, he moved, scrambling over Caesar, who growled again, and snapped. Yusuf knocked his head against the bottom of the table, found a space between drinkers, dove through it, and ended up under the empty table in the dark corner of the room. Panting, undiscovered, and triumphant.

Carried by the elation of victory, he crawled rapidly along the floor to the end of the table, scrambled under the bench, and wriggled toward the doorway into a second room at the back of the tavern. It was easier than he could have imagined. In the time it took a fat farmer to sing one bawdy song, Yusuf was at the door to the second room, with his ear as close to the leather flap that formed its closing as he dared, devoting his entire attention to listening to what was going on.

The end was swift and sudden. A plump, strong hand grasped him by the scruff of the neck and dragged him out from under the bench.

"Rodrigue," shrieked the innkeeper's wife. "I've caught a thief." She took hold of Yusuf's arm while keeping a tight grip on his neck. "Send for the officers!"

The tavern erupted into pandemonium. A loud cheerful voice called out, "Let him go, Mother, and get us another jug."

"Who is it?" yelled one of the more curious.

"Hang the little bastard right now," growled another.

"Anyone got a rope?" cried a wit, and those at his table shouted with laughter.

Rodrigue came out of the kitchen to survey the situation. He began to lumber over, much hindered by the movement of a dozen somewhat befuddled customers. The fat farmer of the bawdy songs stood up and knocked over his bench. Two smaller men landed on the floor with it. When the farmer turned to survey the damage, he collided with the table, dumping the board and all of its contents on the men sitting on the other side.

Yusuf jerked and wriggled and flung himself sideways with all his strength and agility. It was no use. He was caught. He was vaguely aware that the door covering right beside him was being pushed aside. A quiet voice spoke in the ear of Rodrigue's wife. "What have you here, mistress?"

"A thief," said the woman. "I sent the potboy for the officers."

"What profit is there in turning him over to the officers, mistress?" the soft voice went on, speaking quickly. "I'll give you a good silver groat for him—no questions asked."

"For him?"

"He seems a likely lad, and under the dirt, a pretty one. I think I know him. There'll be no complaints, don't you worry." He held out his hand. In the dim light, a silver coin glittered in the palm. Rodrigue's wife let go of Yusuf's arm and reached for it.

Rodrigue, charging across the room like a slow-moving bull, finally reached the center of the action. He slapped Yusuf on the side of the head, making his ears ring and his eyes dance with stars. The blow knocked him against a bench, loosening the grip the woman still had on his neck. He rolled, using his slender weight to break free, bounced to his feet, and ran. He leapt over the overturned bench and table, with one foot landing on each, and sprang onto the stairs.

As he raced down, three steps at a time, toward the door, Rodrigue's wife's furious voice floated after him. "You useless, stupid, interfering oaf. Do you know how much you just cost us?"

Yusuf darted past two customers and out into the dusk. He ran along the street, up one alley, and down another, clinging to the dark walls and staying well away from curious or interfering passersby. At last, past the north gate to the city, he paused. His head was still spinning, and his nose throbbed. Large drops of blood splashed at his feet, and tears streamed from his eyes despite his best efforts to stop them. He tripped and fell, picked himself up, and headed doggedly for the Baths. He opened the door, stumbled down the steps, and threw himself on Big Johan's mercy.

Tomas walked back down from the Bishop's palace and stared across the square. He had been offered every courtesy when he arrived—a comfortable place to wait, refreshment, and means to wash away the dust of travel. Everything he could want, in short, except for the Bishop. The Bishop was on his way back from the convent, and could very well have taken a stroll around the grounds before vespers. "One never knows," the hastily summoned Canon Vicar had said, "with the Bishop. He could be almost anywhere."

"There he is," said a voice at his ear. It was the Canon Vicar again, pointing across the square toward the cathedral. Two men, one bearded, tall and broad-shouldered, and the other clean-shaven, shorter and powerfully built, were strolling, deep in conversation. To judge by their dress, the one who looked like a wrestler was the Bishop.

"Who is he talking to?" asked Tomas.

"I believe it is His Excellency's physician," said Francesc Monterranes. "One Isaac. A very skilled practitioner of the art."

"The two men I wish to see. Thank you, sir, for your courtesy."

"You might mention to His Excellency that his presence in the palace would be greatly appreciated."

"I'll try," said Tomas, and strode away.

In the space of a week, Tomas de Bellmunt had gone from a belief in the honesty of all men—except those officially labeled as His Majesty's enemies—to a confused half conviction that you could trust no one, not even your mother. Therefore, he refused to mention his business until they were seated in Berenguer's private study, the door closed and locked.

Isaac and Berenguer waited, somewhat mystified, for the

young man to speak. "First of all, Your Excellency, Master Isaac, I bring you greetings from your niece and your daughter. They are safe, and unharmed. They are resting at an inn an hour's gallop from here. I have promised to escort them into the city in the morning, if that is agreeable to you."

The color drained from Isaac's face, leaving it ashen, and the other two men rose to their feet.

"My God, man," said Berenguer to Tomas, "fetch a cup of wine. Over there. And the jug of water."

"Hold, friend," said Isaac, somewhat breathlessly. "One moment to compose myself and I am well." He accepted the wine, took a taste of it, and forced himself to smile. "A superior wine, Your Excellency. I apologize for my weakness. I have not paused to eat today—foolishness on my part. But Don Tomas, thank you. With all my heart I thank you. You bring most welcome news. Please, tell us what you know, and how it all came about."

Tomas related the story as he had understood it, dealing briefly with his part in the rescue, and not at all with the matter of Doña Sanxia.

"And so the mysterious Romeu," said Berenguer, "belonged to you. What the devil was he doing wandering around Girona for a week, stirring up trouble, and giving out that he was a gentleman? And why abduct my niece and the good Raquel from the convent? A most shameful act."

"As to the first question," said Tomas unhappily, "I cannot give you an answer. All I know is that the lady wife of an acquaintance at court begged for the loan of Romeu to carry out a delicate mission in Girona. It seemed a reasonable request—he was a very clever and shrewd sort of—"

"Rogue," interrupted the Bishop.

"Your Excellency," murmured Don Tomas. "You are entirely correct. I was the bigger fool for not realizing it. I swear I had no idea that the mission involved carrying off Your Excellency's niece. If I had—"

"You know who she is?"

"I do, Your Excellency," he said miserably, and then forged ahead with his recital. "And I believe I can tell you why they were abducted. Your good daughter, Master Isaac, was taken because the Lady Isabel was ill, and needed care, and there was no woman in the party to look after her, and protect her honor."

"The woman who was to have filled that function was dead, was she not?" said Isaac. "Her throat cut, and her body thrown in the Baths. Do you know why she was killed?"

"No," said Tomas, giving him a startled look. "I only know that Romeu didn't kill her. Or so he declared in dying. He also said I was meddling in things I didn't understand, and that is certainly true."

"But why was my niece abducted?" said Berenguer impatiently.

"She believes that it was the plot of a rich man after her lands. Someone with important mercantile interests who wants to annex her fortune and name to his. And since His Maj—and since her father would never have consented to the match, he chose this method to bring it about."

"Who would dare, and hope to escape retribution?"

"Lady Isabel thought it might be Montbui."

"Perico de Montbui?" Berenguer sounded incredulous.

"She says he is a friend of her uncle, Don Fernando."

"It would amuse Don Fernando," said the Bishop. "Even if Montbui perished in the execution. I don't doubt he encouraged him. If it's true."

"If he intended to enlighten us," said Berenguer, "he failed. I am more confused now than before he spoke." Bellmunt had been sent off to dine, leaving the two men to make sense out of his account.

"It is possible that the Infant's adventure had nothing to do with your niece's abduction," said Isaac. "Because something happens to two of my patients on the same night doesn't mean the events are connected."

"Romeu seems to have been concerned with obtaining

a bride for Montbui—quickly,'' said the Bishop. ''Everything else flowed from that.''

''But why wander around the city raising up a riot?'' asked Isaac.

''To make a great enough disturbance to cover the abduction,'' said Berenguer. ''It was a clever idea, and might have worked.''

''Except that Lady Isabel was near death, and surrounded by an uncomfortable number of witnesses all night.''

''Indeed. Her corpse would have been poor comfort for the hopeful bridegroom,'' said Berenguer dryly. ''But we still don't know what we most need to know. Who murdered Doña Sanxia de Baltier? I can make no sense of it. Why was she murdered?''

''That is true. But I cannot linger here another moment,'' said Isaac. ''I must return home at once and tell my wife the joyful news. She has been very troubled.''

''I shall send an officer with you as far as the gate to the Quarter,'' said Berenguer.

''This time, Your Excellency, I shall not refuse.''

By the time he reached the gate of his house, Isaac was feeling the effects of the last day and a half. In that time he had slept only a few hours, and eaten not at all. He had slaked his thirst with water, and with a half cup of wine at the palace. He was feeling sick and giddy with exhaustion. He knocked at the gate, listening for Ibrahim's footsteps.

''Master,'' said Ibrahim, startled, as if Isaac's return were the last thing he expected.

''Indeed,'' said Isaac. ''Fetch your mistress.'' He walked over to the bench under the arbor and sat, unable to move a step farther.

''You have returned,'' said Judith. Her voice came out of nowhere and roused him from his momentary torpor.

''I have, with the best of news. Raquel and Lady Isabel have been found. They are safe, and unharmed, and will be in Girona tomorrow.''

''The Lord be praised!'' said Judith and sat down. ''I thought she was dead.'' She broke into deep wrenching sobs, unable to say more. "I thought you would not speak to me because you knew she was dead," she said at last, gasping.

"How could I know she was dead and not tell you, my love?" said Isaac gently. "If I had had such dreadful news, I would not have left you here, suspended between hope and terror."

"You have ways of knowing, whether you will tell me of them or not." And she said no more.

"No, Judith. I have common sense and logic. The Lord gives that to all. I told you the conspirators would not harm either one of them. It would not be in their interest. Lady Isabel's family is too wealthy and influential, and while Raquel is with her, she will not be touched."

"Oh, Isaac," said his wife bitterly. "Men call you wise, but there are many things you don't understand. You believe all men are like you, and coldly reason out every action. Most men do what they wish, and reason it out after."

"You may be right, my love," said Isaac. "But in this case, they do not seem to have been harmed."

"Where were they? Who took them?" Her voice turned hard and edged with suspicion. "They've been gone a night and a day. Who were they with?"

Isaac sighed wearily. Now that the crisis was past, Judith was casting about for someone to blame. And some nameless rogue or villain would not do; it had to be someone to whom she could put a face. He thought carefully about his words; one careless statement now and it would be Raquel. She would spend her life under the heavy shadow of her mother's scorn. For in Judith's eyes, the fact that Raquel had been alone and unprotected for an entire night was inescapable. "Lady Isabel was abducted, it seems, by a wealthy merchant who wishes to marry her. Raquel was taken at the same time to safeguard the lady's health and honor. They have not been apart for an instant since being taken from the convent. They have not so much as seen the gentleman in question. The affair was in the hands of two or three of his trusted servants."

"Where are they now?"

"At an inn on the Barcelona road."

"At a common inn? Alone? Surrounded by travelers and vagabonds and soldiers—"

"They have a pair of rooms with a stout lock and a female servant to look after them alone. Don Tomas assured me—"

"Don Tomas? Who is this Don Tomas?"

"He is secretary to the Queen, my dear. He was riding to Girona on a royal errand when he came across the party riding the other way. He said that Raquel attracted his attention, letting him know very cleverly that they were not there of their free will. He rescued them from their abductors, killing one and frightening away the others. He then escorted them to the inn, and established them in comfort and safety." He took care to omit the young man's age and generally handsome appearance. "Are you not pleased to have your daughter restored to you?"

"If you're sure that nothing happened to her—"

"I am sure, my love."

Judith looked up and noticed her husband's appearance for the first time since he'd come in. "You're ill!" she said. "Isaac! What's wrong?"

"Nothing, my love. If I am pale, it is because I have not slept or eaten much, and—"

"Whether you have slept or not, I cannot say," said Judith resentfully, "since you have locked me out of your chamber, but I know that you have eaten nothing. Nothing at all since yesterday morning. Naomi!" she called. And with her usual efficiency and organization, Judith mobilized the resources of the household to provide for the master's return.

Berenguer dispatched a messenger to the Abbess Elicsenda, and then began, painfully and most carefully, to draft another letter to His Majesty. He greeted the knock at his door, when it came, with great relief.

"A messenger arrived, Your Excellency," said the manservant. "He brought you this. It needs no reply, he said."

Berenguer took the letter, looked at the seal, and sighed.
"Wait there," he said. "No—tell them to hold the mes-
senger, and give him refreshment until I have read this.
Then return."

It was from His Majesty himself. It was brief, and to the
point, like most of Don Pedro's communications to him.
The King would arrive, with troops, a day hence. King and
officers would quarter at the palace.

"Find the Canon Vicar, would you?" he asked the servant, who had just come panting back. "Tell him that visitors are about to arrive, and then ask him to come and see
me. And warn the cooks to heat up their ovens, and start
baking." Royal visits were always a curse. Sudden royal
visits could be a disaster.

When Isaac had eaten, and Judith had gone off to super-
intend the evening duties in the household, Yusuf scratched
at the gate. "Master?" he called softly, for he hoped to
avoid the mistress or Ibrahim.

"Yusuf?" said Isaac, and walked over to unfasten the
gate. "You are home late. Have you eaten?"

"No, lord."

"Then eat whatever is left on the table. If there is anything."

"There is a great deal," said Yusuf, looking over the
remains of Isaac's meal. He placed a piece of fish on some
bread and ate it like a starving man. "I have come from
Rodrigue's tavern," he said, as soon as he had swallowed,
"where they were holding a meeting of the Inner Council
of the Fellowship of the Sword."

"That was foolish, lad. Were you seen? Did anyone recognize you?"

"No one, lord," said Yusuf, taking another piece of fish.
"I dressed in my old rags, that Big Johan has kept for me,
and dirtied myself again, and hid under the tables. I could
not hear everything they said, because it took me a long
time to get near the door of the meeting room without being
seen. And after that, Rodrigue's wife caught me." He
stuffed some rice and vegetables into a piece of flat bread,

added a slice of lamb, and paused to eat that, too.

"What happened?"

"Nothing. She wanted to give me over to the officers for thieving, although I hadn't touched a thing, but she lost hold of me and I got away. I ran back to the Baths and Johan let me wash myself clean again, and gave me back my new clothes. And then I came home."

"I see. And what did you hear?"

"Well, lord, first of all, Big Johan told me there was no Sword."

"What were you talking to the keeper about that he should say that?"

"I asked him if he knew anything about the Fellowship—since he hears everything, although he doesn't always understand what he hears. No one watches his tongue in front of Big Johan."

"And did he?"

"I think he was trying to tell me that they made him a member. He said there was a meeting at Rodrigue's—that's how I knew—and they wanted him to be there. But he couldn't leave the Baths unattended."

"That is interesting, lad. And he says there is no Sword."

"Right," said Yusuf, stuffing a honey cake into his mouth. "There will be one someday, but there isn't one now."

"What did he mean?"

"He didn't know. And then at Rodrigue's I heard them say that they were almost ready, and that it would be discussed at the meeting on Saturday night. In front of the group as a whole. And did they all know what they were supposed to say and do. But while they were answering, I was caught."

"Where is the meeting?"

"Someone said it was at the Baths. And someone else asked if Johan had agreed, and the first man said it didn't matter—he would deal with Johan if he became difficult."

"Can you tell me who was there?"

"Five men. While I was listening I heard three names—

Raimunt, Sanch, and Martin. Martin the bookbinder,'' added Yusuf, and shivered. "I saw him. I also saw a churchman, tall and thin, very serious looking.''

"That is Raimunt. He is a clerk,'' said Isaac. "The other would be Sanch the ostler. Nicholau mentioned his name, as well.''

"I know there were two more, but their names were not mentioned.'' He reached for another honey cake, and was forestalled by a shriek from above.

"Where have you been?'' Judith's voice rang like an alarm bell. "Worthless boy! Your duty is to stay with your master, and you have left him to wander about on his own. He has not eaten or drunk all day. And you have only returned to fill your belly.'' Isaac heard her moving quickly down the staircase. "Goodness!'' she said, in a startled voice. "Whatever happened to you? Have you been fighting? Or has someone attacked you?''

"What is wrong with him?'' asked Isaac.

"One eye is swollen shut, he has a cut on his forehead, and a scrape on the side of his face.''

"He has been in the wars, my love, on my orders. I'm sorry, lad. I did not mean you to be hurt.''

"Johan patched me up, lord. He put salve on my wounds that he said you had given him. Is that true?''

"Salve?'' He thought for a moment. "I suppose I did. It was for the ringworm, as I remember, but it won't do you any harm.'' He reached out and touched Yusuf's face delicately, feeling for the swellings and cuts. "I have better remedies than that for your wounds. And while you have been fighting, good news has come. Raquel and Lady Isabel have been found. They are safe, and unharmed, and will return to us tomorrow.''

"Then all is well, lord, is it not? You can have no more troubles.''

TWELVE

Tomas de Bellmunt arrived back at the inn at sunrise as the earliest of the night's guests were leaving. "Landlord," he called impatiently. "I have come to fetch the ladies. Are they stirring?"

"Stirring, sir?" He laughed, and swept up a small pile of coins. "Thank you, sir," he muttered, and turned his attention to Bellmunt. "They stirred some time ago," he said. "They left last night. Before sunset."

Tomas could feel the blood drain from his face. "What do you mean?"

"What I say, sir. The lady's father came to fetch her."

"Her *father*?" said Tomas, trying to imagine Don Pedro, King of Aragon and Count of Barcelona, in all his majesty, at this inn, negotiating with the man in front of him. "Are you sure?"

"The gentleman said he was her father. And he was of an age to be."

"What did he look like?" asked Tomas.

"No beauty," said the landlord, laughing. "On the short side. Well fed, with a rough, pockmarked skin. Brown hair, what there was of it."

"Ah yes," said Tomas.

"You'd recognize him, I expect. He was pleased enough to catch up with her, he said. Paid the reckoning and some over. She and the lady with her were not too pleased to be caught, though, if that's any comfort to you. Your pretty mistress said to tell you she was right about him. She said you'd know what she meant."

"Thank you, innkeeper. I will take some cold meat and bread before riding on. Did they say where they were going?" Coins jingled softly in Tomas's hand.

"Not a word, sir. But in my opinion it wasn't far. It was near sunset when they left, and they were planning to reach their destination before dark." The coins jingled again. "Someone noticed two grays with a litter on the road to Valtierra." The coins swiftly changed hands.

"They took the horses?"

"They said they were theirs, sir. I had no reason to disbelieve them."

"Even the mare?"

"Even the mare."

"Poor Blaveta. Still—I expect I'll get her back."

"I expect you will," said the landlord. "I'll bring you that meat and bread."

The road to Valtierra also led to Doña Sanxia's *finca*. That, without question, was where the young women had been taken. It was not difficult to deduce what had happened, even without Lady Isabel's helpful comment. The description of her "father" had been enough. Romeu's accomplices had followed them to the inn, and reported to Montbui. He arrived, bribed the innkeeper, and carried them off.

Tomas's horse was fresh, the distance was not great, and the sun was just rising. He might arrive at the *finca* in time to rescue them again.

He took the loaf stuffed with meat from the innkeeper, paid him, and rushed out to the innyard. He snatched a mouthful for breakfast, stowed the rest, mounted Castanya, and rode for his life to the *finca*.

•   •   •

"He means to marry me as soon as possible," Isabel had said in a low voice. Two men had escorted them to a large upper chamber at Doña Sanxia's *finca* and locked them in. The housekeeper returned with food, water, and wine, and pointed out a chest filled with clothing. It was the chest that had prompted Isabel's remark.

From the time Montbui and his two assistants had burst in on them at the inn, Lady Isabel had not spoken, and had refused any help but Raquel's. She had struggled painfully in and out of the litter, and then had limped pathetically into the house, drooping like a dying lily. Raquel supported her heroically as Lady Isabel had panted, her hand pressing against her breast, slowly up the stairs. Once in the room, she had fallen into a large chair, her head leaning back, apparently too exhausted to move.

"Did he say that?" asked Raquel, pitching her voice to the same level.

"When could he have said it? I have kept you at my side since they arrived at the inn."

"True."

She frowned, and bit the side of her finger. "But he can do nothing until morning. We are safe until then."

"Are you sure?"

"No priest is going to marry us now. It is too late in the day. No—they will arrive at dawn, and try to take me before a priest. Oh, Raquel—what shall we do? Is it possible to get out of here?"

Raquel went over to the window, undid the shutters, and peered out into the darkness. "No. Even if it were, you are much too ill to climb out of windows. And we are locked in."

"Don't be too sure of that. Did she take the key?"

"Yes," said Raquel. "I looked."

"I am much better," whispered Lady Isabel. "I know I should be worse, from not resting, nor taking care, and from everything that has happened to us, but I'm getting better. My leg doesn't hurt. Look at it."

Raquel set a candle on the floor close by, and knelt on the carpet in front of Lady Isabel. She pushed up her dusty, travel-stained gown. "Then why lean on me like a dying donkey, my lady?" she murmured.

"Because they mustn't know. If we can postpone the wedding long enough, Bellmunt might receive my message, and someone will be sent to rescue us." She paused. "The household appears to be very small. Two servants that we have seen, and perhaps one or two others. And Montbui's two men. One of them is the coward that Don Tomas chased off. Three good knights—or even just two—are all that would be needed to free us."

"Or the brave Don Tomas all alone?" suggested Raquel with a sly smile as she began to unwind the bandaging.

"Don't be foolish," said Isabel. "I have no interest in Don Tomas."

"What would your papa say if you wanted to marry someone he didn't like?" she whispered. "Suppose that Montbui were handsome and young and charming, would he allow you to marry him?"

Isabel broke into laughter, and converted it into a cough. "Probably not," she murmured. "If I fell in love with someone suitable, he might consider him. But someone he didn't approve of—" She shook her head.

"Would he make you marry someone you hated?" Raquel set down the cold poultice and brought the candle up to inspect the site of the abscess.

"You are very curious," said Isabel coldly.

"I'm sorry, my lady," said Raquel, turning red with hurt and embarrassment.

"But it's a question I won't be able to answer until it happens." A board creaked, and she dropped her voice to a soft murmur. "Look at my leg, and say something about how bad it is. They are listening at the door."

"And watching," said Raquel. "My lady," she said, raising her voice, "all this travel has done you no good. Does this hurt?" She pressed down around the site of the injury.

"Aah," screamed Isabel. She flung herself back in her chair in an attitude of helpless abandon.

"Not too dramatic, my lady," whispered Raquel.

"Help," she cried. "Lady Isabel requires assistance."

Feet pounded on the staircase; the door opened with suspicious rapidity, and Raquel began to pour out orders, for infusions, and poultices, and clean linen, and delicate broths, all to be brought at once.

"Wake the priest," said Perico de Montbui, his round pink cheeks turning rounder and pinker with anger.

"It is late," said Doña Sanxia's steward. He resented this evening's invasion. Not only did he dislike Montbui, but he felt deeply aggrieved by the extra work he was creating. His opinions on the little man had a great deal in common with those of His revered Majesty, Don Pedro. Montbui was a nuisance.

"I don't care," said Montbui. "Wake him up. Tell him I will marry the woman tonight. Don't you see, man—if I don't marry her now, she could be dead by morning." He stood up, as if hoping the extra height would move this ridiculous rustic to action. "He can marry us in her chamber. That way, she won't have to leave her bed."

"He won't do it," said the steward. "He did that once, and it went all the way to the Archbishop. They came near to suspending him over it, and he enjoys being a priest. And the marriage was annulled," he added spitefully, and smiled. The tale was a fabrication from beginning to end, but it had a ring of authority to it, and the man had no intention of riding through the night to wake the priest.

Montbui walked rapidly up and down the room. "At dawn, then," he said. "Wake the priest at dawn. Have your wife wake the lady, get her dressed, and we will carry her to the altar if need be."

Castanya was a neat, quick, sturdy little animal, very surefooted, and she arrived at the *finca* still breathing easily, with a light sweat darkening her glossy coat. Tomas slowed her to a walk and approached the estate with caution.

The building was modest in size, built fairly low to the ground, and quiet. Very quiet. A dog was lying in the sun on the east side of the building. He stood up, stretched, barked to warn the house that a strange man and horse had arrived, and then, his duty done, retired back to his comfortable resting place. Other than that, there was no sign of life. All the windows were shuttered, and the door firmly locked. Tomas's heart sank. He had been convinced that Montbui would bring her here. He dismounted and began to search for signs of life, and means of watering his horse.

The picture was more hopeful behind the house. The exquisite scent of lamb roasting on a spit drifted out a window. A stout and capable-looking woman was spreading linen over branches to dry in the sun, aided by a lad of about twelve. "Good morning, Ana," he said simply. "How are you?"

The woman turned, startled, and then curtsied. "Don Tomas! We were expecting you."

"You were?" he asked.

"Yes. With the child. Only—"

"Ah. Yes. I'm sorry."

"No need to be. It wasn't you who slit her throat," said the woman.

"No, it wasn't." He looked around. "Have you had other visitors?"

"You mean Don Perico? Are you a friend to His Lordship?"

Tomas was about to claim undying friendship with the man when he caught the look on the woman's face. "Not at all," he said, firmly. "I have reason to believe that he seized, against their will, two young ladies that it was my duty to escort safely into Girona."

"Well—he's off marrying one of them this very instant," said the woman dourly. "That's his wedding breakfast I'm cooking."

The scene in the church up the road was a curious one. At the altar stood the red-faced bridegroom, sweating nervously and looking angrily about him. Beside him, the white-faced bride sat in a chair hastily procured for her by Montbui's valet. Raquel stood beside Lady Isabel, occasionally whispering a word in her ear and listening carefully to her replies. Missing, among those usually in attendance at a marriage ceremony, were two people: someone competent to give away the bride, and a priest to bless the union.

Suddenly, like Vesuvius, Montbui erupted. "Where is that fool of a priest?" he roared. The sound echoed throughout the small church. It produced nothing but the squeaking of a few bats.

The west door opened, and in walked, not a priest, but Doña Sanxia's steward, now in his office as Cupid, the messenger of love. "We're having difficulty waking Father Pau," he said.

"What?"

"We can't wake up the priest."

"Why not, man? Is he dead? Then fetch another."

"There isn't another, sir. Not for a longish distance. And Father Pau isn't dead. Just asleep."

"Then pour water over him," he said, his voice rising dangerously. "Do whatever it takes. What's wrong with him?" he thought to ask, finally.

"He was celebrating his name day rather late. He's—uh—tired."

"Tell him he can sleep after we're wed. Not now."

The steward nodded, almost respectfully, and left again, grinning.

"I'm hungry," whispered Lady Isabel. "It would almost be worth marrying the disgusting old man just to be able to eat."

"You look very convincingly pale," said Raquel.

"I can't go without food," she whispered. "Hunger makes me turn all faint and giddy. I wonder what's happened to the priest."

"Maybe he's still too drunk to marry you," observed Raquel.

"I hope so."

At that, the west door opened again, and the steward came in, dragging a sad-looking wretch in a black cassock.

"Father Pau," he said, with the air of a conjurer producing a wooden devil out of a painted hell.

Father Pau was lean and unshaven. His eyes were red, and his hair was soaking wet, plastered down against his skull. Water dripped over his cheeks and down his nose. He sneezed pathetically and wiped his face with his hand. He looked as if he wished to speak, but was having difficulty making sounds come out of his mouth. As the two men progressed toward the altar waves of alcohol preceded them. He was indeed still drunk—magnificently, hopelessly drunk. Isabel grinned broadly, and pulled her veil across her face to hide her expression.

"Just give me a hand up the step," he said, staggering and falling against Montbui. "Thank you. Now—take her hand, sir." He grabbed Raquel's hand and tried to move it over Lady Isabel's head to where Montbui stood, speechless with rage.

"You've got the wrong woman, you drunken fool," screamed Montbui. "I'm not marrying that one."

Father Pau peered wetly at the bridegroom. "Then you'll have to come back when you've got the right woman here. I can't marry you if you didn't bring the bride. . . ." His voice trailed off. His eye lit on the stalls behind him. "It would be better anyway. I'm tired, now, too tired—" He fell into the stalls and his snores filled the church.

As Perico de Montbui considered his next move the third interruption occurred. The west door opened for a third time, and a voice cried out, "Fly for your lives! The King approaches with fifty horse, Don Perico, intent on your death!"

It was Tomas de Bellmunt, covered with dust and mud, panting from effort, and leaning against the door in an attitude of physical exhaustion.

The first to react was Lady Isabel. With a cry of terror, she collapsed, falling out of the chair onto the ground in a dead faint. When Raquel knelt beside her on the cold stone floor, her unconscious patient hissed, "Faint, Raquel. It's harder to carry both of us!"

Raquel fainted, on top of Lady Isabel.

Montbui reached for his bride, saw the tangle of women, and cursed. He peered at the west door, recognized Bell-munt, and grew instantly suspicious. "What the devil are you doing—"

He was interrupted by a patter of bare feet racing into the church. "My lord," cried the lad from the *finca,* released from laundry duties for the moment, "my lord, a troop of soldiers is searching the *finca* this very moment. They will soon be riding this way. The mistress sent me to warn you. They asked where you were, and where the lady was. The man who led them said he was her father. The mistress said to run, my lord, as fast as you can. I borrowed a horse to come and warn you—"

"That's enough, lad," murmured Tomas.

"Get the horses," said Montbui to his man. "Our horses."

"What about the ladies?"

"The ladies may join their parents in hell," said Mont-bui, and hurried out of the church.

Lady Isabel and Raquel untangled themselves and rose slowly to their feet. Don Tomas walked toward the altar, barely repressing the desire to run. The priest snored peacefully. All was well.

The hastily assembled wedding breakfast that had been prepared for Don Perico de Montbui and his bride did not go to waste. A smaller, happier party sat down at a table under the trees to a pile of fat trout, chickens stuffed with herbs, nuts, and dried apricots, roasted lamb with onions and garlic, a ham, cheeses, fruits, and all manner of breads, rice, and vegetables. A breeze blew down from the hills, the dishes were savory and tempting, and Don Guillem de Baltier's wine flowed freely. The two hostages and their rescuer were in high good humor; the steward and his wife attacked the banquet with the relish of people who have just done in their dearest enemies.

Then Tomas leaned across the table, with concern etched on his face. "My lady," he said, "a thousand pardons, but you were lately very ill. Perhaps it is unwise to exert yourself so.''

"Would you starve me for my health, Don Tomas?" she asked, smiling.

"Oh, no, my lady," he said hastily. "But yesterday you were—"

"Lady Isabel's health improves by the day," said Raquel, calmly.

"You see, I carry my chaperon and physician with me wherever I go," said Isabel. "And I am feeling much better, thank you. But tell us, Don Tomas, how you came to rescue us so opportunely."

"It was very simple, my lady. The innkeeper is an honest man in his way," said Tomas. "He gave me your message."

"*Honest,*" said Raquel indignantly. "He sold us to Montbui."

"But not for long, Raquel," said her companion. "I suspect he sold us back to Don Tomas."

"I had heard that Montbui had access to Baltier's estate," he said quickly, hoping that part of his story would remain unexamined. "The good mistress here directed me to the church, and young Marc assisted in the performance." He leaned back and smiled, very pleased with himself.

"You were rather casual about the time," said Isabel. "If the priest had not been drunk, you would have arrived rather late to be of help."

"No risk there, my lady," said the steward. "I was with Father Pau for a while yesterday evening, and when I left, he was already much the worse for drink. I knew it'd be a hard task to get him out of bed this morning."

"And assuredly it was," said his wife.

"I brought him a small leather bottle of brandy," said the steward. "In truth, it's the only way to get Father moving. It grieves me to say that in a fit of absence of mind, I handed him the bottle. How could I know he would drink it all?" he added, shaking his head.

"And he did drink it all?" asked Lady Isabel.

"He did," said Tomas.

"And the troop of fifty horse was your invention?"

"I'm afraid it was."

"Don Tomas, you saved me from an unpleasant fate. I am most grateful." She indicated his empty cup to the steward, who made haste to fill it. "A cup of wine is small thanks for all you have done for me, but I must start somewhere," she said, with a glance through her lashes. "I am sure my father will also be grateful."

"Thank you, my lady," he said stiffly. In the merriment of the occasion, he had almost forgotten who she was, until her words firmly reminded him. He could not jest with her as if she were a dairymaid or his youngest sister.

Isabel gave him a calculating look. "You're offended at the pitiful quality of my thanks," she said. "I'm sorry. If I had casks of rubies, I assure you, I would think them a small price to pay for my rescue. Would you like rubies?"

"No, my lady," he said. "Rubies may be beautiful things, but your thanks are enough. I need nothing else."

"I see," she said. "You make a pretty speech, Don Tomas. Did you learn that at court? But you haven't touched your wine. Won't you join me? We don't get such wine at the convent."

He raised his cup and drank. "Would you like to be a nun?" he asked, desperate for something to say.

"What an odd question, Don Tomas. Are you recruiting ladies of good family for a particular order? Or would you like to lock all women away where they won't be troublesome?"

"Neither one, my lady. Of course. But I was told you had long been with the nuns, and I wondered—"

"If I had developed a taste for it?" She paused, and narrowed her eyes. "Does your question have a right answer? Am I to be frowned upon for saying yes, or no?"

"How can I answer that, my lady? I have no right to judge you. But any man might hope that a lady would prefer to stay in the world."

"Ah—I think I understand. To answer you—it is a quiet life, when one isn't being abducted; but I don't think it would suit me for a lifetime. I haven't Lady Elicsenda's tranquillity of spirit. And therefore, I must marry, if I can. If that is what you mean by staying in the world.''

"Do you like the thought of marriage?" said Don Tomas.

"How can I answer that? You saw that I hated the prospect of marrying Don Perico. It depends on circumstances. Someday, perhaps, a man may happen by. And if my father likes him, and I like him, and he likes me enough to put up with my faults, I can marry. Do you think that's probable, Don Tomas? Or are there too many ifs and perhapses in there?"

"My lady, the country must be filled with men of wealth and rank who are clamoring for your hand," said Tomas, struck by a vein of bitterness under the banter.

"Do you think so? Then they must do their clamoring far outside the walls of the convent, for I haven't heard them. Not one single love song has come drifting through the dawn into my chamber."

"Perhaps they are afraid—"

"Of Lady Elicsenda? She can be fearsome at times."

"Of you, my lady, and of your position."

"Not possible," said Isabel. "Take you, for example. You picked me up, and slung me over your shoulder without even an 'excuse me,' and carried me off into an inn. But then, perhaps you are braver than most. You certainly chased off Montbui."

In spite of himself, Tomas laughed. "He's timider than most, perhaps."

"You do him an injustice. He's brave as a lion when faced with two helpless females. But perhaps I won't marry," she said, looking tired again, and restless. "For I will only marry where I love, and I cannot love one who doesn't love me. Do you believe that lovers pine away for someone they cannot have, and die for love of one who doesn't love them? I don't. Raquel," she added, rising, "I confess I am tired. Before we take to the road again, I would like to rest. If that is possible, Don Tomas."

"Anything that will add to your comfort is possible, my

lady," said Tomas, gravely. "When you are ready to travel, have someone to fetch me." He bowed, and stood watching the women move slowly back to the house.

"What do you think of our rescuer, Raquel?" asked Lady Isabel, staring out the window at the orchard where they had been so merry for a while.

"He seems very pleasant," she said. "And handsome, as I said before."

"You are cautious in your praise."

"He's difficult to know," said Raquel. "He seems unhappy—not by nature, but from circumstances that we don't understand. Why does he know all these people? What are they to him?"

"Please don't say that," said Isabel, biting her lip. "I feel as if I am surrounded by schemers and plotters. I don't know who is a friend and who an enemy, because they all fawn and flatter. Except you. Do you think he, too, is only after wealth?"

A knock on the door, followed by the housekeeper, interrupted them.

"I have brought fresh water. Is there anything else, my lady?"

"Thank you," said Isabel vaguely. "Mistress, are you acquainted with Bellmunt?"

"Oh, yes, my lady. I met him at His Lordship's other estate. And Doña Sanxia frequently spoke of him. He worshiped her, you know," she said, lowering her voice to an almost holy hush. "Worshiped her. And she him. Don Guillem is a very strange, cold man—no husband for a passionate lady like her. And Don Tomas would have laid down his life for her. Only she died, of course," added the steward's wife in her normal tones.

"Thank you," said Lady Isabel. "We require nothing more." And she lay down on the bed and stared at the ceiling, not at all satisfied with the conversation.

Once the heat of the day lessened, Lady Isabel—with ill grace, and in a foul temper—climbed into the litter between the two patient grays, and the little procession set out again.

The interruption was sudden and cataclysmic. Over the

horizon a plume of dust arose. It was rapidly followed by half a dozen horsemen bearing down on them at a gallop. In seconds, they were surrounded.

The leader seized Castanya's reins. "Tomas de Bellmunt?" he asked.

"I am," said Tomas stiffly. "And you are?"

"I arrest you in the name of His Majesty, for the crime of high treason, and various other crimes that will be specified. Scize him," he said to his men.

THIRTEEN

Near the bank of the River Ter, upstream from the city of Girona, three men, a tall, grim-faced soldier, a square, red-faced merchant, and an earnest-looking youth, sat in the shade late Friday morning. Their horses grazed a short distance away.

"When do we tell the others? Tomorrow?" asked the young one, looking like a worried lieutenant responsible for the success of a meeting of generals.

"Not at the meeting," said the stocky one. "They'll be offended. As members of the Inner Council, they'll think they should have been part of the decision. Believe me. And if they're offended, we won't be able to count on them when the situation becomes difficult."

"No one will be part of the decision," said the tall one. His harsh voice grated in the peace of the countryside. "It is my prerogative, that decision, no one else's. I am the Sword."

"Hold on," said the stocky one, with an air of good humor. "That'll do for public consumption, but we're alone now. We work for a common cause, and toward a common end. You don't make decisions without us, my friend. And all our decisions are subject to review."

"You will address me as my lord, or as the Sword," the tall one replied. "We are not equals and friends."

"Sword, *my friend*, you can be replaced. No one has seen you, so far—at your insistence, I remind you. There are others who would willingly take your place." He continued to smile in the friendliest of fashions, but in his eyes the younger man saw a glint of steel.

"You will regret those words," said the Sword, flatly.

The young man looked from one to the other and carried on. "Don Pedro arrives this morning, drawn here as we—as you planned, my lords."

"Hardly as we planned," said the stocky one, cheerfully enough. "Doña Sanxia's end was most unfortunate. She should not have been abroad at night when the disturbances were at their height. Someone should have kept her safely behind a locked door." He looked from one to the other, assessing blame. "Her death has attracted unnecessary attention."

The younger man reddened in confusion, as if he had been attacked directly. "I was not in the lady's confidence," he said stiffly. "Romeu looked after those details."

"She adopted the habit of a nun," said the Sword. "It was an evil act, and that was the reason she died."

"It was?" said the stocky man in surprise. "Are you sure of that?"

"That house is a pit of corruption, not a house of the Lord," said the Sword. "From the Abbess to the lowliest servant. She should not have entered it. It was a judgment on her."

"Ah," said the stocky man. "I understand you. Well—Baltier will be easily consoled, and we can survive her loss. She was too easily swayed to be reliable." He looked around briskly. "I propose we convene the Inner Council this evening, unveil our strategy, and introduce the Sword."

"No!" said the Sword. "Unveil our strategy if you wish; flatter the rabble if you must; but I do not appear until the proper time."

"And when is that?"

"When I receive the Word," said the Sword. He whistled for his mount, jumped lightly on its back, and rode off.

"He seems to be taking this very seriously," said the stocky one.

"I'm afraid he is," said the young one. He looked gloomy.

"Cheer up. It's not beyond remedy," said the stocky one. "But then, little is, except death."

"I worry just as much about the Inner Council," said the young man. "They think they should have as much power as their rulers."

"Don't fret," said the other. "They have a very useful function to fulfill. When Don Fernando takes his rightful place on the throne, he will need people he can hang for the deaths of his brother and his poor little nephew. They will come in handy. Just the right number, don't you think?"

Shortly before the bells rang for sext, before the city slowed in preparation for its midday repast, a minor procession—the captain of the Bishop's guard on a large stallion, two lesser officers, and two foot guards—followed Isaac and Yusuf through the streets at a stately walk. The officers did their best to look casual, as if they were making their way through the steep and narrow lanes for the pleasure of fresh air and exercise. They were finding it difficult. The Bishop had been firm. "You are not off to arrest an evildoer," he had said. "You are escorting a small child whose safety is of utmost importance. You don't want to frighten him, or to alarm the neighborhood." He had paused and looked piercingly at them. "And you don't want every person in San Feliu and in the city to know within the hour that the Infant is in the palace."

"Perhaps I should go alone," the captain had suggested. "On foot, or accompanied only by Master Isaac."

"I had considered that," the Bishop had said. "But we can't risk it. Some people may already suspect the truth. They'll be watching for a move like this." And so they had set out, horse and foot, armed to the teeth, for the north gate, and the parish of San Feliu.

The situation worsened when they reached their destination. The Infant Johan decided he was not going to the Bishop's palace, and was not slow to let everyone know it. He was enjoying life with Nicholau and Rebecca. He had established a position of total command over their deeply impressed two-year-old son, and Rebecca's warm kisses and lively stories had almost compensated him for the loss of his nursemaid. He clung to her stubbornly, wailing in distress, until the frantic captain called a council of war.

"I can't carry a screaming child past the gate and through the streets and hope not to be noticed," he said desperately. The Infant was as quick as any child to perceive signs of appeasement; his screams redoubled in violence and intensity, and the assembled crowd gave in.

In the end, Rebecca's son and his nursemaid were dispatched to the care of a neighbor. Rebecca joined the party; the Infant Johan was swept up in front of the captain on the bay stallion, and allowed to hold the reins. Thus, with the Prince in charge, the whole troop moved in state until they were swept inside the palace, to await the arrival of his royal father.

"It is difficult to decide how much a child understands or remembers," said Don Pedro. His retainers had been dismissed, and the two men sat comfortably together. The Bishop nodded his agreement. "I have good reasons for wanting to find out from him what happened. Not only am I concerned for his welfare, but I also believe he knows the man who killed his nursemaid, and would have killed him, if he hadn't been hidden." He paused. "The nursemaid was expecting an attempt on him."

"Had she spoken of it, Sire?"

"Not to my knowledge. But she must have hidden him when she heard her attacker approach. How else could such a small child have escaped?" Don Pedro raised his silver goblet in tribute. "May her brave soul have rest. She was a better soldier than most. Including the two I sent with them to keep guard.''

"Two, Sire?''

"Well hidden within the household. Too well hidden. When danger came, they were busy playing at being friars and stable lads.'' The anger that the King had kept carefully controlled surfaced for a moment, and his cheeks paled.

"And Your Majesty believes that Prince Johan knows his attacker? Or might know him?''

"He knows. He is a brave child, yet every time a man was admitted to my presence today, he shrank in fear behind me until he saw and heard him. Except for you, Berenguer. Perhaps because of your robes.''

"It is comforting to know that the assassin is not a bishop, Your Majesty,'' said Berenguer dryly.

"But less comforting to consider that my son was attacked by someone whom he expects to see close by me.''

"Or someone who looks like one of your counselors or retainers, Sire,'' added the Bishop.

"That is possible. We had decided not to keep him near the court, where conspirators would expect to find him. But it seems he will be safer close to his mother for the rest of the summer. With a public guard. She will not wander off in pursuit of her own interests when her child's life is at stake,'' he added grimly.

"There are always problems with clandestine arrangements, Sire,'' murmured Berenguer. "It is more difficult to mount an effective defense if your soldiers cannot appear to be soldiers.''

"Indeed. Who is the good woman who kept him hidden and safe?''

"The daughter of the physician, Your Majesty. Rebecca, wife to Nicholau, one of the cathedral scribes.''

"Speak to Don Eleazar. He will see that she is well compensated for her pains,'' he said. "We shall visit our daughter when the press of the day's business is over, Berenguer. You might wish to accompany us.''

• • •

"Hola, Johan," called Isaac from the door of the Baths. In the early afternoon a guilty conscience—and the fact that he could not rest with Raquel not yet safely at home—had sent him on a round of visits to his neglected patients. His last case brought him close to the Baths; leaving Yusuf outside to watch for strangers, he went in to tackle the keeper.

"Master Isaac. Sir," said Big Johan, his voice trembling.

"Have you time to sit with me for a while?" asked Isaac.

"Here, sir," he said. "You may sit here. This bench is comfortable." But his voice lacked its usual friendly welcome, and the placid, even-tempered keeper seemed curiously restless.

Isaac sank onto the bench, and set his basket between his feet. "Thank you. Now, Johan—sit beside me. They say you are not looking well. It concerns me, and I have hurried over. Tell me what is wrong."

"Nothing, Master," he said hastily. "Nothing is wrong."

"Then why are you not looking well?" And painfully, step by tiny step, Isaac dragged the keeper through a long list of minor complaints.

"So," he said at last, "you do not sleep with your accustomed ease, and you cannot eat with the enjoyment you used to find in your dinner, and your head aches, and your belly quivers inside with fear, for no reason. And when did this start? Don't tell me. I know. It started the night the nun was killed in your Baths, didn't it?"

"Yes, Master," said Johan miserably.

"And why is that, I wonder?" There was no response. "I am not a spy from your absent master, Johan, wishing to take your employment from you. Nor am I a judge, or a priest. I am only your physician, who concerns himself with your health, not your morals." Still no response. "Then let me guess. Did you let the poor creature into the Baths after nightfall?"

"Oh, no, Master. I didn't do that."

"Did you let a man into the Baths—and that man prob-

ably her murderer—after nightfall, when they should be
locked?''

"Oh no, Master. I didn't let anybody in. I weren't anywhere near the Baths that night, I swear.''

"But you gave someone your key, didn't you? Pedro
used to, they say.''

"No,'' said Big Johan, stung to the quick. "Only three
times have I done it since Old Pedro died. Once I let—''

"Don't tell me,'' said Isaac. "It's none of my business,
and I'm sure this is the first time that any evil has come of
it. A certain amount of sin, no doubt, but not pure evil.''

"It is,'' said Johan in panic. "And I know I were drunk,
Master Isaac, but I swear, I didn't give the key to anyone.
It were magic, that's what. They bewitched me. You un-
derstand magic, Master Isaac. You know how they did it.
I have a little money put by, Master Isaac. I will pay you
to protect me from them and their spells.''

"Keep your money, Johan. Someday you will want it for
better purposes. Did anyone ask you about the key?''

Johan thought. "That Romeu did. The one who bought
all the wine. He asked about the key. I showed it to him,
and said I always kept it about me, on its chain. But how
did it get from my chain into the water of the bath? Except
it were demons who put it there.''

"If it were demons, Johan, they were human ones. I
don't think you should worry about that.''

"But, Master Isaac, they want me to open the Baths tomorrow for a big meeting. And they say if I won't, they
can make the locks spring open with their spells. I'll never
keep my post if they hold a big meeting in the Baths after
nightfall. You can't keep that quiet. But what can I do,
Master Isaac? I can't fight against magic.''

"Now listen to me, Johan,'' said Isaac. "This is what
we will do.''

Late in the afternoon, Isabel d'Empuries limped slowly up
the stairs to the infirmary, assisted by Raquel, leaving the
Abbess and her dozen nuns behind, tormented with curiosity. "Are you in great pain, my lady?'' asked Raquel.

"Because I can send to my papa for more soothing drafts."

"No, I'm not," said Isabel. "But if they think I'm better, they'll bother me until they've wrenched from me every detail of what happened to us. I'm tired and miserable, but not in pain." She stopped in the corridor to look at her companion. "I wish you could stay. Otherwise I have no one I can talk to." She opened the door to the infirmary. "Good evening, Sor Benvenguda," she said pleasantly. "The Abbess would like to speak to you."

"Thank you, Lady Isabel," said the sister, and bustled off.

"I can't spend the entire evening looking at her sour face," said Isabel. "Can you stay?"

"I should go home for the Sabbath," said Raquel uneasily. "And that means I must leave soon. My mother will be upset if I am not there—but if you truly need me, my lady, I will stay."

Lady Isabel sat down on the edge of her bed. "I don't *need* you, Raquel." She tried to smile, but tears began to well up in her eyes. "It would be easier for me to bear being here if you could stay. When can you come back?"

"Mama wouldn't let me leave the Quarter until sundown tomorrow. Maybe I could talk Papa into coming to see you then—"

"I'll need him. I am so unhappy, Raquel." Tears poured down her cheeks. "How could they arrest Tomas? How can they be so stupid? He didn't kidnap us. I'd be married now to that disgusting man if he hadn't rescued us. Montbui only wants my mama's money. He and his friends need it to depose Papa and put my uncle Fernando on the throne. Everyone knows that." She picked up the end of her elegantly long sleeve and mopped up the tears from her cheeks with it. "Don't tell anyone you saw me do that," she murmured.

"Why do they think Tomas kidnapped us?" said Raquel, glancing out the window. Shadows were lengthening. "We told them he didn't. Can the Bishop do anything?"

"Uncle Berenguer? Yes. And Papa, if I can get word to

him. Oh, Raquel—please! Will you take a message for me?''

''Yes, my lady,'' said Raquel, looking out the window again. ''But hurry. It is close to sundown, and I must be home by then.''

''We need paper, and ink, and a pen. Raquel—find one of the other wards. A young one. Tell her I need writing things. Quickly!''

The declining sun had turned from pale yellow to gold before Raquel breathlessly reported success.

''Where is she, then?''

''She has to find them, my lady, and then bring them here. And avoid the sisters, who seem to be everywhere.''

''She'll know how to do that,'' said Isabel confidently. ''It's the first thing you learn.''

But the footsteps in the corridor did not belong to one of the convent's young wards. There was a sharp rap and the door was flung open by Sor Marta. ''Good evening, Lady Isabel. The physician is here to see you. And your father is in Lady Elicsenda's study with the Bishop. He will come to see you later. His Majesty would like to speak to Mistress Raquel. Now.'' She nodded magisterially and turned to go.

Isabel went white. Raquel's cheeks flushed scarlet. ''I will try to come tomorrow night,'' she whispered in terror, and left.

The sun hovered, a fiery orange-red globe, just over the horizon when Isaac and Raquel finally left the convent.

''What is the hour?'' asked Isaac.

''The sun is near setting, Papa. We must hurry.''

''Where is Yusuf?'' asked Isaac.

''Here, lord,'' said the boy.

''Who is this, Papa?'' said Raquel, looking suspiciously at that battered face.

''He has been my eyes since you have been gone. But he is just a boy, and cannot be my hands, as well. I am pleased to have you with me again.''

''Now that your daughter has returned, will you no

longer need me, lord?'' asked Yusuf. There was no expression at all in his careful voice.

"A man cannot have too many pairs of eyes," said the physician. "I need you both. He will run errands for you as well, Raquel. He is quick."

"And fond of fighting," she remarked.

Jacob saw them approach and held the gates open. "Hurry, Master Isaac," he called. "The sun is almost gone." They sped through, and rushed down the streets toward the house. Ibrahim stood at the open gate to the courtyard, waiting. It, too, banged shut behind them. They were home.

"Make haste to wash," said Isaac, and everyone flew in a different direction.

They were seated, breathless and flushed, at the table when Judith entered. "Raquel," she cried, dragging her up from her place and enveloping her in a tight embrace. "I expected you this morning," she said, angrily, pushing her out at arm's length to look at her. "Where have you been?"

"Oh, Mama," said Raquel helplessly. "It's so—I'll tell you later."

Judith backed away, lit the candles, and began the prayers.

"I have fathered a hellishly unreasonable daughter," Don Pedro said to Berenguer, once he was comfortably settled in the most luxurious accommodation the episcopal palace had to offer. He had chased away his attendants, except for his secretary, Eleazar ben Solomon, and his watchdog, Don Arnau. The three men stirred uneasily.

"Her mother, as I remember, was also strong-willed," said the Bishop, cautiously. "She found it impossible to hide—or feign—her affections or her dislikes. It was one of her charms."

"That is true. And you do well to remind me of it, Berenguer," said the King. "What connection has my daughter with Bellmunt?"

"None, Sire," said the Bishop in astonishment. "She has been most closely guarded with the sisters, I assure you.

Until this horrific event, she has not been outside the walls of the convent unaccompanied.''

"Then you would believe her, if she said that she met him yesterday for the first time.''

"I would. I would also find it impossible to believe that she had contrived to meet him earlier. And last night Bellmunt slept here under my roof,'' he added, "leaving the palace at dawn to fetch the two ladies and return them to the convent.''

"What did he tell you of their acquaintance?''

"He appeared to be very frank and open. He told me that while he was resting his horse, he saw a party on the road, made up of a closely curtained litter, a lady on horseback, two servants, and a gentleman. Then he saw that young Mistress Raquel was tied to her mount, and that the 'gentleman' was his own servant, dressed in his clothes, and wearing a sword. He challenged him, his servant drew on him, they fought, and the scoundrel was killed. He escorted the ladies to the inn, saw them comfortably settled, and on the advice of your daughter, came to see me.''

"That was what she told me, as well. And so did Mistress Raquel,'' said Don Pedro. "Then how do you account for this?'' He gestured toward his secretary, who produced a letter. "Give it to the Bishop, Eleazar.''

"Certainly, Sire.''

Berenguer read through the letter that the hapless Tomas had written with so much agony to his uncle, right down to those last damning words, *I fear I have been led into treachery.*

"You see, Berenguer. He confesses it himself.''

"Well—to some extent. He confesses that he doesn't know what's going on. And after looking at this, I must admit that I share his feeling. It is most strange, Your Majesty. And what does Castellbo say? I presume that he gave the letter to Your Majesty.''

"You would be wrong, Berenguer. Castellbo's secretary gave it to Don Eleazar. The Count has been on a confidential mission for us.''

"His nephew didn't know that he was away?''

"Every effort was made," said Don Eleazar, "to prevent anyone from finding out that he was not simply suffering from a bout of illness."

"You succeeded with the nephew," said the Bishop. "But perhaps that wasn't difficult. He seemed to me to be a pleasant young man, but somewhat gullible. He confessed to being at sea in the politics of the court."

"You knew that he was Her Majesty's secretary," said Eleazar.

"I did," said Berenguer.

"Unfortunately, the young man appears to have condemned himself with his own pen," said Don Pedro, cautiously. "But see that he is kept in comfortable quarters and treated well, in case there is some merit in his defense. We will try him tomorrow."

FOURTEEN

News that Tomas de Bellmunt, son of Don Garcia de Bellmunt and the late Doña Elvira de Castellbo, was to be tried for treason was a delicious morsel of scandal to top off a week of alarming rumors. Not that Don Tomas was of any interest to anyone. Her Majesty's youthful secretary came from a good and honorable family, but one that the winds of fortune had stripped of power or wealth, leaving them with little but rank and name to keep out the winter cold. And they were from some far-off and obscure part of the kingdom.

The fascination lay in the charge, and gossip was growing more improbable and fantastic by the minute. Women and common folk whispered in the market of unspeakable deeds involving Her Majesty, while grave wealthy merchants spoke solemnly in the Wool Exchange of conspiracies—complicated plots by the English to incite civic unrest, and by the French to murder the Infant Johan, and thus, in some mysterious way, destroy the demand for local wool. They shook their heads and fretted about prices. Long before the hour of sitting was reached, the courtroom was filled.

The benches allotted to spectators were all occupied. The

bells rang out the hour and the prisoner was brought in. A surprised murmur rose from the crowd. Its usual thirst for vengeance was, to a degree, tempered by pity when it saw how handsome the young man was. The color had drained from Tomas's face, except for dark hollows under his eyes, but he walked to the chair set out for him with his head high. The constantly shifting winds of favor that made up the politics of the court may have been beyond his grasp, but the implications of a charge of treason were not. He had been questioned, and had answered truthfully; he could think of nothing else to tell his interrogators but the truth as he knew it. But he had wit enough to realize that every word he had spoken had been damning. Today they would bring them out, and use them against him. He had no hope of escape.

The clerk was seated at his handsomely carved table, organizing his documents. He glanced up, noticed that the prisoner was regarding him fixedly, reddened, and looked hastily away. Tomas politely turned his attention to the walls. A panel of four advocates arrived, splendid in the long robes of those skilled in the law, and talking in low tones together, sat at a bench on one side. Two of them had spent long hours the evening before, questioning Tomas, but they scarcely seemed to notice his presence.

Finally, the door opened to permit the entry of the judges. The noisy crowd rose hastily, and then sudden silence filled the room. A tall man, dressed in sober black, and like a warrior just off the battlefield, walked into the room and took the central place on the bench. He was followed by two judges, both robed like peacocks in comparison. Court was being taken by Pedro of Aragon himself.

The younger justice nodded to the clerk. "Read the charge."

"Your Majesty, Your Lordships," murmured the clerk, and read out the solemn formulas that charged Tomas de Bellmunt with treason, in that he had conspired with other unnamed persons to seize the heir to the throne.

"And what says the prisoner to the charge?" asked the King.

One of advocates rose, consulted a piece of paper in front of him, and spoke in the round and solemn tones of his kind. "Your Majesty, the prisoner avers that he is a true and loyal subject to the King, and that his complicity in this plot was unwitting." He did not sound convinced.

"And has the prisoner made a statement concerning the charges?" asked the younger justice.

A second advocate stood, and bowed to the bench. "He has, Your Majesty, my lords," he said, and began to read Bellmunt's painfully full and detailed account of the affair. Tomas felt curiously divorced from the scene, like a spectator at an entertainment. In spite of occasional inaccuracies, it was an admirably good rendition of what he had said. He could see with brutal clarity the strength of the case against him. If he had been a stranger in town, come in out of curiosity to watch the trial, he would have concluded that the prisoner was either a fool, too dangerous to live, or a reckless villain, so hardened in villainy he was careless of consequences. He wondered briefly if anything could have lessened the impact of the facts. Perhaps if the court had seen Doña Sanxia, her hard, lying eyes, and her bewitching hair, they might have understood his ready acquiescence to her request. But Doña Sanxia was dead. With his newly won wisdom, he realized that even if she were alive, she would never have risked her own neck to save his.

Moreover, Tomas had suppressed only two facts in his long statement, and the relationship between them was one of them. Like some knight out of the old tales, he was determined to shield her, even in death, from the crude sniggering of the crowd. And he shrank from admitting his sin and folly in a public place, in case Lady Isabel should hear of it, and think less of him. He had also failed to mention the connection between his uncle and Romeu. It was no secret, but it could only have brought harm to his innocent patron—the brother of his dead mother. He would go to his death, he thought grimly, accepting responsibility for his own actions, and not pull anyone else, alive or dead, down with him.

To his astonishment, the statement ended with the discovery of Doña Sanxia's body and his tardy return to Barcelona. Nothing of Lady Isabel, or Montbui, or the killing of Romeu. He started up from his seat to protest, and was hastily pushed back. "The prisoner will remain silent," said the clerk in his dry little voice.

The second advocate rose to his feet, enveloped in confidence, bowed low to the bench, and began to set out the case before the judges. It took no time at all. It began with a short preamble, and ended with the letter that Tomas had sent to his uncle, containing those damning words, *I fear I have been led into treachery.*

It was so simple, thought Tomas. Everything else had been mere elaboration. He had penned his death warrant on that night in Barcelona.

His uncle's confidential secretary was called, looking dustier and more dried out than ever, and delivered a precise and monotonous account of receiving the letter.

"And how was it that you received and opened a letter that was addressed to the Count?" asked the advocate, who appeared, in some way, to be representing Tomas.

"The Count was some distance away on a mission of great secrecy for His Majesty. I was instructed not to let anyone —neither closest family nor dearest friend—know that he was away from the court. I let it be rumored that he was suffering from sickness. Otherwise, I would never have opened a letter from his nephew."

"What did you do then?" asked the junior justice.

"I opened the letter the next morning, Your Lordship. By then, Don Tomas had already left Barcelona. For Girona, I now understand."

"On instructions from the Count?" asked Don Pedro suddenly.

"No, Your Majesty. Not that I know of. I believed at the time that he was traveling with Her Majesty's retinue."

Tomas raised his head indignantly, ready to object to the lie. But it was a small lie, he realized, offered to protect his uncle's reputation. He subsided into apathy.

A small group of witnesses were brought forward to place Tomas on the road to Girona, rather than with Her Majesty's retinue, and the case against him was complete.

The only witnesses who could have sworn—if they had wished to—that Tomas was an unwitting pawn in the plan to seize the Infant Johan were dead. And the prosecutors, clever men that they were, had charged him with nothing else. They had no reason to. A man has only one head to lose.

His Majesty rose, and with him the rest of the court, and retired to consider the facts.

"Mama has gone to her room to rest. I could read to you, Papa," murmured Raquel as the endless Sabbath afternoon lazed before them, quiet and sunny. "Yusuf could fetch the book, if I told him which one." They were sitting under the arbor. Only the muted splash of the fountain broke into the silence of the hot afternoon. The cat slept; the birds had ceased their quarreling; even the rumble of carts and voices from outside the Quarter had died away, fading into a universal somnolence.

"Are you sure?" said Isaac, in tones of mock terror. "Perhaps we might risk a page. Of something suitable to the day, of course."

"Of course, Papa. Where are the twins?"

"I was told the twins are sleeping," said Isaac. "So, if you must read, be sure to speak softly. It would be wrong, at their tender age, to expose them to depravity."

"It is not that I must, Papa," said Raquel, uncertainly. "I thought it would ease your worries." Raquel, who took her father very seriously, found his tendency to self-deprecating humor unsettling. Did he want her to read to him on the Sabbath or not? Her father was a profoundly religious man, and yet as her mother was fond of pointing out, he was often careless in matters of observance. This time, she took matters into her own hands, and beckoned to Yusuf to follow her into the study.

Isaac heard the soft rustle of his daughter's skirts as she

moved across the courtyard, heard her push open the door
to his study. While her eyes were searching for something
suitable he fancied that, through them, he could see the long
row of precious books again, in their dark and solemn bind-
ings, and he wondered idly which one she would select.

"I chose Boethius, Papa. *De consolatione philoso-
phiae.*"

Isaac was not surprised. It was one of Raquel's favorite
works: the first "difficult" writing she had learned to read
and understand.

"What does that mean?" asked Yusuf.

" 'On the consolation of philosophy,' of course," said
Raquel.

"May I stay and listen, lord?" asked Yusuf.

"You won't understand it," said Raquel, with more than
a touch of superiority. "It is written in the language of
learning."

"I understand some of that language," said Yusuf. "The
clerk I traveled with taught me. I will listen quietly, and
not ask questions. Then I will go into town and find out
what you wish to know, lord."

"You may stay," said Isaac, doubtfully. A certain jealous hostility seemed to be springing up already between
those two strong and demanding minds, and it made him
uneasy. In the past few days, Yusuf had won a small place
in his life. He had started to form plans for the education
of the Moorish boy, and overcoming Judith's suspicions
was going to be difficult enough. If Raquel turned against
the boy as well, the peace of his household could be shat-
tered by open warfare between his two unlikely apprentices.
"But don't disturb Raquel."

Then in her soft and pleasant voice, Raquel began to read
the measured verses. The imprisoned philosopher, Boethius, laments the cruelty of his situation; it has robbed him
of his youth and strength, making him old before his time;
death is imminent, and poetry—which was once his
delight—has failed to console him. Yusuf watched intently
as her lips formed the words; Isaac listened to the familiar
lines with the pleasure he always took in the beauty of

sound, and permitted his mind to wander over the extraordinary events of the last few days.

Raquel finished the poignant lines in which the philosopher rebukes his friends for having boasted in the past of his good fortune. Her voice faltered for a moment, but she drew a deep breath and went on. The Lady Philosophy made her sudden appearance in the prisoner's cell, majestic, tattered, and acerbic. Raquel could no longer enjoy the scene; it was all too close to reality. She closed the book and handed it back to Yusuf. "Why did they arrest Don Tomas, Papa? You must have heard something."

"Not much, my dear," said Isaac cautiously.

"It seems very unjust to me. He risked his life twice to help us. And he had nothing to do with our abduction." She kept her voice quiet and low, but she could not prevent it from shaking with indignation.

"I understand that it was his servant who abducted you and the Lady Isabel. That would be reason enough to arrest him."

"Is that the law?" she asked. "If little Yusuf here went to the market and stole a cake, would you be sent to prison?"

"If I had sent him to steal it, and he brought it home for me to eat," said Isaac. "If it were his own greed that prompted him, then it would be his body in prison."

"It would still be my body in prison, lord, whether you sent me to steal the cake or I went on my own," said Yusuf promptly. "They would take me, whether it were judged your fault or not."

"True," said Isaac. "And so with Tomas. The servant must suffer the punishment for his deed, but if it is judged that the master ordered him to do it, then the master, too, must be punished. And by rights, more severely. And you may leave now, Yusuf. Quietly."

The boy rose silently to his feet, and then stood in front of Isaac, clearly loath to leave such an interesting conversation.

"Wait," said Raquel. "If you're leaving the Quarter, I might have a message for you to take."

"Tomas knew nothing about what happened to us that night," said Raquel, as soon as Yusuf had settled back down on the ground beside Isaac. "He came to help us when he saw me with my hands tied."

"Did he say that?"

"No. I saw him lying there, down by the river, watching us—not spying intently, but like someone resting, enjoying the day. He had almost let us pass quietly by, when I saw a startled look on his face. He was staring at my hands, Papa. He drew his sword, came running up the hill, and made Romeu fight. He killed him in front of me."

"That could have been a clever ruse on his part—to convince you and Lady Isabel that he was innocent. Perhaps he had decided that the abduction was a failure, and he needed to remove himself from the plot."

"Oh, Papa! He was truly astonished. I don't think he could have feigned that expression. He is not a devious man," she said firmly. "If you knew him! He is so lacking in guile and cunning he couldn't even imagine a scheme that wicked. And if he tried to carry it out, he would turn scarlet with shame. I don't know how he has survived this far," she added, with a hint of scorn and pity.

"You remember, my dear, I spoke to him. He impressed me as a young man of singular honesty and directness. But he may be embroiled, without realizing it, in something far too dangerous to escape from."

"But, Papa—he is the soul of innocence."

"And how does it happen that my daughter knows the secrets of his heart so well? And why does she plead his cause so fervently?"

"Oh, Papa," said Raquel impatiently. "Anyone can know the secrets of his heart after a moment of conversation with him. He's too guileless and open for my taste. He has no sense of humor—or not enough, and not a very subtle mind," she added, and then felt ashamed. "Except that I think he's worried or unhappy about something. But I believe Lady Isabel has fallen in love with him, although she denies it. And he with her. I'm sure of it. He blushes a charming color when he speaks to her. But he has made no advances to either one of us. He is a most proper gentleman. Almost too proper, in fact," she added.

"I'm sorry for that," said Isaac. "Not that he is too proper, but that Lady Isabel loves him. It is most unfortunate. She would do well to prepare herself for the worst. The young man has placed himself in an impossible position. And even if I could help him in some way, I can do nothing today. Tomorrow it will likely be too late to save him."

"But, Papa—it's not right. Surely the Lord would not wish a man to die unjustly for want of a word of help on the Sabbath." She dug her fingernails into the palms of her hand to keep herself from tears.

"My dear," said Isaac, "if I knew that my help would keep him from an undeserved death, Christian or not, Sabbath or not, I might attempt to intervene," said Isaac. "But I do not believe there is anything I can do."

"Why must you always be so cautious and careful, Papa?" She stopped to gather her determination together. "If you will not help him, then I will. If Lady Isabel asked her father, he would help, but I'm sure she has no idea of the peril he is in. The nuns won't tell her anything. That place is like a prison, in some ways." Raquel grasped her father tightly by the arm. "Papa—I must go and see Isabel."

"Now?" said Isaac.

"I cannot wait until sundown. May I send Yusuf with a message for her? And then I shall leave."

"You propose to go through the streets and out to the convent all alone?"

"I thought that perhaps you could let me have Yusuf to accompany me," she said uncertainly.

"Alone, with a boy? He is quick and clever, but he is not much protection for a woman alone. And how will you return?"

"I shall spend the night at the convent, and return in the morning. I will tell Mama something when I get back."

"First let Yusuf go to the convent and deliver your message. That way he can also find out what is happening to Tomas.''

''Shall I return the book to its place before I go, lord?''

''Yes,'' said Raquel. ''And I will write a short message to Lady Isabel.''

As the spectators gossiped, and the officers of the court speculated on how quickly they would be able to get to their dinners, a small boy slipped in a door that had been opened to catch a breeze. He hid himself behind group after group, working his way into the courtroom, where he melted into a dark corner behind a bench, and prepared to watch. In a matter of minutes, the panel of advocates entered again, the court straggled to its feet, and His Majesty returned, his train of judges behind him. ''Does the prisoner wish to say anything on his own behalf?'' he asked in a conversational tone, bending forward to look at the young man.

Tomas bowed. ''Your Majesty. I know now that, blinded by foolishness and inexperience, I was led into the worst of crimes. God knows there was no treason in my heart, but I am appalled at the evils my actions might have unloosed, and I accept the consequences without complaint. I beg, not for your pardon, but for your forgiveness.''

''Brave words, bravely spoken,'' said the King, with no change of expression. ''Tomas de Bellmunt, you are guilty of treason. On Monday next, you will be handed over for execution in a manner befitting your station in life, and your goods will be liable to confiscation.''

The words disappeared in the roaring in his head; he bowed to His Majesty, and was led away.

FIFTEEN

Yusuf slipped out of the courthouse, heading for the plaza in front of the Bishop's palace. Once there, he scrambled up the wall, and crawled gingerly over an adjoining roof. He went from roof to courtyard, to another wall, until he was peering down into the Quarter itself. Then a shutter slammed open, and a loud cry of outrage told him there was no retreat. He eased himself down from the top of the wall, and jumped onto a roof in the Quarter. After that, it was easy. At the roof of Isaac's house, he let down his guard, sliding down the tiles, bringing one with him, and pitching into the courtyard, doubled up, with the wind knocked out of him.

As Yusuf fought to get his breath again Isaac murmured, "Surely it was not necessary to fly over the rooftops of the Quarter. Once inside, we ordinary mortals are allowed to use the streets. What is your news?"

"It was faster, lord," he gasped, "once I was up there. I have a message from Lady Isabel, mistress. She wishes you to come to her as soon as you can. And the news from the court is very bad."

• • •

"Condemned!" said Raquel. "And to die on Monday. I can't believe it. Oh, Papa. This will kill Lady Isabel!"

"Yes, go to her," said Isaac. "It won't kill her. She'll be bitterly unhappy, but she's not one to fade away and die when life turns its ugly side to her. But she'll need you."

"When?"

"In good time. I'll take you. We'll all escape together, but I must wait until your mother comes down before I leave. Put on a dark cloak and wait for me in the doorway across from the gates. I have my own ways of entering and leaving——just as effective as Yusuf's, but more costly."

Raquel changed into her simplest gown, of sober gray, with plain, narrow sleeves, and a darker surcoat. She threw a veil over her head and, ignoring the oppressive heat in her shuttered chamber, wrapped a light cloak around her shoulders. It occurred to her that, in spite of her defiant speech of justification, she was disguising herself as if she were planning to steal a purse, or commit a murder. And she felt as guilty as if those were her intentions. All you're doing, she said to herself, is taking a pleasant walk to visit a friend. It didn't help.

The streets of the Quarter were quiet; here and there from unshuttered windows came small, domestic sounds—babies crying, being hushed by soft-voiced mothers, and small children whimpering over hurts, real and imagined—but the workday bustle was stilled. Stifling hot air hung over the city. The quiet, which ordinarily she found soothing to both soul and body, felt ominous. Every window seemed to harbor a spy, wondering where she was going, what she was doing. Menace lurked in every doorway, and up every lane. When she reached the bottom of the dark narrow stairs that led to the gate, she wrapped her cloak tightly around her, shivering.

The sound of unfamiliar footsteps drove her into a neglected doorway; she shrank into a corner and drew her veil over her face. A roughly dressed, red-faced man turned the corner, peered at her, and seemed as if he would stop. Something made him change his mind, and he carried on his way. The incident was nothing, and yet Raquel's heart pounded in fright; it was as if a mask of smiling innocence had slipped from the face of the city she loved, exposing its evil, lecherous grin. A world that could condemn an innocent man to death with no more ceremony than a hasty trial, to which she—a principal witness—was not called to testify, was a world in which justice, and virtue, and rule of law were a mockery. Tears flooded her cheeks; she was grateful for the thickness of her veil.

She fled up the steps before fear could drive her home again.

She heard her father approaching long before she could see him—his firm footsteps, the tap of his staff on the cobbles, and mixed in with them, Yusuf's quick, light steps. "Are you there, my dear?" he asked as he approached the gate.

"Here, Papa," she said, in a voice that she could not keep from quavering, and stepped out of a dark corner into the late-afternoon sun.

Isaac was dressed as always for a visit to a patient. Yusuf, looking serious, walked beside and somewhat to the front of him, carrying the basket with herbs and remedies. Seeing the boy in her role, with as intent and solemn an air as she must have had when Rebecca's mantle first fell on her, made Raquel gasp in pain. Was the pain nostalgia for her girlhood, she wondered, or was it possible that she could be jealous of this child? Resolutely, she tried to blink the world back into focus.

Isaac reached out for her hand and grasped it firmly. "Raquel, my child, you're trembling. What's wrong? Did something frighten you?"

She wanted to scream out, Yes, Papa, yes, I'm frightened. The whole world is wrong, but here in the sunlight of a quiet Sabbath afternoon, she felt embarrassed by her fear, so irrational and unwarranted. "No, Papa," she said. "But standing here, waiting, I began to think about poor Tomas, and—" Tears sprang up again and she could not continue.

"Of course, my dear. Now—let us talk our way out of

here." Isaac whistled softly. A young lad appeared, and unlocked the gate. The physician dropped some coins into the lad's outstretched palm and they walked out into the city.

They paid their toll and passed the north gate in silence, and were crossing the bridge over the Galligants before Raquel dared to speak. "How did you explain my disappearance?" she asked at last.

"I didn't, my dear. You are feverish, because of your dreadful experience. I have given you a powerful sleeping potion, and it would be most dangerous to disturb you before morning."

"Papa, you are so clever. And wicked."

Isaac had his own reasons for having to be outside the city before the setting of the sun. He and Yusuf accompanied Raquel over the bridge and along the road by the river as far as the convent. "Good-bye, my dear," he said. "Remember—you must return very early in the morning, before your mother is awake and stirring. I will send Yusuf to fetch you; cover yourself closely as you walk through the city."

"Yes, Papa," said Raquel, meekly.

"Do your best to console Lady Isabel. There you will be of more use than I am. But if her general condition is worse—if she is feverish, or light-headed, or in pain—send for me. I'll be at the Arab Baths. You must make the decision before nightfall; after that, it may be too late."

"Why at the Baths, Papa? Is Johan ill? And why so late?"

"Shh, my dear. I have business of my own to take care of. Take the basket. You may need it."

"Hola, Johan," murmured Isaac at the door to the Baths.

"Master Isaac," said Johan. "You came at last. With the boy," he added, in a puzzled voice.

"He is my eyes, Johan. But he is small, and will not take up much room. Is everything prepared?"

"Yes, Master," said the keeper. "What you asked."

"Take me to the place where I may wait."

Johan took the physician by the hand and dragged him around to an alcove at the side. "Here," he said. "Behind the dresser. Where I keep the linens after they dry." He thought for a moment. "Where I hide when I need to sleep. No one ever found me here." He pulled him farther along, and then pushed him down. "There's a stool to sit on, Master Isaac."

"Can I be seen, lad?"

"No, lord," said Yusuf. "Except for a bit of your tunic. Let me push it out of the way. There. Now you are invisible."

"Thank you. Johan. Yusuf will go outside and wait for someone to come by. When he whistles, you are to go out, and lock the door as always. Say something to the passerby so he will remember seeing you lock it, and then go home and stay there."

"Can I not go to Rodrigue's for my supper? I always go to Rodrigue's after I lock the Baths."

"That's even better. Go to Rodrigue's tonight. Do what you always do, then go home, and go to bed. Yusuf?"

"Yes, lord." And Yusuf's soft footsteps whispered and echoed through the high empty spaces of the Baths.

A low, plaintive whistle drifted inside. To Isaac, it sounded like the melancholy cry of some strange night bird, blown by a high wind from a distant country, and lost in the hills of Cataluña. Big Johan picked up his bundle and walked out into the evening. "Pere," he said to a bandy-legged man leading a donkey that was carrying a huge load of wood.

"Johan. You work late on a Saturday night."

"And you, Pere."

"If there's light to work by, Pere is working. They need bigger fires in the palace kitchens. There are grand happenings there tonight."

Johan nodded, and locked the door to the Baths. The key was firmly attached to a chain that looped around his waist.

"You're not staying for the excitement?" asked Pere, with a careless gesture in the direction of the Baths.

"I lock her up, and she stays locked up," said Johan, falling into step with the man and the donkey. He towered over both.

"Wise man," said Pere. "Such affairs bring nothing but grief. You're too young to remember the crusading shepherds," he remarked. "Came down through the mountain passes, crying out slogans, looking like an army of barbarians, killing lepers, breaking into churches, destroying holy things. All in the name of God. Hanged, most of them. I saw it when I was a boy." The donkey stumbled. "Courage, Margarita," he said. "We're almost there. Stay a moment, Johan, while I stable the beast, and drop this load off to the palace, and I'll join you in a cup or two at Rodrigue's, friend. I'd just as soon be somewhere public tonight, innocently drinking, when the trouble starts."

Without a word, Johan untied the straps, hoisted the two bundles of wood up on his own shoulders as if they were so many bundles of rags, and waited for his friend. Together they walked up to the Bishop's palace and delivered the wood to keep the cooks' ovens hot for His Majesty's dinner.

"Lord?" said Yusuf in a quiet voice. Even so, the word echoed in whispers around the Baths. "Where are you?"

"I am where you left me, Yusuf," said Isaac. "What are you doing in here? I told you to stay out. These men love neither one of us."

"I could not leave you alone. They are too dangerous, lord."

The first members of the Fellowship of the Archangel's Sword arrived before the last bloodred rays of the evening sun faded from the sky. They stood on the other side of the door, laughing and talking, making no attempt at concealment. After a short time, one of them tried the door, and cursed loudly. "That fool of a keeper locked it!"

"That is Sanch the ostler who speaks," whispered Isaac.

"I have a key," said another voice.

"And that is Raimunt the scribe, who seems to have made another key to the Baths. So much for opening the doors by magic," murmured the physician with satisfaction.

"Magic?"

"They told Johan they would use magic to open the door—and also to hunt him down—if he refused to leave it open." A key screeched in the lock and the door opened, letting in the noise of a small crowd outside. "But now we must not talk," he whispered, "not until they are so many that their noise will cover the sound of our voices."

Yusuf crouched down in the corner beside Isaac without another word.

It was five men, Isaac judged, who came in at first. Sanch, Raimunt, Martin, and two with unfamiliar voices, one deep and confident, the other light and worried. "How many will come?" asked the worried one.

"Thirty, I reckon," said Sanch. "I counted all them that I talked to, and that's what it were. Maybe one or two more. Is that enough?"

"For now," said the confident one. "The place won't hold many more. If each man brings another to the plaza, we'll have enough. Reinforcements are waiting. They will join us as soon we enter the palace doors."

"How do we get in?" asked Sanch.

"Don't worry about that," the confident voice continued. "Many inside the palace have no love for the Bishop, and are sympathetic to our cause."

"Who has the hoods?" asked the worried one. He was clearly the detail man, checking off possible problem areas.

"I do," said Martin.

"One to each as long as they last," said the detail man. "Those in hoods will be in the front ranks."

"And Raimunt," said the other, "you stand beside friend Sanch, and see you recognize each man as he comes by. You'll have a torch and the moon to see their faces by."

"Why?" asked Martin suspiciously.

"We want no spies here," said the confident one easily. "And later, Don Fernando will want to know what men were with the movement from the first, for they shall be rewarded first."

They poured into the Baths, first a few subdued ones, and then a nervously chattering group, and soon a boisterous crowd. The temperature soared and the sound level became deafening.

"How many are there?" whispered Isaac into Yusuf's ear.

"More than I can see," said Yusuf. "Wait a moment." The boy disappeared, leaving Isaac crouched on his low stool, squeezed in behind the dresser. He tried to concentrate on what was being said, but the atmosphere—heat, noise, and an overpowering smell of sweating humanity—drowned his senses and distracted him.

Then as suddenly as he had disappeared, Yusuf appeared again, pressed against his knee. "There are thirty or more crowded into the big hall," he whispered, "and the doorway is filled with men so tightly packed I cannot count. Perhaps ten or twenty more. They have fired torches, and set them in the walls. And now they are broaching a keg of wine, and passing out cups for all to drink from. They have brought forward a platform, and the red-faced man is going to speak."

"Then we must be very quiet, and listen."

The address to the crowd started in an almost conversational tone. It was the confident man who spoke, and he began talking about the town—her prosperity, her trade, her importance, and the wealth of her citizens. Then he stopped. "But not of all of her citizens. Is that not true?"

"True, true," shouted the group, breaking into excited babble.

"We all know what has happened to some of us—I give you Martin, the honest bookbinder, who has lost his custom, and Raimunt, the scribe, half of whose work has been taken from him, and many others in this good and hard-

working company who have similar stories to tell. We all
know to whom the work has gone, and we know who has
given it to them.''

The shouts and yells grew in number and increased in
volume, until Isaac's head began to ache with the noise.

''At the head is the King, who surrounds himself with
Jews as counselors, and uses our wealth to promote a false
heir.'' A roar went up from the crowd.

''Aided by the Bishop, who with the help of the Jews,
grows rich on our toil, while we work and grow poor.''
The roar doubled, and redoubled.

''And the Canon Vicar—'' The list continued, name after name, each one producing its roar of approval. The
room grew hotter and hotter.

Yusuf pressed closer to his knees; Isaac could feel him
trembling. ''What if they find us, lord?''

''Can you crawl under this dresser?'' asked Isaac.

There was a pause as Yusuf calculated the room. ''Yes,
lord.''

''Take this ring,'' said Isaac. ''Listen carefully. If things
become''—he paused to find the right word—''difficult—''

''What do you mean, lord?''

''Don't speak. Listen. If things become difficult, you will
know it. Then, if you can escape from here, go to the
Bishop and tell him what is happening. If you cannot get
away, stay hidden. Johan will let you out in the morning.
Crawl under the dresser. Now. And make sure that not one
edge of your tunic is visible. Leave when you can. Don't
wait for me.''

The crowd in the room swayed and moved, some to get
closer to the podium, some to get close to the wine, a few
to get nearer the door in hopes of air. Two or three stumbled, or were pushed back into the dark alcove where Isaac
and Yusuf were hidden. Isaac heard confused footsteps
close by—much too close—and muttered curses. He heard
the slap of a hand striking a body, a grunt of pain, and then
suddenly, a hand pressed down hard on his shoulder for
support.

"By all that's holy, there's someone here," said a voice. "Look."

"A spy, planted by the Bishop. Drag him out."

Isaac was pulled to his feet and yanked a step or two forward.

"It's the magician," said another voice.

"Isaac the Jew," said a third.

"Hold him down or he'll fly away."

Fingers dug into Isaac's shoulders; someone dragged him out of the alcove. His hands were roughly tied behind his back and he was pushed down on his knees against the edge of the makeshift podium. His overwhelming impression was of being trapped within a massive press of sweating humanity with very little in mind, ready to explode, destroying all in its path. Including him.

"Kill him," said a loud voice, slurred with wine. "Filthy spy."

"Put him to torture," said another. "Find out what he's here for."

The first blow was a powerful kick in his side. Pain flooded out in every direction from the site of the blow, and he tried to roll away from the attacking feet. It was impossible. A volley of blows hit him from every side, some halfhearted, some vicious, some well placed, some harmless. There was a momentary pause, and then a crushing kick landed squarely in the middle of his ribs. The medical man in him noted sparely that at least one rib could well be broken; a blow like that to his head and he would not survive.

"What are you here for? Speak."

"You know why he's here," said another. "Kill him. Get it over with."

"Kill him!" said five or six more, and a huge shout went up.

"Burn him before he bewitches us," shrieked a particularly shrill voice.

"Hold!" The voice cut through the pandemonium. "Loose that man." It took several moments for the crowd,

drunk with wine and mayhem, to respond, but then hands
hurriedly fumbled about Isaac's back to free him of his
bonds, and pull him to his feet.

The last shred of hope died in Isaac's heart as soon as
he heard those words. This sudden respite was no miraculous rescue. Even in the echoing turmoil inside the Baths,
he recognized the Sword's harsh voice.

The room fell silent. The voice lashed out, pouring its
contempt on the crowd. "Think what you do, fools! What
use can come from kicking the man to death? Do we want
to know why he came? What he knows? Who else knows
he is here?" The questions pounded at them like blows
from a hammer. "Then you must be able to ask him. A
dead man can be more dangerous than a live one."

Pain was spreading throughout Isaac's body, growing
and flowering like a noxious weed. His ears rang, and his
body rocked with dizziness. From a long distance away, he
heard an uneasy murmur rising from the crowd.

"Do you want to endanger tonight's enterprise?" The
muttered response was vague, and embarrassed. "Then
give the man to me, and I will examine him at my leisure."

Raquel—with her basket of remedies to cleanse poisons
from the body, and soothe troubled spirits—had had little
trouble talking her way into the convent. Sor Benvenguda
was ready to hand over responsibility for Lady Isabel's condition without a murmur.

As soon as she saw Isabel, Raquel understood why. It
was evident that someone had told her the verdict; she was
shaking with despair and rage.

"How can they, Raquel?" she sobbed. "I counted on
Papa and my uncle to help. Who else is there? What am I
to do?"

"Won't your father—"

"My father is the person who heard the lying evidence
and believed it, and who passed that sentence on the most
innocent human being I have ever met. Don't you believe
him innocent?"

"I do," said Raquel. "With all my heart, I do." But

neither one was foolish enough to suggest that anything
remained to be done to help him.

Raquel steeped herbs in a kettle, and coaxed Isabel to
drink a little of the infusion. "Will you stay with me, Raquel? I cannot bear to be alone," she said. "Or surrounded
by inquisitive sisters."

"Of course I'll stay," said Raquel. She helped Lady Isabel out of her gown and into bed. She sat by her side, and
listened while she raged, and then cried, and raged again,
until she became drowsy. Her eyes closed, and she drifted
into sleep.

At that moment, a roar of people shouting came through
an unshuttered window, died down, and was quickly followed by another roar, louder this time. Raquel pushed
back her chair, ran to the window, and leaned out.

The movement woke Isabel. She climbed unsteadily out
of bed and followed. A low-voiced babble filled the heavy
night air. "That's strange," she said, carefully. "It's coming from the Baths. They should be closed."

"The Baths?" repeated Raquel, panic-stricken. The
scene, river and trees and the building itself, lay half-
revealed between deep shadow and the ghostly pale light
of the full moon, still low in the sky.

"Yes. There are lights. See, down there, across the
river?" A roar of human voices burst in through the window.

Raquel grasped Isabel around the shoulders and helped
her back to bed. "Lady Isabel," she said, breathless with
fear, "I'm sorry, I'm very sorry, but I must go. My father
is there—"

"At the Baths?"

"He was going to see the keeper when he left me here.
And now the Lord only knows what is happening. He could
come to some dreadful harm. Please forgive me."

"Then go. Of course you must go. Will you come back
tomorrow?"

"I will," said Raquel. She grabbed her cloak and ran
from the room.

•   •   •

Raquel convinced Sor Marta to let her out, swearing that her father and his servant were waiting for her just outside the convent gate. The rising moon was full, but in the shade of the convent the road was no more than a thick black ribbon in a slightly paler landscape. She waited until her eye could pick out shapes, and then stumbled ahead until she passed out of the shadow. She paused to consider what she was doing, took a deep breath to steady herself, and then ran along the moonlit road to the bridge, where she stopped again.

The crowd was pouring out of the Baths. She backed into the shadows of the church of San Pere de Galligants, watching, and hoping to catch a glimpse of her father. There was no sign of him. At last, when everyone seemed to be outside, she heard the door being pulled shut. But at least one torch still burned inside the building, casting the light from its darting flames up and out the windows. Pulling her courage about her like a second cloak, she walked across the bridge.

The noise of the men leaving the meeting had given way to the usual quiet of the night, punctured by the small chirps and squeaks of night creatures. But as she approached the building she picked up the sound of an animal in distress. With a sinking feeling in her belly, she realized it was muffled sobbing, coming from the deep shadows on the other side of the path. She took a step into the profounder darkness and bumped into a small warm shape that made a familiar noise. "Yusuf?" she whispered.

"Yes, mistress."

"What has happened?" she asked, her voice tight with fear. "What are you doing out here?"

"The demon that came to Valencia and killed my father—" His voice cracked and went silent.

"Yes? What about that demon?" asked Raquel, grasping his shoulder.

"He is in there, with Master Isaac. And he will kill him, too." Yusuf began to tremble violently.

And gradually, Raquel coaxed the entire story from the boy. Of the man in black, with a sword at his side, and

armor on his breast and back, who had been following the
physician ever since that night that Yusuf first met him.
And who had talked to Master Isaac in the field just over
there, and had seized him when the crowd was going to
kill him.

"But perhaps he is a good man, Yusuf, who means no
harm."

Yusuf's trembling grew worse. "No—he is not," he said
emphatically. "He is a demon. Believe me, mistress. He is
evil. I know his evil deeds."

"Are they alone in there?"

"I think so."

"Then we must go in."

"I cannot," said Yusuf, in a cry of pure panic. "He is
bathed in blood; we will not escape this time. He said so,
when he killed my father. As I ran away he said he would
come back from hell for me."

"Well, he didn't say he'd come back from hell for me.
Surely he wouldn't kill an innocent woman. I'm going in."
And she marched bravely enough up to the door, but it was
with great caution that she tried to push it open. Not that
it mattered. It was locked.

"Yusuf," she said earnestly, back at the spot where the
terrified boy still lay huddled. "Do you know where Johan
lives? The keeper?"

"Yes, mistress."

"Take me there. We must get the key."

SIXTEEN

"Johan, please," begged Raquel. "We need the key to the Baths."

The keeper, roused from a sound sleep, stared at her in mute incomprehension from the door of his hovel.

"Papa is in there, Johan, with men who hate him. You know my papa. Isaac the physician." Trembling with frustration, she turned to Yusuf. "Talk to him, Yusuf," she said, grabbing him by the arm and shaking him. "Talk to him or I'll beat you. Tell him what is happening."

But Yusuf hung back in the shadows, trembling and pale with fear, and stayed silent.

Raquel mastered her panic and turned back to the keeper. "Johan," she said quietly. "Yusuf says Papa is in there with a demon. A wicked man, who will kill Papa if we don't stop him."

Johan shook his head. "Kill him?" he said slowly. Tears filled his eyes. He brushed them away. A wail of pain broke from his lips, his face twisted with fury, and he roared, "No!"

Raquel jumped back in surprise.

"He will hurt Master Isaac?" he added, in confirmation.

"Yes, Johan," she repeated. "If we don't stop him, he will."

Johan picked up a long wooden staff, and headed out for the Baths.

"You are a man of many surprises, physician," the Sword remarked. "And not many men can surprise me." He had pushed Isaac down onto a bench in a quiet corner, and stood over him, so close that Isaac's foot and knee brushed against his body. Whether the Sword was protecting him or guarding him, Isaac could not tell, nor did he care. Pain had usurped both reason and emotion; it throbbed heavily, constantly, radiating from the site of the first blow, encompassing his entire body. It stabbed to the heart every time he drew breath. "Does that please you?" asked the Sword. Does what please me? he wondered. But answering the question seemed to be more trouble than it was worth. He stayed silent.

Far off in the distance, the voice of the orator flowed on for the length of time it took Isaac to say over his evening prayers in silence. Then he noted, vaguely, that the speeches were over. The meeting had been turned over to the detail man. He was instructing them to be at the top of the steps to the cathedral, in the plaza of the Apostles, at midnight, when the bells rang for matins, and to bring a reliable friend to join in the battle.

The shouts of the crowd belonged to an alien world. Isaac adjusted his position as much as he could to ease his throbbing body, and retreated into the world deep within his mind. Time disappeared, and the Baths, with all their noise, and hate, and violence, faded into the insubstantial distance.

Then it occurred to him, from that distant place in his mind, that the crowd had left in a more substantial sense, taking the burden of their hot, stinking bodies with them. A rush of cooler air replaced the last group to leave, easing his feeling of sick dizziness. The Sword closed and locked the door.

"I would not like to be interrupted," he said.

Isaac made no reply. He wondered if Yusuf were still under the big dresser, and thought it a pity that he should witness this.

"It may puzzle you that I stopped those oafs from kicking you to death. It wasn't out of pity, or some other fine feeling. Nor was it to extract knowledge from you. You know nothing that interests me. Can you answer me?" he asked suddenly. "I find it irritating to speak to a dumb man, like an old woman mumbling to her cat."

"I can answer," said Isaac, drawing breath with difficulty. "I saw no reason for it."

"Indeed. I had a much more important reason for saving you from the rabble." He paused. "You do not wonder what it is?"

But Isaac, shaken by the sudden realization that he had no idea where he was, nor in what direction he was facing, had stopped listening. He feared disorientation more than any physical harm; he feared it as some fear enclosed spaces. It induced panic in him that blanked out rational thought. Then, in the silence, he remembered that the madman had asked a question. He should listen. It might be important to have listened.

"You are destined to be part of my own salvation. That is why I saved you." The Sword's voice was reasonable in tone, as if he were explaining the cost of something to a potential client. "And to do that you must die in blood. In your blood, and in the blood of the usurper King, and his spawn, and the false Bishop, there lies my salvation. I shall be swept up to heaven on a river of the blood of the unrighteous. Do you understand?"

Isaac fought his panic and his pain for the breath to speak. "You make yourself clear."

"Your death does me no good. It is your blood I need. The blood of those two vile women—the false nun, and the Jezebel nursemaid—that was not enough. Three nights ago, the Archangel spoke to me again. He stood on my own mountain peak that rises into heaven and, looking down into the rich valley, said to me, 'Stay your course to

the end. None can be spared. All must die. . . .' '' His voice
drifted away dreamily.

Isaac was overcome by the absurdity of the situation—
to be locked in the Baths, trapped by a madman, a self-
appointed priest, who preached to his sacrificial ram as it
lay stretched out on the altar of his delusions. How could
anyone die for such a sad little cause—as an offering to a
madman's private demon, who visited him in the guise of
an angel of the Lord? Yet it would happen. This man was
going to kill him, as he had killed Doña Sanxia and the
Crown Prince's brave nurse, and only just failed to kill
young Prince Johan. And then he remembered once more
that Yusuf was somewhere nearby, cowering under the
dresser.

Anger, like a small fire fed with dry sticks, grew in his
belly, consuming his pain and his fear. Because of this
man's insanity, Isaac had placed Raquel, and Yusuf—innocent pawns, both of them—in jeopardy. Yusuf was still
a child, not yet thirteen, and he had already lived through
more than Isaac could even guess at; it was an obscenity
to subject him to this.

But Isaac himself was alive and unfettered. In spite of
his aches and bruises, he was a strong man, and if he only
knew where he was, he could fight back. It was possible
that the Sword had pushed him down onto the same bench
where he'd sat yesterday talking to Johan. The material
under his hands had a very familiar feel. That bench had
been careless work—done by an apprentice, perhaps, and
sold cheaply to a penny-pinching steward of the absent physician who controlled the Baths. He ran his fingertips over
the roughly shaped wood, exploring its surface patterns. It
was the same bench. He found the marks of the ax, and the
sharp hollow where the carpenter's adze had slipped.

At once, the whirling chaos around him formed itself into
a vast ordered pattern. He knew where he was in relation
to the Baths, to the city, to the county, to the sea. That
meant that Yusuf was no more than four or five paces distant from him now, listening to every word. The fire of
rage spurted up again; in one blast it burned away his re-

maining confusion and died, restoring icy clarity to his thoughts.

The Sword ceased his diatribe. In the silence, Isaac could hear his own heart beating, and his own breath moving quietly in and out. Close by, he was aware of the Sword's ragged, nervous breathing. With Yusuf but four paces away, he should be able to feel a third presence in the room; he did not. Not the slightest movement, not the faintest breath, not even the strange and yet firm conviction that another being was nearby.

Yusuf was not there. If he had been discovered, and dragged away, or killed on the spot, the clamor and shouting from the crowd would have been as exuberant as when he himself had been found. Yusuf was out of the building, with the Bishop's ring. A thousand mischances might prevent him from reaching the palace, but the Bishop's officers could be on their way. Having just laid down his arms and accepted death, Isaac was astonished at the ferocity with which, suddenly, he desired life. His mind, moments ago dull and slow with shock and despair, now raced at breathless speed, calculating, appraising, spewing up ideas.

"I find it difficult to believe that the blood sacrifice, once accomplished, should have to be repeated," said Isaac coolly. "According to your Christian belief, the ultimate blood sacrifice—the death of Christ—has been made, has it not? To require it from further victims smacks to me of paganism. Have you considered that?"

"Paganism? You have the effrontery to call my sacred mission pagan?" said the Sword, his voice rising angrily. "You are the pagan."

"Jew," corrected Isaac, in a mild tone. "Not pagan. You should know that."

"The Archangel came to me in all his glory, and spoke." He grasped Isaac's shoulder and gave it a shake. "He told me what must be done, and he swore to come to me again before the end of the world is accomplished."

"How do you know his appearance is not a delusion?" said Isaac. "It is common enough. Especially to peasants and milkmaids."

"I *know*," said the Sword, his voice becoming terrible in rage and indignation. "How dare you speak of me as a peasant, Jew? Do you not realize who I am? What I am? The noble blood of the Visigoth conquerors runs in my veins. My forefathers freed this land from the Moors with their own powerful swords. If my great-grandfather had been a schemer and a plotter like Pedro of Aragon, I would now be a king as well as he!"

"But he wasn't," said Isaac.

"Quiet! And I have walked through the night on my holy errand and remained invisible, as the Archangel promised me. It is not a delusion."

"Are you sure?" asked Isaac.

"I am. Find a man who has seen me at night, or heard my horse. You cannot. I am invisible when on the Archangel's work, and silent as a shaft of light glittering from his sword."

"No, you aren't," said Isaac. "Not to me. In the dark I see as well as you, sir, and I know when you are there. You followed me on the eve of the feast, didn't you? As the midnight bells rang you left your horse and followed me from the city gate to the Quarter. The sound of your footfalls, and the smell of your clothing, your armor, and your own body are as distinctive to me as a man's face is to you."

There was no sound except the harsh breathing of the Sword. "It cannot be," he muttered at last. "I was promised."

"It was a false promise, friend," said Isaac. His voice was at its kindest, and most gentle. "A delusion."

"You are not a friend!" The Sword's voice rose to almost a shriek. "It is because of your magic spells that you could see me," he said, his speech becoming quicker, and more urgent.

"You know I have no magic spells. Would I be here, in your power, if I did? Have you never wondered if your angel could be a demon, come to tempt you to terrible sin? A demon can take many guises, some of great beauty," said Isaac.

"You are the demon," screamed the Sword. "You are the tempter, sent to divert me from my path." His voice dropped to a mutter of self-justification. "That is why you must die, and die before your words crawl into my bosom, and eat away at my faith and reason. I knew there was a motive for killing you," he added, his voice rising in wonderment. "The women I understood—there is a pure and holy joy in killing an evil woman of great beauty—but I was puzzled that I was to waste my powers on one so insignificant as you, physician." Then his voice rose to an uncontrolled shriek. "I thank you, Lord Michael! Come down once more and aid me in your work."

But in the background, under the noise of the Sword's invocations, Isaac could hear footsteps, and scraping, and the movement of metal in the lock.

The door burst open, and Johan came in, his staff upraised, followed by Raquel. She saw her father in the flickering torchlight, his clothing torn and muddied. Behind him stood a tall figure in black. He clutched her father's chin and beard in his left hand; in his right he held a knife. Isaac's strong hands were pushing the black-clad arms as his body twisted violently to deflect his aim. The man swore, and raised his weapon.

"Don't you touch him," screamed Big Johan, and swung the staff in an arc above Isaac's head.

The Sword threw down the knife, wrenching his arms out of Isaac's grasp. He stepped back, and caught the tip of the staff in a grip of steel as it came by. He drove it at the keeper, knocking him back, and while Johan was off balance, yanked it out of his hands. "Always prepare for the counterattack, my friend," he said mildly. "Tell me, what is the hour?"

"It is an hour or more since the convent bells rang for tierce," said Raquel, too astonished to do anything but answer.

"I must go," he said. "I am sorry to leave our business unfinished, but a king and a prince must die before you tonight. Not to say a bishop. I am expected at the palace for matins." He smiled.

He picked up his dagger, and walked over to the other side of the Baths. There, he sheathed the dagger, set down Johan's staff, and picked up a white cope of rich and splendid design. He put it on over his black tunic and light hauberk. "Farewell," he said. "I shall see you again." And without even a glance backward at its confused and startled occupants, he strode from the building.

"Raquel. Johan, my friend," said Isaac. "You are here and safe. Thank the Lord. I am grateful for your help. I was just discovering how reluctant I was to give up on life. Surprisingly so, considering how I feel," he added wryly. "Have you seen Yusuf? Do you know if he is safe?"

"He was with us until a moment ago," said Raquel, looking around. "I'm sure. I thought he was behind me."

"How did it happen that he was with you, my dear?" asked Isaac. "He was to go to the Bishop."

"I don't know," said Raquel. "I was at the convent until I heard the shouting. I came at once, and found him outside."

"Yes," said Isaac. "They shouted with great joy when they found me. He was with me then, but well hidden."

"He was too distressed to move when I found him," said Raquel, with considerable delicacy. "The door was locked, and we knew you were inside, and so we went to Johan for help—and the key."

"Then you didn't send him for the officers?" said Isaac, feeling somewhat baffled. "Somehow I was expecting armed men, not one man and a girl, to come to my rescue."

"He ran off, Master Isaac, Yusuf did. Toward town before we left my house. I saw him," said Johan.

"He is terrified of the Sword, Papa," said Raquel. "And he has reason to be. He cannot bear even to look at him. Don't be angry. He will be hiding somewhere around here."

"Possibly," said Isaac, "or he may have gone at last to tell the Bishop."

"Let us go home, Papa," said Raquel.

"There is too much to do before that," said Isaac ruefully. "I must go to the Bishop. Give me your hand, friend Johan," he asked. And supporting himself on the keeper's hand, he pulled himself to his feet, and staggered dizzily.

Johan caught him around the waist and held him up. "I will take him to the palace, mistress," he said.

"Not without me, Johan," said Raquel, looking out into the darkness.

In a room in the palace, the Infant Johan stirred, and murmured. Rebecca awoke at once and, throwing a shawl over her shift, went to sit by him. He tossed his head restlessly, and then cried out in terror. She picked him up, holding him close. "There now," she murmured. "It's all right, darling. You're safe."

"He was chasing me," said Johan, his eyes wide with fear. "I couldn't run."

"No one can chase you here," said Rebecca, mopping his damp forehead with a clean linen square. "There are two big strong men, Papa's soldiers, outside the door. You're safe. Shall I light another candle?"

Rebecca put him down, and lit a second candle from the one that burned in a wall sconce. She set it on the other side of the room, to banish the shadows there.

"See soldiers, 'Becca," he demanded.

She placed her finger on her lips. Johan climbed down from the chair and took her hand. Together they tiptoed across the room. Rebecca picked up the Prince, pulled open the door, and they both peered out into the corridor. It was empty except for a man lying on the floor, fast asleep.

Furious, she set the Prince down behind her and shook the guard vigorously by the shoulder. He stirred, and belched, breathing out a cloud of wine fumes. "Drunken sot!" she cried. "Guard!"

Footsteps raced up a short flight of stairs near the room. Two men, awake, alert, polished, and armed, rounded the corner. Rebecca pointed down. "He won't be much help in trouble, will he?"

They looked at her, and then down at the wide-eyed heir to the throne.

"Here are your soldiers, Johan," said Rebecca sweetly. "They will keep us safe. Won't you?"

"Yes, Your Highness. Yes, mistress," said the captain of the watch.

Rebecca picked up the Infant Johan once more. "Good evening to you, officers," she said, and swept back into the room.

"You," said the captain, rapidly, "go and fetch Ferran. And when you get back, the two of you will keep watch at this door. I will stand guard until then. No one enters but His Majesty. You hear?"

"Yes, Captain. Sir."

"And if the Queen of Sheba comes by in her shift and offers you wine, you don't touch it. Understand? Nothing stronger than water, no one in but the King. Not even me. I will deal with this one and his mate—wherever he is— as soon as you return. Be quick about it."

Isaac and Johan made their way slowly across the plaza of the Apostles toward the Bishop's palace, followed by a nervous Raquel. Clouds danced across the surface of the moon, alternately showing them the way and plunging them into darkness.

Johan stopped at the foot of the steps, intimidated by the sounds of revelry from the evening's banqueting. "I have no business here, Master Isaac," he said. His voice was choked with fear.

"You have every reason to be here, Johan," said Isaac. "You saw the man who calls himself the Sword, you and Raquel. I did not."

At the sound of his voice, a small figure uncurled itself from the porch, and raced over. "Lord," he cried. "The demon did not kill you!" He caught him by the hand and broke into tears of pain and relief.

"As you see," said Isaac. "What are you doing out here, Yusuf, my little friend? Did you not carry my message to the Bishop?"

"They would not let me in," said Yusuf. "I was waiting until I could creep by the guard on the door."

"Then let us find out if we have more success now."

"Master Isaac!" said Berenguer. "You are hurt. Let me ring for—"

"There will be time for that," said Isaac. "We have much to tell you that must be said quickly. We have just come from the Arab Baths, where a meeting was held this evening. . . ." And Isaac began his account as they walked slowly to a comfortable room on the ground floor.

"This must be told to more important listeners," said the Bishop, interrupting the physician shortly after he began.

Don Eleazar ben Solomon was the first to arrive, bringing his scribe with him. "Master Isaac," he murmured, "I have heard your praises from many lips. Tell me, what have you discovered that has alarmed my lord Berenguer so much?"

Isaac tasted a small amount of watered wine that the Bishop urged on him, and began his tale again. For the next quarter of an hour or more, though his back ached and every deep breath cost him a sharp jab of pain in the ribs, he gave a detailed description of the meeting. Don Arnau, with hauberk and sword, boots and spurs, came in after a few minutes, bringing one of his junior officers. Shortly after that, Eleazar sent his scribe out with a hastily scribbled message.

"Perhaps we could wait a moment," said Eleazar. "Your account is wonderfully clear, Master Isaac. I would like others to hear it." He came over and sat beside the physician, where they could speak in relative privacy. "It is your opinion, Master Isaac," he murmured, "that the man is mad?"

"The Sword?" said Isaac, cautiously. "He has madness in him, indeed. But he can also speak perfect sense."

"This is a deliberate, assumed madness?"

"It is difficult to be certain. I think he half believes his own ravings, yet knows, in some way, that they cannot be true.''

''And the others you spoke of. Are they mad?''

''Oh, no, Don Eleazar. Their minds are as cool as yours or mine.''

The door opened and His Majesty, Don Pedro, walked in. ''Do not rise,'' he said. ''If, as I understand, time is of the greatest importance, I wish to hear your account at once, Master Isaac.''

And for the third time, Isaac quickly summarized the events at the Bath. ''Unfortunately, Your Majesty,'' he said as he finished his description, ''I am unable to put a name to the three most important participants—the Sword, and his two lieutenants. I would recognize their voices if I heard them again. But the Keeper of the Baths, Johan by name, came into the building along with my daughter Raquel, to rescue me. They saw the man who called himself the Sword. They are waiting outside the room now.''

Johan and Raquel were fetched in. Johan gulped, and turned scarlet, and tried to speak. ''He were very strong, my lords,'' he said. ''He took my staff and 'most knocked me over, like.''

''Thank you,'' said Eleazar, when it seemed unlikely they would get a much more coherent statement from the terrified keeper. ''Mistress Raquel,'' he said, ''can you describe the man?''

And once more, Raquel faced the King. ''He is tall, Your Majesty, and his hair is black. His face is thin.'' She closed her eyes, desperately trying to dredge up details. ''There was only one torch burning in the Baths, and he was never standing in its light. I remember his eyes—they seemed to burn. And before he left he dressed himself in a long white robe, all embroidered with gold and scarlet threads.''

''Were there scars on his face, or other markings?'' asked Eleazar, who, discounting the burning eyes, could put a dozen or more names to the description. Tall, thin, and black-haired, indeed.

''The light was too dim to be able to see, my lord.''

"He has a limp," said Isaac. "I don't know if it is very visible, but it can be heard."

"Thank you," said Eleazar, and Raquel and Big Johan were released.

"It is perhaps a father's foolishness, but I feel uneasy about my daughter Rebecca and the Prince," said Isaac quietly.

"They are lodged in safety, my friend," said Eleazar. "Well guarded."

"That is enough talk," said Don Pedro. "It is time to act."

While that meeting was going on, a door opened in the back wall of the palace; one black-clad figure, in tunic and boots, armed, slipped past another black-clad figure, in cassock and sandals. He nodded and set off through the kitchens toward the apartments where distinguished guests were accommodated.

The armed man moved with the confidence of one who knows where he is going and the absolute confidence that he has every right to be there. He recognized the captain on guard by the Infant Johan's door; they had fought side by side in Valencia, and ridden the same road many times in the service of the King. He nodded to him, and reached out his hand to open the door. The captain stepped forward rapidly and interposed his body between the door and the man in black. "My profoundest apologies, my lord," he said. "But His Majesty's instructions were most precise. I would have thought you had heard them," he added reproachfully. "No one, not even yourself, or His Excellency the Bishop, is to enter the room with the Prince and his nurse."

"My apologies," replied the man in black cordially. "I forgot. I had a message to deliver to the nursemaid," he said. "But it will wait." Then, without warning, he thrust the dagger concealed in his short cape under the captain's breastplate. It angled up under the ribs and struck his heart. "I am sorry, Captain," he said, with real regret in his voice. "You were not supposed to be here."

He pulled his knife from the captain's chest and let his body slump to the floor. He wiped the blood from it on the captain's cloak, and slipped it back into its sheath. His hand had just touched the handle of the door when rapid footsteps made him look up. Two guards rounded the corner. They saw their captain on the floor and broke into a run.

The man in black turned in the other direction and melted into the shadows. By the time the guards grasped the situation and gave chase, he had disappeared into the farthest recesses of the building. The entire incident took less time than would be required for a man of moderate disposition and habits to walk from one end of the corridor to the other.

The plaza of the Apostles, lying between the cathedral and Bishop's palace, was silent and empty. The moon was riding high above it, but her face was thinly veiled with cloud, looking blurred and imprecise in the watery atmosphere. A lamp burned on the altar in the cathedral, shining like a beacon in the darkness, but the ecclesiastical palace, its sumptuous dinner over, was black and shuttered for the night. Then, from the main steps up to the west door of the cathedral, dark shapes began to move into the darkness of the square. Soon it was filled with people; the forty or fifty souls who had been at the Baths were reinforced with fifty or sixty more. The plaza was filled with the sound of the silent crowd—a hundred or more breathing, shuffling, jostling beings—as they gathered on the south side of the cathedral. Then, at the back of the crowd, two flaming torches appeared. Almost at once, their fire passed from torch to torch until the blaze seemed to rival the day. A line of torchbearers moved up through the throng, their beacons lighting up the hooded faces of those near the cathedral.

In the silence, a single tenor voice of great beauty rose in song, chanting the first line of "Tibi Christi, splendor patris." A few more voices joined in. The venerable hymn swelled in the quiet of the night; gradually the steady but muffled beating of one, then six, and finally some twenty drums picked up the rhythm and overwhelmed the voices.

● ● ●

News of the captain's death spread through the palace with
the urgency of a call to arms, and those who could not or
should not fight had been hastily ushered into the Bishop's
study. "His Majesty tells me that your daughter's quick wit
has saved the Prince's life," said Berenguer. "He is grateful, and they are somewhat better guarded now," he added
dryly. As he spoke he stood by an unshuttered window to
watch the drama below.

"Thank you, Your Excellency," said Isaac wearily.

"What are they singing, Your Excellency?" asked Yusuf
in a small voice. He sat on a cushion beside Isaac's chair,
close to Raquel. Big Johan was with the cooks, being
calmed and rewarded with the Bishop's wine.

" 'Tibi Christi,' " said Berenguer, absently. "A hymn
for the feast of Saint Michael."

"When is that?"

"Not until the twenty-ninth day of September," said the
Bishop. "They are somewhat beforehand with their dem-
onstration, Yusuf, my little friend."

"What are they planning to do?" asked the Canon Vicar,
leaning forward from behind Berenguer to catch a glimpse
of what was going on.

"Storm the palace, and murder us all," said the Bishop
calmly. "I suspect there's a crowd at our doors right now.
That gathering by the steps is a distraction. They want us
to believe they will attack the side entrance to the cathedral.
Don't worry, young Yusuf," he added. "This door is thick,
and it's locked and barred." He looked out again. "It irks
me to be cooped up in here doing nothing. But His Majesty
was most insistent."

On the ground floor, a silent drama was being acted out in
front of a silent audience. Each time the moon ducked behind the gathering mass of cloud, the watchers surrounding
the palace moved closer. Inside, four armed officers were
positioned at each entrance, ready for the attack. Three
young priests, who had been arrested as they struggled to
unbar and open the doors to the invaders, waited under
guard in the cellars.

• • •

In the plaza, the singing and the beating of the drums continued. Clouds blackened out the skies; the air had become heavy and menacing. The watchers from the palace saw a tall man in a white cope, with a bishop's mitre on his head, threading his way through the crowd and mounting the steps to the south door of the cathedral. He stood with his back to his followers, and raised both arms high in supplication to heaven. A gust of wind scattered the clouds from the face of the moon, and she lit up the figure of the Sword in his splendid vestments. A muted roar swelled up from the massed participants. Then she disappeared behind another fast-moving cloud, leaving darkness and the flickering torchlight behind.

"Francesc, look at that," said Berenguer. "By Saint Michael himself," he murmured, "that's my cope the treacherous bastard is wearing. How did he come by it?"

The Canon Vicar looked out the window. "I believe it was taken away to be laundered. I must find out who recommended it be done," he added.

"And I want to speak to that laundress," said Berenguer grimly. "She seems rather free with my garments."

Minutes passed by. From their vantage point above the scene, the watchers from the palace were just able to make out more dark figures entering the plaza from every side. "Look at that," said the Canon Vicar with wry amusement. "Even in the middle of insurrection, someone is out for profit." He pointed to a figure carrying a large jar. "He must be selling wine." The man with the jar was moving as quickly as possible up the steps to where the Sword was still standing with his arms raised to heaven. More dark figures appeared on the edges of the throng. Thunder rumbled from the hills outside the city and the Sword abruptly lowered his hands. Somewhere to his right, another noise reverberated, that of a weapon striking against the edge of a shield.

The man with the jar moved closer, as if to offer his leader wine. The torchbearers drew nearer to their leader, and the jar was set down. The Sword struggled to draw his weapon, sadly hindered by the thick folds of the Bishop's cope.

"He cuts a poor figure for a man who calls himself the Sword of Michael," said the Bishop dryly. "He should have practiced."

"He is the Sword, do you think, Excellency?" asked the Canon Vicar.

"Without a doubt. He donned my cope at the Baths, remember."

At last, the figure on the steps raised a heavy sword high above his head. With a forward gesture, he turned in the direction of the palace.

He was met by the King leading a troop of horsemen poised to ride down the throng. As Don Pedro raised his sword to signal the attack, a panicked cry arose from the edges of the crowd. The contingent led by Don Arnau had moved in from the rear. The Sword paused, uncertain, and glanced around him. His two lieutenants stood on either side of him, each bearing a flaming torch.

A sudden wind howled around the cathedral. A huge bolt of lightning split the sky. A crash of thunder seemed to rock the stones beneath everyone's feet and a horse screamed in fear. The torchbearers scrambled back hastily. The Sword lifted his arms to heaven, and cried, "Saint Michael, deliver us once more from evildoers!" A torch seemed to fall, and a huge flash of fire and noise filled the space in front of the cathedral. When the throng in the plaza regained the sight of their dazzled eyes, flames were consuming the body of the Sword.

"It is the vengeance of the Lord!" screamed someone, and everyone turned in panic, and ran. Lucky ones slipped away into dark corners and open doors; others fell into the arms of the waiting troops. Rain began to patter down on the cobbles, hissing as it struck the flaming body.

"Did you see that?" asked Berenguer. "One moment he was there, and then he was on the ground in flames."

"I did, Your Excellency," said Francesc Monterranes,

whose eyes were as good as any man's. "It was almost as if a bolt of lightning had sprung up from the ground. I thought he might have stumbled into a blazing torch, but the fire was too bright."

"Perhaps a blazing torch stumbled into him," said Berenguer.

Isaac turned his head toward the open window and sniffed. "That bolt of lightning had a strangely sulfurous smell," he said. "I think it might repay further investigation."

SEVENTEEN

Few people in the palace slept that night. Men-at-arms, wet and hurrying, tramped in and out of the building, seeking orders, giving reports. The public rooms had been commandeered for an inquiry into the night's events. The twenty-four drenched and frightened citizens who had not succeeded in melting into the darkness after the lightning struck were huddled under guard in the hall, explaining to anyone who would listen that they'd gone to the plaza to hear the drums and music.

While Don Arnau organized the hunt for the rest of the conspirators, Don Eleazar caught the harassed officer who was attempting to coordinate the inquiry. "There was an Inner Council of six," he said. "We have three names. Find out if any of them are in that group," he added, handing him a list. "Get more names if you can—someone should be willing to trade a traitor or two for his neck—and send them over to Arnau."

"I am not from Girona, sir," said the officer. "I could use one of the local officers to put names to people. It will save time."

"Arnau has all the locals," said Eleazar. "Let me see. Too many of the priests are in it up to their chins. His

Excellency and the Canon Vicar are with His Majesty." He considered who was in the building. "There's one Johan, but he won't do. And the girl's being sent home with her father. But their young servant lad can help." He turned to go. "He's frightened," he added. "Keep him hidden. And take my scribe. You'll find him useful."

"A child?" said the officer in surprise. "Well—better an honest boy than a man who lies. Thank you."

And so, fortified with fruit and bread and cheese, Yusuf was taken, still trembling, down to the room where the prisoners were being questioned. One by one, they came before the scribe, who wrote down their names, occupations, and reasons for being in the plaza. And one by one, Yusuf looked at them from the dark corner where he sat, almost hidden behind the officer. "Will they know I have been here?" asked Yusuf.

"No one knows you are here except Don Eleazar. And me," said the young man. "And he didn't tell me your name."

Rodrigue was the first to stand before the scribe. He gave his name, occupation, and a self-righteously indignant account of his evening's activities. He had been at the tavern, serving. "Although, God knows," he said, "I might as well have closed. I didn't sell enough wine to drown a fly in. And then I went up to the plaza because I heard the drums."

"Is that his name?" murmured the officer.

"Oh, yes," said Yusuf. "And he wasn't at the meeting."

And thus it went, with Yusuf separating the goats, who had been at the Baths, from the sheep, who had come out later. With only three men left, Yusuf pulled delicately on the officer's sleeve. "He lies," he said, nodding at the man standing before the scribe, smiling and sweating. "His name is Sanch, and he is one of the Inner Council."

"Excellent, lad. What about the two still waiting?"

"That one is Martin. He is of the Council," said Yusuf. "The other wasn't at the meeting."

"It's time you were in your bed, lad," said the officer.

"This is for you." He slipped a penny in Yusuf's hand and went to deal with Sanch.

Yusuf bowed and left. He tossed the penny to a beggar huddled on the porch, and fled unobtrusively through the night to the physician's house.

Only Sanch the ostler and Martin the bookbinder had been captured. The two speakers at the meeting and Raimunt the scribe had disappeared. Throughout the rest of the night, Martin sweated and swore that the Fellowship was a group of skilled tradesmen, interested in improving their lot, and owing a particular reverence to their patron, Saint Michael.

And more than that he would not say.

Sanch the ostler would have said more—much more— if he could. He told them everything he knew, and a few things he invented, but he had no idea who the two strangers were. "They never said. They weren't the Sword," he said. "We were the Sword. The Sword was the group."

"Who was the man who spoke last at the meeting?"

"Last?" said Sanch.

"Yes. The one who stopped you from kicking the physician."

Sanch stared at him as if he had seen a ghost. "Were you there?" he whispered.

The officer smiled.

"I don't know who it was," he said, his voice rising to a squeak. "You mean the big man who talked like a lord? Dark, thin? With a limp?" he added, as if the more details he could find, the purer his heart would seem to be. "Maybe Raimunt knows—he's a scribe, a learned man. I don't see him here," he added maliciously.

A voice from behind the officer broke in. "Tell me, Sanch the ostler, what the purpose of the group was." And Don Eleazar took over the interrogation, with his scribe back at his side.

When the officer left to see to his men—gratefully, for this kind of work was not to his taste—the talk had dropped to a whisper, and the names and words that he heard as he walked away made him shudder.

• • •

The body of the Sword had been laid out in a room in the cellars, well lit with candles. On the floor beside it lay a heap of blackened fragments. "What is that?" asked Berenguer.

"Clay. Parts of some kind of jar—an oil jar, possibly, Your Excellency. They were everywhere around the body," said a soldier. "And in his flesh. I thought it might be important."

"And so it might," observed the Bishop, picking up a fragment. "I believe I saw that jar standing beside the man last night." He sniffed the piece in his hand. "It smells of the pits of hell," he remarked.

"It smells of thunder powder that the Moors of Algeciras used to shoot hot iron balls at us," observed the soldier. "Anyone wounded by it died within seven days. It's fearsome, Your Excellency. I was there. And I haven't seen anything like it until tonight."

"Do we know who he is?" asked Berenguer.

"Not enough face left to tell, Your Excellency," said the soldier.

Strong hands helped Abbess Elicsenda, Lady Isabel, and Raquel dismount from the military horses that had been sent to fetch them from the convent. It was late morning; the curiosity seekers were all crowded into the cathedral, and the plaza was almost deserted. Except for a blackened patch on the south steps, the storm had washed away all traces of last night's violence and confusion, leaving the place bright with sun and holy peace. Nevertheless, the armed officers who had formed their escort into the city turned them over to an armed foot guard, and they made their way across the plaza and into the palace surrounded by eight burly men and an officer. No precautions were being omitted.

After a few hours of disturbed sleep, Raquel had returned to the convent early in the morning. In the midst of a late breakfast that neither she nor Lady Isabel could eat, the summons to come at once to the Bishop's palace—no reason, or apology, or explanation offered—arrived like a bolt of lightning. "What do they want with us?" asked Raquel, nervously.

"Who can say? Perhaps another innocent person is to be condemned for treason," said Isabel bitterly. "Something to do with last night."

The Abbess was standing by the main gate, waiting for them, with nervous apprehension etched across her face. By the time they reached the plaza, Raquel's stomach was churning with curiosity and fear. Lady Isabel, hollow-eyed and deadly pale, walked toward her uncle's residence with the steady resolution of a martyr heading for an arena full of particularly hungry lions. Raquel gathered up her skirts and bravely followed.

Raquel shivered as she stepped from the sunny porch into the vast and daunting room. It was dark and chill, filled with elaborately carved, heavy pieces of furniture. Isabel's father and uncle, deep in conversation, were seated at the far end. The King's secretary sat on his right-hand side, looking through a sheaf of documents and organizing them into piles. Beside him sat the scribe, with paper, pen, and ink in readiness. Several handsome chairs waited, empty.

A faintly clerical-looking servant ushered Abbess Elicsenda to a bench against the wall, in front of a large tapestry depicting the fall of Jerusalem. Raquel waited, uncertainly. Isabel laid a hand on her arm, and then walked boldly forward until she was directly in front of her father. She fell on her knees, and tried to speak. But tears covered her cheeks, and her voice dried. "Your Majesty," she whispered. "Papa. I—"

"Come, my dear. Up from your knees," her father scolded gently. "Sit here beside me. Your uncle will give you his place for a few moments, will he not? We are all friends here."

"Thank you, Papa," she murmured as she rose and took her uncle's hastily vacated chair.

"Now, daughter," said Don Pedro, patting her hand reassuringly. "Once more tell me everything that happened to you from the time you awoke—in a stable, was it?—until our soldiers happened upon you. Every small detail. You have brought the Abbess and your admirable nurse, I see." He raised a hand, and the servant came near to pushing Raquel across the room.

Rendered mute with nervousness, she dropped her deepest curtsy.

"Excellent. Come here and stand by Isabel. I shall have questions for you as well. Come, child. Speak, and loudly enough for the scribe to hear."

Isabel started with the loft in the stable.

"How many men were there?" He turned to Raquel.

"Four, Your Majesty," said Raquel, with another curtsy. "The owner of the stable, one who appeared to be a gentleman—Romeu—and two grooms."

"Thank you. Continue."

And Isabel went on until she became hoarse, and turned even paler. Wine was sent for, and a mint *tisane*. She took a sip and continued. Time after time, Don Pedro stopped her, checked with Raquel, asked for clarification.

Don Eleazar consulted his documents and whispered in the King's ear. Don Pedro nodded, and turned back to Lady Isabel. "Why were you sure that the plot to abduct you originated with Montbui?"

A flush spread over Isabel's cheeks. She clutched her trembling hands together, and cleared her throat. "Someone approached me at the convent, not long ago, on behalf of Don Perico, Sire," she said in a low voice.

Abbess Elicsenda went pale; Berenguer leaned forward, frowning.

"Who approached you?" asked Don Pedro calmly.

"A nun who was staying with us. She told me her name was Sor Berengaria, and that she was from the mother house in Tarragona. She said that Don Perico was desperately in love with me, and desired my hand, but that he feared Your Majesty would not approve."

"What did she ask you to do?"

"She wanted me to run away with him. Only a married

woman, she said, could be free of the constraints of the convent, and enjoy life."

"A strange attitude for a nun," murmured Berenguer. "Although not unheard of."

"But, Papa, I didn't agree," said Isabel, anxiously scanning his face for signs of disapproval. "I had no desire to leave or to marry him. I knew from other wards at the convent that Montbui was no friend to you. And that he was old and ugly," she added, and reddened with embarrassment.

"But you told no one?"

"I meant to, Sire, but soon after I became very ill, and it passed out of my mind." She coughed, and looked wretched.

"There now," said Don Pedro, "don't fret. Take some wine, and rest a moment. Lady Elicsenda, who was this sister from the house in Tarragona?"

"Your Majesty, we have no Sor Berengaria in the convent. It was not Sor Benvenguda who spoke to you, Lady Isabel? She is from Tarragona."

"Oh, no, Mother. I know Sor Benvenguda. This was quite a young nun. I had never seen her before," said Isabel. "Shall I continue?"

And on the story went, back and forth. To Isabel's surprise, the eminent audience was transfixed by her account. No detail was too insignificant, no word too banal to interest them. When she finished, Don Pedro looked around at his advisers. No one spoke. "We need nothing more from you, my dear. Or from you, young Mistress Raquel. We thank you. If you are weary, you may retire. If you are curious, you may withdraw and sit in comfort, and listen to the proceedings."

"We would like to stay," said Lady Isabel firmly. And the three women were ushered into comfortable chairs in a large alcove hidden behind *The Fall of Jerusalem,* from which they could hear, but not see.

"What is happening, my lady?" asked Raquel softly.

"I don't know," said Isabel. "I'm bewildered. He's been

tried, and condemned, and now they are questioning the witnesses. The world is mad.''

Abbess Elicsenda held her tongue.

The next person to arrive was Isaac the physician, leaning heavily on Yusuf. As soon as the streets had quietened down the night before, he had been borne to his house on a litter, dizzy with exhaustion, and aching in every limb. Once there, he allowed himself the luxury of giving up. Raquel and her mother had wrapped his limbs in hot cloths soaked in healing salts, and rubbed arnica and soothing liniments into his bruises; they had tied a smooth cloth around his ribs, and given him herbs in wine mixed with water. Finally they allowed him into bed. In the middle of their ministrations, Yusuf had crept back to the house.

Isaac had awakened late in the morning, bruised and aching still, but with his head clear, his bones unbroken, and extremely hungry. He had scarcely finished breakfast when the royal summons reached him.

"You are welcome, Master Isaac," said Don Pedro rapidly. "Your daughter and our son send you greetings. They are safe and well. It should be noted that this is not a session of the courts, but a gathering of friends to consider the events of the last five days. It would be improper to hold a judicial session on a Sunday, would it not, Berenguer?"

"In this, as in all things, Your Majesty is correct," said Berenguer.

"Thank you, Your Majesty," said Isaac. "May I be permitted to ask whether the man who died was the Sword?"

"As far as we can tell," said Don Eleazar, cautiously.

"And do we know the cause of his death?" asked Isaac.

"The general opinion," said the Bishop, "is that he was struck by lightning. That means he died, appropriately enough, at the hands of God. He burned, as you know. And there was lightning."

"Not to say a strong smell of sulfur about him," said Don Eleazar.

"So it was firing powder?" asked Isaac. "I thought it might be."

"The lightning bolt makes a more acceptable solution," said Eleazar. "And the hand of the Lord is in all things."

"Indeed. And do we know the name of the man behind the Sword?"

The Bishop leaned forward. "No, Master Isaac," he said, "we don't."

"Bring in Don Tomas de Bellmunt," said Eleazar.

Isabel and Raquel's surprise at receiving a summons to the Bishop's palace was nothing to Tomas's astonishment at learning that he was to report to His Majesty.

A reprieve, with its blinding hope, was the first thought in his mind; a moment later, reason returned, and he understood. He sat down, clutching his hands to keep them from trembling. Throughout the long night, he had listened to constant movement—horses, footsteps, muted but urgent conversation—the sounds of crisis. War, or insurrection, had broken out, and they had decided to execute him before His Majesty rode off. He prayed briefly for strength, and walked out of his unlocked door to meet his fate.

Don Pedro nodded to acknowledge Tomas's presence, and sat back to watch the proceedings through half-closed eyes.

"I'm sorry to disturb your Sunday," said Eleazar briskly, "but important matters have arisen that you may be able to shed light on."

"I will do what I can, sir," said Tomas, in polite desperation. "I was quite unoccupied."

"Indeed. Tell us again, Don Tomas, if you please, why you sent your servant Romeu to Girona."

Tomas reddened. "Doña Sanxia de Baltier begged me to release Romeu to help her carry out a very delicate mission for Her Majesty."

"Why were you so obliging?"

"Doña Sanxia was Her Majesty's lady-in-waiting." He stopped. "That was not the only reason, my lords. But since the truth might blacken the lady's reputation—"

"The lady's reputation cannot get much darker, Don Tomas," said Don Eleazar. "But you still say the mission was to protect the Infant Johan."

"I truly believed at the time that it was to protect the Prince."

"Why did you return to Girona?"

"On my uncle's instructions, sir."

"You spoke to him?"

"No. His secretary wrote me a letter."

"Do you have it?"

Tomas looked like a drowning man whose last support had just sunk to the bottom. "I penned my reply on the foot of his letter," he said.

"Then tell us, Don Tomas, how Romeu came into your service."

"My uncle arranged it—Romeu's horse, suit of clothes, and first year's wages all came from my uncle. He has been most generous to me."

"Indeed. You refer to Count Hug de Castellbo?" Tomas nodded. "But who engaged him, Don Tomas? You? Or Castellbo?"

"The Count, sir," he said. "Romeu had served my uncle since childhood. The Count thought I needed a servant who knew the ways of the court to keep me out of trouble." Surreptitious smiles flickered over several faces.

"He hardly managed that, did he?" murmured Berenguer.

Don Eleazar paid no attention to smiles or murmurs. "Thank you. Now tell us why you expected to find Lady Isabel at Baltier's *finca*."

"It was the place where I was to take the Infant," said Tomas, and added a careful summary of his discoveries and conclusions.

"What was Doña Sanxia doing at the convent of Sant Daniel?"

"The nuns gave her shelter, and she had a trusted friend at the convent."

"Who?"

"Someone she had known since childhood, sir. That is all I know."

"Why disguise herself as one Sor Berengaria and attempt to lure Lady Isabel from the convent?"

"She did? I didn't know." Tomas stared at him in astonishment. "May I ask a question, Don Eleazar? Your Majesty?" he added in confusion. He had forgotten that Don Pedro was there.

The King nodded.

"Who killed Doña Sanxia? With his dying breath, Romeu denied it."

"She was murdered by the Sword of the Archangel Michael."

"The Sword of the Archangel Michael? Who is that?" said Tomas.

A burst of laughter erupted in the room.

"As the only man left in Girona who has not heard of the Sword," said Don Pedro, smiling, "you should stay and find out. Don Eleazar?"

"In five days," said the secretary, "the city's peace has twice been marred by rioting. Depositions from several citizens agree that neither disturbance was spontaneous. The first was instigated by Romeu; the second by two strangers. Master Isaac can tell us much about both events."

"The first night of rioting was to cover Lady Isabel's abduction from the convent—and, it would seem, the abduction of the Infant Johan," said Isaac. "Both attempts failed. Lady Isabel was too well guarded, and the Infant's nursemaid kept the child safe. At the cost of her life."

"Who was the assassin?" asked Tomas.

"The man who called himself the Sword," said Isaac. "He told me as much last night, before leaving for the palace to kill His Majesty, and the Infant, and His Excellency the Bishop."

"Instead, he killed a fine captain," said Don Pedro, "and escaped."

"Escaped only to suffer the vengeance of heaven," said Berenguer. He turned to Don Tomas. "He was struck by lightning. Or something similar."

"Who was he?" asked Tomas again.

"The chief conspirator?" asked Isaac.

"Not the chief conspirator," murmured His Majesty, dryly. "But his chief lieutenant, perhaps."

And for a moment, the hovering presence of Don Fernando, the King's half brother, seemed to fill the room.

Isaac bowed in the direction of the King. "I believed last night that I had told Your Majesty everything of importance the Sword had said to me. But I fear that last night I was not myself. In the peace of morning, I've remembered a few things that might help someone to identify the man."

The people in the room seemed to draw themselves into a tighter space. "Yes, physician?" asked the King.

"He said he was from a noble line, descended from the Visigoths."

"So claim half the families in the kingdom," said His Majesty.

"Indeed, Your Majesty," said Isaac. "He also said that if his great-grandfather had been able to"—Isaac considered the word *scheme,* and replaced it—"had been a more skilled politician, he, the Sword, would now be a king. He didn't say of which kingdom."

"That brings it down to a mere hundred families," said Berenguer rather sourly.

"And then he said that the angel Michael spoke to him from the top of his own mountain peak, while looking down into his rich valley."

"If he's as important as he thinks he is, Your Majesty, then he holds considerable land in the north," said Eleazar. "There are a few who might fulfill those requirements."

"A thousand pardons, my lords, but I know who he is."

The treble voice silenced the room. Everyone turned as Yusuf ran forward, fell on his knees, and bowed until his forehead touched the cool tiles. "Your Majesty," he said.

"Rise, child," said Don Pedro. "Tell us what you know."

Yusuf scrambled to his feet again. "Your Majesty," he said, looking steadily at him. "First I bring you greetings from my father, who from the far side of time wishes you and your subjects long life and prosperity. He was a friend to you and your interests."

"And who was your father, to send us greetings from his grave?"

"My father was emissary from the Emir Abu Hajjij Yusuf, great Lord and Ruler of Granada, to the Governor of Valencia," said Yusuf.

"Did you know this?" said Berenguer to Isaac, in the pause that ensued.

"No," said Isaac. "I knew only that he came from Valencia."

"Why did you leave Valencia, child?" asked Don Eleazar. The busy scribe made a note of the question.

"My father knew that traitors surrounded the King and the Governor. Before he could speak, he was murdered. They would not let me see the Governor, and so I came north to warn the King."

Don Pedro gave Berenguer a startled look, and leaned forward. "May we ask the name of your noble father?"

Yusuf looked from one man to the other in mute horror. "I cannot say it," he whispered.

"When did this happen?" asked Eleazar quickly.

"In the year of the fighting in Valencia, and the great pestilence."

"Surely this must be the child of Hasan Algarrafa?" murmured Eleazar.

"Or of one of the others in the Emir's party," said the King.

"Lord," said Yusuf to Don Eleazar, "as soon as the Sword spoke to my master, I recognized the demon who killed my father."

"You saw him do this?" asked Don Eleazar gently.

Yusuf nodded, biting down on his trembling lips. "He is a great noble in Your Majesty's service. I came to tell you that he intended to betray you, so I could see him punished. I have his name here," he said, touching his breast. "Written down in a letter from my father to Your Majesty."

"Let us see this letter, child," said the King.

Yusuf pulled the leather purse out from under his tunic, and took it off his neck. With trembling and awkward fingers, he untied the cord that fastened it tight, and drew out a crumpled piece of paper. He straightened it with care, fell on his knees again, and presented it to Don Pedro.

"It's in Arabic," said the King, showing it to his secretary. "I admit to being somewhat slow in making out the words."

"Indeed, Your Majesty. I will gladly—"

"I can read it," said Yusuf. "If it pleases Your Majesty."

"Just read me the name if you can, child," said the King. "And Don Eleazar will do a fair copy for me of the rest. It is badly stained."

"With my father's blood," said Yusuf. "I took it from his body." He took back the paper, and fell back down on the floor, where he crouched and, using his finger as a guide, traced his path through the letters. "Your Majesty," he said uncertainly, "I think his name is Lord Castellbo."

"My uncle," whispered Bellmunt, horrified. "It can't be true." But as he spoke the words everything fell in place, and he knew that it was.

"He was not a kind protector to you, Don Tomas," said Berenguer. "I would waste no tears on him."

"My God in heaven," said Tomas, "what a fool I have been."

"There are more fools than one, Don Tomas," said Don Pedro. "Count Hug de Castellbo was the man I sent into the country to guard my son."

Yusuf stood in front of the King, confused and unhappy. "Have I done wrong, Your Majesty?" he asked, holding out the letter.

"Not at all, my brave child," said Don Pedro. "I shall keep this letter, if I may, and cherish it."

"It was written to you, lord," said Yusuf simply.

Don Pedro took the worn piece of paper, and bent toward the boy. "It is not fitting for you to be reduced to servitude, child," he said, "If you wish to join our court, we will make arrangements with your master. Is that agreeable to you, Master Isaac?"

"Yusuf is free, Your Majesty," said Isaac, as evenly as

he could. "He did me a service, and in return I gave him shelter, but I make no claim to him. If he wishes to stay in my household and be taught, he is welcome. If he prefers a place in court, he will go with my blessing."

"Then let the child decide," said His Majesty. "He remains under our protection as long as he is in our kingdom."

"You may sit, Yusuf," said Don Eleazar. "With the physician."

EIGHTEEN

The door to the study closed on the three men. "What do we do with Bellmunt?" said the King to Berenguer and Eleazar. "His crime seems to have been a single act of unbelievable stupidity."

"I believe he has learned a very hard lesson, Your Majesty," said the Bishop. "About women, and the world. And I confess to liking him."

"Her Majesty finds him charming and modest—as well as useful," said Don Eleazar. "And he seems to have courage. His rescue of Lady Isabel had a touch of brilliance to it."

"He's a good strategist," said Don Pedro. "But it's unfortunate she was left in Montbui's power for two days. There is already gossip."

"Marriage would cure his stupidity about women," the Bishop suggested, "and the gossip about my niece. I would stake my life that the rumors have no foundation," he added. "But scandal cares nothing for truth, of course."

"He's poor," said Don Eleazar.

"From a good family," said Don Pedro. "And my daughter seems pale with love for him. But he has been convicted of treason. That's a problem."

"Through the machinations of your enemies, Sire," said the Bishop.

Then Don Eleazar cleared his throat, a sure signal that he had found a solution. Everyone turned to him. "A clear message is what is needed," he said. "A pardon by itself is not enough. All his life the cloud of treason will hang over him, and that can make a good man dangerous. Behead him tomorrow, or elevate him at once. Valencia is in need of a new governor, Your Majesty. It will tell your enemies that their plots have failed if you appoint Bellmunt to that position."

Don Pedro stared off in the distance for a few moments. "We could give him Castellbo's lands and goods. They are forfeit to the crown."

"Perhaps, Your Majesty, one half of them would be sufficient," murmured his secretary. "There is the Genoese campaign to finance."

"Excellent," said the King. "That solves his poverty."

Don Eleazar made a note.

"We'll send Arnau to Valencia with him—he's cautious and sensible. And it will get him out of my hair. All this, of course, if Bellmunt consents."

Don Eleazar made another note. "And if he doesn't?"

"Oh, I think he will. But he can always choose the alternative." His Majesty rose to his feet. "So, gentlemen," he said, "we have a new governor in Valencia. My daughter will be pleased."

The royal party rejoined the gathering. The Bishop murmured a word in an attendant's ear, and within seconds, servants poured into the room with trays piled high with delicacies, and ornate silver pitchers overflowing with wine. Don Eleazar drifted over to speak to Master Isaac about the Infant, and the Bishop moved close to Tomas de Bellmunt.

The tapestry was drawn back to let the Abbess, Lady Isabel, and Raquel join the others. The ladies curtsied; the gentlemen responded. Tomas looked horrified, His Majesty genial, and Lady Isabel distraught.

Berenguer drew Bellmunt aside. "It gives me great plea-

sure to see you, Don Tomas,'' said Berenguer. ''My niece
has made a remarkable recovery in these last few days,
hasn't she? But then she has an excellent constitution, and
a skillful physician.''

Tomas gave him a desperate look. ''She is lovely beyond
compare.''

''Any flatterer can say that,'' said the Bishop. ''Although
I agree with you. Would you say she appears to be good
and virtuous as well?''

''None more so in all Cataluña,'' said Tomas.

''I'm glad you think so. Because already foul slanders
are being spread about her. They are saying she eloped with
Montbui, and was dragged forcibly back. I'm afraid the
convent may be the place for her. Unless she is willing to
marry, and soon, before the slanders can grow.''

''To whom is she promised?'' asked Tomas, for whom
misery seemed to build on misery.

''No one at the moment. See—there she sits, alone and
looking very sad. You might speak to her, and cheer her
up.''

''I doubt if the words of a condemned man will cheer
her very much, Your Excellency.''

''Ah, yes. Those were interesting charges,'' said Berenguer. ''You realize, Don Tomas, that you were convicted
on one point only, that of giving help—in the shape of your
servant, Romeu—to a group you ought to have suspected
of treachery. Of course, you acted in ignorance. Perhaps
even in good faith. But there is a fault there to expiate,
shall we say.''

''I haven't much time for expiation,'' said Tomas.

''That depends,'' said Berenguer, looking off into the
distance. ''At the moment, His Majesty is in need of a man
of principle, courage, and absolute loyalty. A man prepared
to live and, perhaps, die for the crown.''

''A life for a life?'' said Tomas, cautiously. ''What
would this man have to do?''

Berenguer explained.

Tomas stared incredulously at the Bishop. ''You laugh
at a dead man,'' he said at last. ''You offer power, and

your niece, and say it requires courage and loyalty to accept? You are amusing yourself at my expense.''

''Not at all. Valencia needs a governor who can be trusted. And His Majesty will not force a choice on his daughter. You must win her. If you don't . . .'' He spread his hands.

Tomas paused. ''I understand,'' he said, thoughtfully. ''But why would she consider me? I have nothing to offer her but poverty and disgrace.''

''She's a grateful creature, by nature, and you did her a good turn. She finds Montbui abhorrent. And if you win her, Valencia is yours, along with a portion of your uncle's estate. There she is. You may have a quiet corner of the room and the afternoon to make your case. I wish you well.''

Don Pedro rose. ''My good Bellmunt,'' he said, ''I believe my daughter wishes to thank you for the service you have done her.'' He gathered up Eleazar and the scribe with a glance, and left the room.

Lady Isabel beckoned her uncle over. ''What did Papa mean by that?''

''He meant,'' said the Bishop, quietly, ''that he is neither heartless nor blind. If you want the young man, you may have him. Arrangements will be made for a suitable position for him. Your father has a soft spot in his heart for marriages of affection.''

''But he has been condemned—''

''Look at him. Do you think him a traitor?''

''Certainly not, Uncle.''

''Neither does anyone else. So unless he does something to prove us wrong, his head is fairly safe.''

''But perhaps he won't want to marry—''

''You look pale with the heat, my dear. I suggest you take your companions and sit by that window.'' It was more a command than a suggestion, and Isabel obeyed.

The three women sat by the window at a table now set out with fruit, and wine, and cakes. They were silent—the Abbess and Isabel were too deep in thought, and Raquel too tired to make conversation. Don Tomas walked up to them with the air of a man heading into battle against overwhelming odds.

"How did you come to be your father's assistant, Mistress Raquel?" said the Abbess, turning to her with sudden interest. "Surely that is a rare privilege for a woman. Or is it a tradition among your people?" She rose and glanced out the window.

"Not at all, my lady," said Raquel, rising as well. "My cousin Benjamin had been his apprentice, but—" And the Abbess drew Raquel some distance away, in order to listen to her account.

Bellmunt asked after Isabel's health, and ran out of conversation. He stood motionless, his eyes fixed on the wall, on her uncle's back, anywhere but on her face.

After a few silent moments, Isabel rose from her chair. She walked over to a window; Tomas trailed behind. "Look, Don Tomas," she said. "There was a riot there last night; the plaza was filled with hate and violence. Mistress Raquel's father, a good and harmless man who saved my life a few days ago, was injured. A madman—your uncle— tried to murder my father, my uncle, and my brother, and was burned to death. Those honest citizens we see out there were screaming for the blood of those dearest to me a few hours ago. And yet it seems so peaceful."

"The world is filled with deception and treachery, Lady Isabel," said Tomas, standing behind her. "I would have staked my life on my uncle's loyalty to the crown."

"But what can we do? When a man pursues me, what am I to think? Consider Montbui. Why did he want to marry me?"

"Your Ladyship is beautiful and charming," said Tomas awkwardly. "Any man would pursue you."

"That's foolish," she said, glancing back at him. "He'd never seen me. What he'd seen were descriptions of my lands, and how much they brought in each year. Do you know what he wanted my money for?"

"To destroy your father," said Tomas. "Yes—I realized it at last."

Isabel looked back out the window. "We are not as merry as we were in the country, Don Tomas," she said, unhappily. "You talked to me much more freely than you do in town."

"In the country it was easy to forget my poverty and insignificance," said Tomas in a low voice. "I was not surrounded by kings and bishops and abbesses in the country. And I had not been tried—"

"Don't speak of that," said Isabel, her eyes filling with tears. "I cannot bear to hear anyone say it of you, even yourself."

"My lady, please—do not cry. *I* cannot bear to see you suffer for an instant because of me. I am not worth your tears," he added angrily. "How do you know that I'm not another Montbui, pursuing you for gain?"

"I don't, except that you neither look nor behave like him." She stopped, and appeared to be absorbed in the quiet scene outside. At last, she shook her head and half turned toward him. "What would you do if I said that I cannot love or trust any man, and have decided on the convent?"

"I would go to my death as firmly as I could, hoping that you might pray for my soul, my lady," he said, refusing to meet her eyes. "And wishing you a life of tranquillity and peace."

"I think you might, at that," she said.

"Is that your decision?"

"I'm not sure," said Isabel. She took a deep breath, as if she were trying to shake off her melancholy. "I've been at Sant Daniel for some time now. The nuns are kinder to me than the world is, and I'm used to it."

Tomas winced, as if he'd been struck a painful but invisible blow. "Then I wish you every happiness, my lady." He bowed, and walked away.

"Don Tomas." The touch on his arm, as light as a butterfly landing, stopped him. "Don't leave, Don Tomas, not yet." She had followed him those few steps from the win-

dow embrasure, and she tightened her grip as she drew him
back. The hand that held his forearm trembled, but stayed
where it was until he returned with her to the window. "I
have a question to ask you that has been troubling me since
we were in the country."

"I am at your disposition, my lady." Using his body to
shield his action from the rest of the room, he placed his
own hand on top of hers. She left it there.

"Will you sit with me, Don Tomas, and take a cup of
my uncle's excellent wine? The last time I offered you
wine, I'm afraid I offended you. Am I forgiven now?" She
gently loosed her hand, and placing it on top of his, allowed
him to lead her to a chair. She nodded, and a servant appeared with a jug of wine and two silver cups. As he moved
to pour the wine Isabel frowned. He disappeared like a puff
of vapor in the wind.

Bellmunt stood in front of her, frozen with indecision.

"But perhaps after being forced to spend so much time
in my company, you would rather talk to someone else."

"Forced?" he said, with vigor. "My lady, I can think
of no better way to spend any moment than in your company." He placed a chair next to her and sat down hastily.

"I understand now," she said, shaking her head. "You
will happily spend a moment in conversation with me, if
you can then pass on. You tire very quickly of a lady's
company, Don Tomas." She poured wine into two cups,
holding the heavy jug with great care.

"You misunderstand me, Lady Isabel."

"I don't think so. It's my hair, isn't it? Neither black
like the raven nor red like fire. Just brown."

"You were listening to my testimony," he said, with an
accusing look. "Listening to me make a fool of myself."

"If a fool, then at least an honest one," said Isabel.
"Perhaps you are mourning for her yet. It was thoughtless
of me to laugh."

"Mourn! I was a fool, my lady, and she was a scheming,
heartless—"

"I know what she was, Don Tomas. I didn't know if you
knew as well."

"And your hair is not brown," he added stubbornly. "It is the color of wheat in August, or beech leaves in November. My mare has a brown coat; your hair is golden." And he blushed, but held his gaze.

"I remember your mare very well. She has a charming coat. But tell me, honestly and without flinching, whether you loved Doña Sanxia de Baltier or not. I want to know."

At that moment, honesty seemed the most important quality in the world. "For one dazzling moment, I loved her," he said slowly, "until I saw that I meant less to her than the clever laundress who could wash clean a silk gown she prized. Then she gambled with my life and my honor. No—after that first moment, I didn't love her. And I'm ashamed I ever had."

And the strange bewitching creature beside him smiled. "I am very happy for that," she said. "I had been concerned about your judgment. And do you love anyone else?"

"Lady Isabel, you must know the answer to that question."

"Well, I don't. Or at least I'm not sure of it. But I must marry now, they say, and unless I can marry someone I love, I shall have to join Lady Elicsenda at Sant Daniel. Would you prefer to have me in the convent for the rest of my life? I won't marry anyone else."

"I beg your pardon?" he said.

"Is that an answer to an honest proposal of marriage, Don Tomas?" she asked. "Will you drink a cup of wine with me?" She picked up the cup with shaking fingers. It splashed over the rim.

He took it from her wine-stained hands and drank.

NINETEEN

Monday, June 30, 1353

Jubilant crowds gathered in the plaza of the Apostles to say farewell to their king and his heir—many of them the same people, with the addition of their wives and children, who had gathered on Saturday night in hopes of witnessing the excitement of his overthrow. Don Pedro smiled and acknowledged the crowd; Don Arnau and his officers remained tense and wary, keeping themselves and their edgy mounts prepared for trouble, as they searched for signs of another rapid shift in the public mood.

Rebecca danced gleefully down the steps, holding the excited Infant by the hand. She was going home at last to her husband and baby. A new gown, and countless other luxuries, lay tucked into the bodice of her gown in the shape of a well-filled purse from His Majesty. She embraced the child, told him—automatically—to be a good boy, and handed him to an officer who lifted him up to his father's stallion. He settled himself on the saddle in front of the King, and a look of complete happiness spread across his face.

"Bye, 'Becca," he said, and waved, and the royal troop left the city for their summer quarters.

The crowd, deprived of the beheading of a noble traitor, had to make do with the hanging of a bookbinder and an ostler, and a few fistfuls of silver coins tossed by the royal party, which sent the children—and some of their parents—scrambling wildly over the cobbles.

Everyone agreed it was a wonderful day.

Abbess Elicsenda returned to the convent after a brief conference with Berenguer and His Majesty on the subject of Isabel's marriage. It was to take place as soon as the details of the settlements could be argued out, written down, and signed. That responsibility would soon be over. She stood in the doorway to her study, looking tired and saddened, waiting.

"Agnete," said Lady Elicsenda, "could you give me a moment? I would like to talk to you."

"Yes, Mother," said Sor Agnete. "Certainly. Shall I bring in the accounts?"

"Not yet. We'll deal with them at another time." The older nun followed the Abbess into her study. "Sit down, Agnete," she said quietly, and waited until Sor Agnete was seated. "I would like to return this to you," she said, placing on the table a small dark book in a heavy leather binding. "It was found on Saturday. I believe it's yours. It has your name on it."

"Oh!" said Sor Agnete, and picked it up. "Thank you, Lady Elicsenda," she said. "I've searched everywhere for it. It was a gift from my father, and very precious to me. Someone must have borrowed it."

"Had you left it in the library, where such things belong, it would not have been lost, Agnete."

"Yes, Mother," she said. She nodded in submission, but her hands tightened possessively around the book. "I will place it there. Where was it found?"

"In a chest used for storing old garments. The chest from which you took two threadbare habits for two very tall sisters to wear."

Agnete looked directly at the Abbess and then dropped her eyes in humility. "Oh, no, Mother," she said gently.

"I would never have given those habits to anyone without your permission. And never to someone who wanted to harm one of our wards."

"How did your book come to be in there?"

She shook her head with a puzzled air. "I don't know, Mother. Someone must have taken it—"

"Who could have taken it, Agnete? Where did you leave it?"

Sor Agnete's hands, folded quietly on her lap, began to tremble. Her pale cheeks turned red, and she raised her chin, looking defiantly at the Abbess. "Why was it in the chest?" Thirty years of deference dropped away like a snake's old skin, and her voice turned cool and arrogant. "Because I couldn't carry the habits and the book at the same time, Lady Elicsenda. Unfortunately, I forgot that it was there." Then suddenly, as if her moment of rebellion had been too overpowering, she buried her face in her hands.

"Tears won't help anything," said Elicsenda coldly. "Your obligation now is to tell me who involved you in this plot, and which other sisters knew about it."

Agnete drew herself upright again, dry-eyed. "I feel no guilt or remorse for what I did, Lady Elicsenda. It was right and just—except that I was forced to lie," she said, with the same cool arrogance. "Our country is being destroyed by money-grubbing peasants. You may not see it, but if you knew how it is out there—how it was with my family—" She leaned toward the Abbess. "Our lands are barren; our crops have failed. My brother owes his very soul to Jewish moneylenders. We are noble, my lady, as noble as yourself, and the merchants and traders—jumped-up beggars' brats, all of them, bred in the mud—have sucked us dry, stolen our goods and our places in court."

The Abbess said nothing.

"What are you going to do, Mother?" asked Agnete.

"Nothing, Agnete," said the Abbess. "Not yet. I will wait for you to tell me who else is involved. Meanwhile, you will pray, and work, and hope for amendment in this life, and forgiveness in the next. I know more about the world than you imagine, and no matter how much you felt you were provoked, what you did was very wrong." She stood up to signify that the interview was over, and Sor Agnete swept out of the room.

"And so it was Sor Agnete," said Berenguer. "I'm astonished."

"So was I, for a moment," said the Abbess. "I should have considered who her family was. She and Sanxia's mother were friends, I remember, and distantly related. And although she brought a substantial dowry into the order with her," she said, with the air of one whose dowry had been much more substantial, "since then, drought, poverty, and pestilence have almost destroyed her family. They must have had moments of regretting that dowry," she added grimly. "She seemed so efficient and even-tempered that it never occurred to me she could be brooding about it. It was remiss of me."

"We can't see into other people's hearts, Lady Elicsenda," said the Bishop. "And for the most part, it's a fortunate thing. Is the physician coming? I had hoped to speak to him this afternoon."

"He's here," said the Abbess, resuming her own calmly efficient manner. "He wished to see Lady Isabel, and satisfy himself that she is in good health after all she has suffered. I asked him to join us as soon as he was through."

A soft knock on the door of the Abbess's study, and the entrance of Sor Marta, heralded Isaac's visit. "Master Isaac," said the Abbess warmly, "how are you? The Bishop is here, and we are delighted to see you. How is our ward?"

"In remarkably good health. She seems to thrive on adversity," said Isaac. "Perhaps being kidnapped, and traveling all over the countryside, and falling in love are to be recommended as a treatment for high fevers caused by pustular sores."

"My niece is very strong, as well as charming and intelligent," said Berenguer. "But I am sure it was your treatment that brought her through her ordeal. With the help of

God, of course. We have much to thank you for."

"And so it seems to be ended," said Isaac. "But there are many questions that remain, I'm afraid. And one of them is the stain on your convent that my inquiries were intended to remove."

"That mystery is over," said Elicsenda, and gave Isaac a brief summary of Agnete's confession.

"Sor Agnete," he said. "How extraordinary. I am humbled by the news. I felt such suspicion, and guilt, and hostility in Sor Benvenguda that I was sure she could not be trusted with Lady Isabel, and yet it was the other all along."

"Benvenguda was jealous of your skills, I expect," said the Abbess calmly. "Think how difficult it was for her to be moved into a group of women who have known each other—living, praying, and working together—for years."

"And Sor Agnete brought me the vial, saying that she had found it on Doña Sanxia. Shrewd of her, but I should have suspected her involvement from that moment. Because it was obvious that only a nun could administer the potion."

"It was disturbingly calculated and deliberate on her part," said the Abbess. "We shall have to consider what is to be done with her, Your Excellency. She may still be a danger to us."

"Perhaps we can leave that question for the motherhouse to decide, my lady," said the Bishop.

"Indeed. What is to be done with the other conspirators, Your Excellency?" asked the Abbess.

"That remains to be seen," said Berenguer. "Word reached the King this morning that Baltier and Montbui have fled toward Castile, where they hope to receive protection from the King."

"With their treasure chests?" said Isaac dryly.

"I would think so," said Berenguer. "I suspect they are hoping to buy themselves back into favor as soon as there is another crisis."

"And it is disgusting to think that they may succeed," said the Abbess.

"I believe I admire Castellbo more than his less dangerous colleagues," said Berenguer. "He at least was prepared
to die for his principles, no matter how mad and uncomfortable they were. The Baltiers and Montbuis of this world
are interested only in filling their purses and bellies."

"Is it better to die at the hands of a noble madman, or
a greedy jackal?" said Isaac. "The jackals have little
charm, but I fear them less than the Castellbos. They don't
seek to destroy you and everyone near you unless it brings
them gain. Will His Majesty pursue them?"

"Within the kingdom? Yes—and relentlessly," said Berenguer. "But not beyond the borders."

"I don't understand where that strange group came
from," said Lady Elicsenda irritably. "The followers of the
Archangel's Sword. How can something appear so quickly?
One day no one had heard of them, and the next, they're
on every tongue. Are they a new wave of Cathars, or some
other heretics?"

"I believe they are as Christian as most of my flock,"
said Berenguer cautiously.

"Then why support Fernando on religious grounds?"
said the Abbess, who had a tendency to demand clarity
from the murkier aspects of existence. "If they're Christians. So is His Majesty, Don Pedro."

"It's more complicated than that," said the Bishop. "As
I understand it, they were a small group that came together
last year to celebrate the feast of Saint Michael, and the
raising of the siege of the city in our grandfathers' time—a
couple of my seminarians, and some tradesmen with grievances against the municipal council and the church, mostly
because they weren't making enough money from city and
church business. They met once a month at Rodrigue's tavern to eat and drink and complain, and talk about petition-
ing for redress of their grievances."

"Did you know about them?" asked Elicsenda.

"I'm ashamed to say that I did not. But in those days,
they were no danger to anyone. They were happy enough
complaining that something should be done to make them
rich, and spending their coin on Rodrigue's food and drink.

Then Castellbo, Romeu, and the two others arrived from Barcelona. They worked them into a frenzy against the King, and helped them recruit more hangers-on. That was when the group came to our attention. You know the rest. The men from Barcelona were agents of His Majesty's affectionate brother, Don Fernando. They set up Castellbo as the Sword—''

"Was there a Sword before he arrived?" asked Isaac.

"No," said Berenguer. "As the group saw themselves, the sword was not a person, but a group protecting the city, as Saint Michael's Sword protected it—and heaven. But Castellbo and his friends must have decided that it was easier to rally people around a central figure.''

"Big Johan had insisted that there was no Sword. I didn't believe him. I did him an injustice.''

"They were attempting to lure His Majesty here by seizing the Infant, with the intention of slaughtering them all— His Majesty, the Queen, and the Infant.''

"And the kidnapping of Lady Isabel had nothing to do with them?" asked the Abbess.

"I think Lady Isabel was the prize that Montbui was promised if he came in on the plot," said Isaac.

"But their luck ran out every way they turned," said the Bishop. "Although my poor Isabel was very nearly sacrificed to her other uncle's desire for a throne.''

"Luck had nothing to do with it," said the Abbess firmly. "His Majesty and all his family are under the special protection of Saint Daniel; we pray for them daily. How could Don Fernando prevail against that?''

"How could he indeed?" said the Bishop. "Come, Master Isaac, I will walk back with you and your daughter as far as the Quarter. I have something to discuss with you.''

"Will I ever see you again, Raquel?" said Lady Isabel.

"It seems impossible, my lady," said Raquel, taking Isabel's hands in hers. "But our lives have taken so many strange turns lately that I can believe anything now. When do you leave for Valencia?''

"In a week. My uncle is to marry us on Monday, I think,

and we will travel to Barcelona after the wedding. Oh, Raquel,'' she said in a whisper, "I cannot bear to wait that long. I can hardly breathe when I think of him. When he touched my hand I thought I would faint, I felt so sick and dizzy with love for him. What will I do if something happens to prevent the marriage?''

"Nothing will stop you marrying," said Raquel, letting go of her hands. "My papa is sure—and he always knows these things.'' She smiled. "I envy you. I wonder if I will ever be able to feel like that.''

"I'm sure you will," said Isabel, with the fervor of the newly converted.

"I'm not. My sister Rebecca was always in love. She fell in love with our cousin Benjamin, who died of the plague. And then six months later, when she was helping Papa, she met a scribe who had a fever, and fell madly in love with him. Only he's a Christian, and there was a terrible battle. Then a year or so later, she ran off with him, and Mama refuses to see her, or her husband, or their baby. I've never met anyone I would do anything like that for. I'm talking nonsense,'' she said, "and I'm sorry. But I'm very happy for you. Don Tomas is the sweetest and kindest and noblest man I've ever met. You deserve each other. I shall miss you, Lady Isabel.''

"Oh, Raquel. I shall miss you, too. Why can't you come to Valencia, and be my companion and physician?''

"I can't leave Papa, my lady.'' Her eyes filled with tears. "I must go now.''

Lady Isabel wrapped her arms around her in a tight embrace. "I'll never forget you, and what you've done for me. Good-bye, Raquel.''

Silence reigned in Rodrigue's tavern when Johan and Pere mounted the stairs. They peered around in the gloom. "Marc, Josep,'' said Pere. "You were so quiet I thought the place was empty.''

"You're here early," said Marc.

"Everything's slowed down, hasn't it? Who needs my wood today? All the important people have gone—no one's

cooking except for themselves. My arms and Margarita's
back can use the rest," he added philosophically.

"It seems odd in here without Sanch and Martin," said
Marc, in a curiously neutral voice, as if he were trying to
judge people's reactions.

"A good deal more peaceful, if you ask me," said Pere.

"They might have paid what they owed me for wine
before going off rioting," said Rodrigue. "We'll never collect it now."

"We won't lose much money with them gone," said the
tavern keeper's wife, poking her head around the kitchen
door.

"I was getting tired of their endless complaining," said
Pere. "I come here to forget my troubles, don't you, Johan?"

Big Johan smiled. "I don't have troubles," he said.
"The Bishop said it weren't my fault they had that meeting
in the Baths," he added in a whisper. "He'll tell the master
that."

"The less said about that the better," said Josep. "There
are some who'd like to pretend it never happened. Eh, Rodrigue?"

"Me?" said Rodrigue. "I was nowhere near the Baths
that night. I know trouble when I see it."

"You wouldn't know trouble until it bit you." The shrill
voice of Rodrigue's wife drifted out from the kitchen. "I
wouldn't let you out the door, if you remember."

A burst of laughter greeted her remark, providing a welcome to another thirsty pair coming up the stairs. "Where's
Raimunt?" asked one of them. "I had something to ask
him about."

"You'll look long and hard before you see him here,"
said Rodrigue. "He's a marked man."

"They say he left the city when the lightning struck,"
said Marc. "Always was afraid of thunder," he added, with
a low chuckle.

"He never did any harm," said one of the newcomers.
"Why can't they let people alone to live their lives?"

"That's it," said someone else, just walking in. "I was

talking to this man in the market, and he said that the devil
appeared to him, and told him that the King—''

"Not again," said Pere. "How many men do you have
to see hanged before you stop listening to madmen?''

"I'll drink to that," said Marc.

"We'll all drink to that," said Rodrigue, and began pouring from the pitcher in his hand. "And put your money
away!''

"Rodrigue!'' The furious scream from the kitchen echoed through the room, and was answered by a loud shout
of laughter.

The evening light began throwing shadows over the courtyard, where Isaac sat at table with Judith, Raquel, and the
twins, Miriam and Nathan.

"Ibrahim went to see the men hanged, Papa,'' said Nathan. "I want to go and see someone hanged.''

"So do I," said Miriam.

"You can't. You're a girl, and girls can't—''

"Quiet," said Judith, in her voice that meant trouble.
"If that's all you can talk about, then it's time you were
in bed. Leah!''

The nursemaid slipped quietly down the stairs. "Yes,
mistress.''

"Take them to bed." And in spite of a long howl of
protest, the twins were whisked up to their room, leaving
the courtyard in peace.

"Is it dark?'' asked Isaac. "The birds seem quiet tonight.''

"No, Isaac, it's just past sunset. It's the heat that keeps
them still." Judith's voice was tranquil. "Where is Yusuf?''

"I am here, mistress,'' said a small voice from across
the courtyard.

"Come here, Yusuf,'' she said. "Let me see you.''

The boy walked across the courtyard and stood in front
of her.

"I thought you were riding off with the King this morning.''

"No, mistress. Master Isaac said that I might stay if I wished."

"Ride or not, things have changed," she said thoughtfully. "It is not right for you to be a servant. You are here to learn now, since you decided to stay with us. You'll need a teacher."

"I will teach him, Mama," said Raquel. "As far as I can."

"That won't do at all. It's time you were married, Raquel," said her mother.

"Married?" said Raquel.

"Reb Samuel received a letter for me from my sister Dinah in Tarragona, saying that Ruben, her husband's nephew, is in need of a wife."

"Tarragona!" said Raquel. "No! I don't want to go that far away, Mama. Papa, tell Mama that I can't go that far away!"

"Take Yusuf and teach him something," said Judith impatiently. "I want to talk to your papa."

"She is almost seventeen, Isaac. And in Tarragona they will not have heard of her disgrace."

"Disgrace! She has not been touched, Judith. And she behaved with courage and modesty. I am proud of her."

"That may be, but the rest of world will not see it that way."

"I will not make a decision right now, Judith. I insist that we wait. I may be going to Tarragona in a year's time. I will consider it then."

"Why would you go to Tarragona?"

"The Bishop has asked me to be his personal physician. But you see, my dear, the Archbishop has summoned him to a general council of the church next year. It's being held in Tarragona, and he wants me to accompany him. If I do, Raquel can come with me. And whether I accept the post or not, I cannot do without her until Yusuf is skilled enough to take her place. That will not be for a while."

"The Bishop's personal physician," said Judith. "Does this mean that you will sleep at home at night?"

"Yes, of course." He paused. "Unless our neighbors call for me. Or my other patients." In the dusk, a bird suddenly decided to fill the courtyard with song, and Isaac stopped to listen. "Judith," he said at last, "come and sit with me by the fountain. I want you to consider something, and I want you close to me while you do it."

"What is that, Isaac?" Judith rose from the table, came over, and took her husband by the hand. They walked to the fountain and sat down.

"It's Rebecca. Wait—don't say anything until I've spoken. Rebecca misses her mama. She would like to see you and to show her baby to you. That is all she asks for now. Don't decide yet, because you will say no, but think of it from time to time."

"Rebecca is dead."

"You may say that all you like, but she isn't, Judith. She is alive, and well, and leading a useful and virtuous life. And she misses you. There is no harm in forgiveness. Judith, my dear," he said, taking her hand in his, "this is very important to me."

She laid her other hand on top of his. "I will think of it from time to time if you wish me to, Isaac. I don't understand how I could change my mind, but I will think of it."

The darkness gathered in the courtyard. From the top of the house, the sound of the twins quarreling faded away, and was replaced by the voices of Raquel and Yusuf as they went over the letters of the Latin alphabet. "I was talking to the rabbi's wife, Isaac," said Judith softly. "She thinks she's having another child. She said you told her she was carrying a child, a healthy boy, before she knew it herself. How did you know?"

"Did I say that?" said Isaac.

"You did."

"I must have been mad. But I remember that something in her way of talking made me think she was with child. But to tell her it was a boy, and healthy—this must stop. Do you understand me?" he asked curiously.

"No. But I never understand you, Isaac," she said humbly. "I'm only glad this week is ended. It was a painful time. And you seemed so far away. I missed you." She touched him gently on the face. "How are your bruises? And your rib?"

"Painful, as well. But I suffered more from missing you during those nights alone, my love. You are a good and loyal wife, and a very beautiful woman."

"But you cannot see me."

"I can, my love, and I do. Passion is a clever physician—he gives sight even to the blind man."

Judith rose and took her husband's hand. "Come to bed," she said softly.

NAMES AND OTHER
HISTORICAL NOTES

The characters in the novel would have spoken a version of Catalan similar to the language of present-day Catalunya, where the cities of Girona and Barcelona are located. In giving these characters names, I have generally used the Catalan version, spelled according to fourteenth-century usage. Thus, the young prince, Johan, would now be called Joan (pronounced Joe-ann, with a *J* like the *s* in *pleasure*). The earlier spellings, as well as being authentic, are often closer to their English counterparts—in this case, John—and are therefore easier for English readers to pronounce. But in the interests of clarity and ease of reading, I have exercised the writer's prerogative to be inconsistent in my choices.

Those who are familiar with Catalan may be puzzled at my giving the two royal brothers, Pedro and Fernando, Spanish (Castilian) names, rather than calling them Pere and Ferran. My only excuse is that the Spanish names are so well known in the English-speaking world that I did not like to risk confusing those readers who are familiar with the fascinating history of the Iberian peninsula, but who do not know Catalan.

I humbly apologize to the late and most worthy Bishop of Girona, Berenguer de Cruilles, for high-handedly attaching various lively members to his family. He existed; his sister and her daughter should have, perhaps, but didn't.

Whether the great and revered mystic, Blind Isaac, could reappear a century after his death as a physician in Girona is for the reader to decide.